A WICKED MERCY

HARRIET QUINN BOOK 1

BILINDA P. SHEEHAN

Previously published as The Hanging Time

ALSO BY BILINDA P. SHEEHAN

Watch out for the next book coming soon from Bilinda P. Sheehan by joining her mailing list.

A Wicked Mercy - Harriet Quinn Crime Thriller Book 1

Death in Pieces - Harriet Quinn Crime Thriller Book 2

Splinter the Bone - Harriet Quinn Crime Thriller Book 3

All the Lost Girls-A Gripping Psychological Thriller

A WICKED MERCY

CHAPTER ONE

THE MESSAGES WOULDN'T STOP. The incessant bleeping of the iPhone as it sat on the nightstand was like a pneumatic drill driving straight through her skull.

Buzz. Buzz. Buzz.

It touched off the side of her can of pop and the vibration intensified growing tinny as it continued to buzz.

"Shut up!"

Fear overwhelmed her and she lashed out at the phone. It hit the soft fuzzy pink carpet next to her bed.

The noise dulled but only marginally.

She didn't need to look at the phone to know what was being said. To know just what they all thought of her.

Whore. Slut. Slag.

Sian didn't know which was worse, the constant noise in her head or the vitriol being dripped through the messenger app.

Creak.

The familiar sound of the third stair from the top caused her to pause. Her mother was out for the day with Nigel. Simply thinking about her stepfather turned Sian's stomach. Not that she could tell anyone why he gave her the creeps. They wouldn't believe her even if she tried. There was only one person who had believed her. One person who had listened and now he was gone.

"Mum." Her voice was nasally to her own ears and she hated it. No wonder everyone thought she was a worthless piece of shit.

Silence slid back in around her, leaving her in no doubt that she was, in fact, still alone with her own misery.

It wasn't the only thing which had fallen silent either. Leaning over the edge of her mattress, she stared down at the phone which had slid partially beneath the bed.

Tentatively, she reached for it. The voice in the back of her head warned her of the risk she was taking.

Of course, she knew there was nothing lurking under the bed, waiting for her to reach down. Nothing awaiting its opportunity to lunge out and drag her into the gaping void that the immature part of her brain believed existed amongst the dust bunnies and the boxes of mementos from her childhood that she didn't have the heart to dump.

Quickly, she fumbled across the floor for the phone and when her fingers finally closed over the hard shell she retreated to the relative safety of the bed.

Ever since she'd been little, there had been some small part of her that feared dangling her limbs over the edge of the bed. It was an irrational fear. Yet it was one she hadn't yet managed to shake.

Perhaps she never would.

The home screen lit up and Sian found herself face to face with her heartbreak.

There in all its digital glory sat the photograph of her and Aidan. His arm slung around her neck—typically protective of him—his lips pressed to the side of her head as he held her close.

Tears dripped, blurring his face. How was it possible that he was gone?

It seemed like some sort of cosmic joke, a sickening nightmare that at any moment she would wake from and everything would be as it should be.

Aidan shouldn't be dead. He was supposed to be alive. Supposed to be prepping for exams just like she was. He wasn't supposed to leave her alone and abandoned. He was the only one who knew the truth and truly understood. The only one who knew her secrets and her darkest shame.

"Together forever," she murmured beneath her breath.

The phone buzzed, sending a jolt through her fingers.

Without thinking about it, Sian clicked through to the message and scanned the screen.

Bile raced up the back of her throat.

"You deserve to rot in hell for what you did to him, you fucking bitch!!!"

Sian's hands shook so badly she dropped the phone onto the coverlet. How could they all think she was the one responsible for his death?

Aidan had committed suicide.

The phone let go another plaintive bleep and the message that flashed on the screen this time left Sian in no doubt as to the depths of her so-called friends' hatred.

"You should kill yourself, Slag!"

Closing her eyes, she drew her knees to her chest and wrapped her arms around her legs. Gently, she rocked back and forth on the bed.

It wasn't fair. She wasn't the cause of this. She hadn't done anything wrong. The lies they'd made up about her were just that—twisted and bitter lies. She loved Aidan—would never cheat on him.

"Please just stop," she whispered under her breath as another message slithered through.

Sian opened her eyes and peered down at the phone screen.

The snapchat icon bore Aidan's name and Sian's heart stalled in her chest.

"I'll always be here for you."

It wasn't possible. He was dead. He couldn't be sending her messages.

"I love you. Together forever."

She scooped the phone up and replayed the message. It couldn't be Aidan...

Creak.

The noise was closer, practically outside her bedroom door. Sian would have known the sound anywhere. It haunted her waking hours and kept her from sleeping most nights. She'd lain beneath the bedcover she was currently perched on top of enough nights and listened to that noise.

Fear wrapped icy fingers around her heart.

"Aidan, is that you?" The moment the words left her mouth, she felt stupid. Aidan was gone.

She glanced down at the phone but it had fallen silent. The messages he'd sent were gone. But hope made her brave as she slid to the edge of the bed.

Silence swept back in around her. *He* wasn't here and she was just imagining the noise.

She had to be.

Sucking in a deep breath, Sian pushed up from the bed and crossed to the bedroom door. Steeling her resolve, she jerked the door open and peered out into the darkened hall.

Nothing.

The landing was empty. Stepping out into the hall, she scanned the staircase and found none of the imagined horrors waiting for her there.

"Hello?"

The house tossed her voice back to her in the form of an echo. Even that mocked her. Drawing her courage around her like a mantle, Sian moved to the top of the stairs. The house really *was* empty; her mind was just creating scenarios that would bring Aidan back to life again.

Retreating back to the safety of her bed, Sian sat on the edge of the mattress and picked up her can of pop. The fizzy liquid slid down her throat causing her to cough. She finished the drink and slipped fully clothed beneath the bedsheets and tugged them over her head.

Her tongue tingled with the remnants of the bubbles.

At least the other messages had slowed to a trickle.

Sian watched the fading afternoon light drift across the floor as her body grew heavy. She couldn't even pull a sickie in the morning. Nigel would be here all day and the last thing Sian wanted was to spend the day alone with him. It would simply be the icing on an already shitty cake.

Not that she had any intention of going into school either. Facing the music wasn't her jam. No instead, she would go to their place. Their hideaway from the world. And it was there she would stay until this all blew over.

Satisfied with her plan, Sian ignored the creaking of the house and pulled her locket from inside her shirt. Popping it open, she stared down at the small image of Aidan she kept there—always closest to her heart.

Tears soaked into the pillow beneath her cheek, their salty taste coating her tongue as she closed her eyes. Perhaps if she slept, she would see Aidan again. If they couldn't be together in this life, then at the very least they could be together when she slept.

AIDAN SWUNG HER AROUND, his arms tight on her waist as he smiled down at her. There was a sharp sting in her neck, reminding her of a bee-sting she'd experienced as a child. She jolted in his arms but Aidan continued to smile at her, seemingly oblivious to the pain she'd felt.

When she awoke, the pillow was damp and cold beneath her face from the tears she'd shed in her sleep. Sian fumbled to draw the quilt back over her frozen limbs but her fingers lay frozen next to her face. She tried to stretch her cramped legs out toward the end of the bed but there was no response.

Fear gripped her heart as she realised she was no longer alone in the dark.

The soft murmur of voices from downstairs

caught her ear and Sian tried to open her mouth and found herself unable to. She willed her body to move but nothing happened.

As she lay on the bed with her eyes half-lidded, she watched the shadowy shape of something move softly around her private domain.

The shape picked up one of her teddy bears from the dresser where she kept them stacked, turning it over in the half-light that crept in through the blinds. Sian's eyes slid shut. Her throat was dry, and her head was beginning to pound.

"Just wake up."

Willing her eyes to open, she was pleased to find her eyelids at least obeyed. The figure melted from the darkness and crept toward the bed.

It was a nightmare. It had to be.

It was residual trauma after everything that happened.

Were the monsters beneath the bed real after all?

It was all nonsense but Sian struggled to make sense of what was happening. Her mind, as well as her body, was sluggish and refused to cooperate.

She fought to send the signals to her arms and legs to move but there was no response. Despite the fog clouding her judgement, Sian was acutely aware of how exposed she was without a quilt to hide beneath.

"Please, just wake up."

The monster crossed the room and crouched

down next to her. She tried to cringe away as a gloved hand came out of the darkness and brushed over her hair, pushing it out of her face.

Footsteps on the stairs. The shadows froze.

Sian's eyes drifted closed of their own volition and she struggled to open them again.

Creak.

The same floorboard she'd heard earlier. Only this time, she knew who had paused outside her bedroom door.

Sian could imagine her mother standing there. They shared the same blonde hair and blue eyes.

The weight of the duvet slipped over her icy body and the stranger tucked it up around her chin, careful to ensure she could breathe.

Sian's tongue stuck to the roof of her mouth as she struggled to cry for help. If her mother would just come in, if she would just push open the door, she would know something was wrong.

But Sian knew she wouldn't.

They'd argued about it often enough. In her mind, Sian could hear her words echoing back to mock her.

"Can't I have any privacy in this house?"

There was a soft knock on the door and Sian's heartbeat hammered against her ribcage. Her lips felt as though they were glued together—vocal cords petrified—the only sound that slipped out was a low moan. But it wasn't enough.

"Sian, it's Mum. Do you want to come down for some dinner?"

In her head, Sian was screaming but her useless body refused to cooperate. Her mother wouldn't come in and for the first time in her teenaged life, Sian wished she would ignore her commands to respect her privacy and throw the door wide open.

She wanted to thrash and scream, anything that would raise the alarm.

"Please, Mum! Please!"

There was a pause and Sian felt her hope rise. The floorboard outside her room creaked again as her mother's weight shifted.

"Please, Mum, just come in."

"All right then, love, I'll leave something for you in the microwave in case you get hungry later."

Sian's fingers spasmed against the bedcovers as her mother's footsteps receded back down the stairs, leaving her alone in the dark with the shadow.

Footsteps scuffed over the soft carpet and the sound of excited breathing caught Sian's ears. The mattress dipped as the monster sat on the edge of it.

Closing her eyes, she willed it to leave.

Leather gloved fingers brushed against her cheek.

"Good girl." The voice was gruff, breath moist against her cheek as the monster leaned over her. "It'll be over soon. And then it won't hurt anymore. It's what you want isn't it?" It paused as though expecting an answer and in the half-light through the blinds Sian watched it cock its hood-covered head to the side as though it were listening to something only it could hear.

"I'll make it all better. I won't let him hurt you anymore. I'll take the pain away. Just like I made Aidan's pain disappear."

Terror gripped Sian as the meaning of the words sank in. It turned her limbs to jelly and a tremor started up in her body.

Aidan.

Aidan had committed suicide. Hadn't he?

The monster lay down on the bed next to her, wrapping its arms awkwardly around her body, pinning her beneath the duvet.

Flashes of memory made her think of Nigel and his excitement in the dark.

Breath moist on her cheek, the weight of his body holding her down. His whispered platitudes and threats in the dark.

Who would believe her?

There had been a time when Sian had welcomed the safety of her bed. When she had loved the weight of her quilt as she curled up beneath it.

But not now.

Now it was a tomb and as she lay in the dark, tears trickled down her cheeks and into her ears.

She was trapped.

The monster had killed Aidan.

There was something terribly defeating in her

thoughts as they swirled in her head. The knowledge that someone as strong as Aidan couldn't prevail against the monster who now lay in her bed was crippling. If he couldn't stop the inevitable. Then what chance did she have?

Because in the dark she was at the monster's mercy.

Sian knew where that kind of mercy would take her and she was helpless to stop it.

CHAPTER TWO

DETECTIVE INSPECTOR DREW HASKELL propped his elbows on the roof of his BMW and buried his face in his hands.

Suicide.

The word tasted of bitter ashes in his mouth. He was only too familiar with the pain and confusion that followed such an act. That was the problem with gaining first-hand knowledge of something.

Pushing his emotions aside, Drew straightened up and scrubbed his hand over his mouth. The days-old stubble prickled beneath his palm and he sighed. There would be no getting home early for a wash and a quick kip.

He glanced over in the direction of the back garden as the SOCO's with their large cases headed around the side of the two-storey white rendered house.

It looked so ordinary, so unsuspecting. He'd practically driven past the place when he'd gotten the call.

Death was a normal part of life. The job had taught him that long ago. But suicide was different. There was no rhyme nor reason to it. The convoluted inner workings of the human mind were a mystery to him at the best of times but when you added a suicide into the equation it left him feeling utterly at sea.

Just what could be so terrible about their lives that they felt the need to end them? When you were a teenager you had your whole life ahead of you. You'd barely scratched the surface of living at the tender age of fourteen.

It was a question he'd asked himself more than once.

The senseless death of one teenager was one too many as far as he was concerned. But to find himself called out to the third one in so many months was too much. There was something going on here but he was damned if he knew what it was. And if there was one thing Drew hated, it was feeling like he was out of the loop on something vital.

He'd known the moment he'd received the call exactly what would await his arrival.

The muffled scream of anguish that rose from the house sent a shiver down his spine. Christ, if he had to look into the face of one more set of parents as he questioned them about their child's state of mind, he was going to scream himself.

"Sir, should we go in?" The softly spoken uniformed officer that paused next to him fidgeted nervously. Clearly Drew wasn't the only one who didn't want to step inside the front door.

He sucked in a deep breath and squared his shoulders. Standing around out here like a plonker wasn't going to make going in the house any easier.

"Give me a minute, would you?" he said, making up his mind to head around the back of the dwelling. If he was going to talk to the parents, then the least he could do was see what they had seen.

The path that led down the side of the house opened up into a wide-lawned garden at the rear of the property. Drew had the sneaking suspicion that in the summertime the place would be a veritable paradise, with the tall ash trees that lined the back wall of the space lending pools of dappled shade.

But the brisk autumn wind that tunnelled at his back now had ripped most of the leaves from the trees and left them discarded like yesterday's rubbish across the neatly mown grass. Drew's gaze was drawn inextricably toward the trees, their thin skeletal branches reaching toward the grey sky like the long fingered limbs of a monstrous creature.

And it was there he saw her, body stretched out

on the grass beneath the trees. Her skin was the unnatural colour that came from death and even from this distance he could see the evidence of petechial haemorrhaging. Her tongue was clamped between her teeth. Blood and foam had dried to her chin and lips. Drew tore his horrified gaze away from her but not before his eyes slid over the deep furrow —so purple it was practically black—around her delicate throat. From the corner of his vision, he spotted the frayed rope that had been ripped from her throat and tossed aside.

Only those who were truly desperate would ever subject themselves to such a torturous end. But she was just a child. What could have been so terrible in her life that this had become the answer to her problems?

Ducking his gaze away, Drew turned to the find the uniformed officer hovering near the corner of the house.

Shaking his head, he moved back toward the front. "We should go in now."

"Why go back there?" The female officer asked.

"Crandell isn't it?" he asked, his voice as weary as he felt.

"Yes, sir."

"I went back there because if I'm going to face that girl's parents, then I need to do it on an equal footing."

She creased her brow. "I don't understand."

"They called the ambulance this morning, correct?" he said.

She nodded.

"So they found their daughter out there. The rope isn't around her neck anymore, so my best guess is they cut her down and tried CPR on her. I can't begin to imagine the horror they faced finding her like that. The least I can do when I go in there is have a working knowledge of their daughter's end. That way I can fill in some of the blanks without forcing them to relive that torture in minute detail."

"Isn't that wrong?"

"What's wrong here is that a young girl is dead. Took her own life and hung herself in her own yard. As far as I'm concerned that's wrong. Everything else is just a matter of form, Officer Crandell."

She blushed, a becoming shade of red that spread all the way up into her blonde roots.

"Sorry, Sir, didn't mean to question you."

Drew shrugged it off. Everyone was on edge, there was no point in adding fuel to the fire by carrying the argument on.

"Let's just get this over with, shall we?"

She nodded and lead the way back to the front of the house.

Pausing on the front porch, Drew took one last deep breath of fresh air.

"Once more unto the breach," he muttered beneath his breath, drawing a speculative glance from the young female officer who had paused next to him.

That's great, Drew, have the uniforms add mentally disturbed to their laundry list of problems they've got with you. He smiled tightly at the officer and gestured her to head inside.

CHAPTER THREE

THE INCESSANT SHRILL ringing pulled Harriet Quinn from her thoughts. Tilting her head to the side, she let the sound wash over her as she struggled to pinpoint just what she was hearing.

It took a couple of seconds for the penny to drop and when it did she scrambled through the pile of academic paperwork spread out over her living room floor.

"Crap, crap," she swore violently as she slipped on an errant page on patient behaviour. At the last second, she managed to catch herself and she narrowly avoided doing the splits between her coffee table and the couch. It had been a long time since she'd been flexible enough to do something as demanding as that and she winced as her sudden movement tweaked a muscle inside her groin.

Banging out through the living room door, she

made it into the kitchen in time to hear the answering machine kick in.

"Hi, Harri, it's me. Just giving you a quick buzz to see how you're getting on. I'm hoping you're really out on a hot date and not on the couch with your head stuck in a musty old book. Anyway I—"

Harriet scooped the receiver up from the cradle and dropped down onto the chrome stool next to her breakfast counter. Considering she'd been living here for three years and she hadn't yet had breakfast at the counter could she really in good conscience call it a breakfast bar? She eyed the stack of psychology books piled neatly in the corner.

"I'm here," she said, her voice a little more breathless than she was comfortable with and she found herself wondering when she'd last been to the gym. Was it one month, or two? Not that spending forty minutes huffing and puffing away on a treadmill was conducive to fitness. Not when she spent so many hours with her head buried in a book.

"Damn, and here was me thinking you'd finally got sense and went out with one of those guys hankering after you from the college."

Harriet rolled her eyes, despite knowing Bianca couldn't actually see her.

"Nobody is hankering after me. Or at least not for a very long time."

"You don't sound too broken up about it," Bianca said, sounding a little worried. "Please don't tell me you've turned into one of those oddball feminists who see all men as the enemy."

Harriet smothered that bubble of laughter that poured out of her.

"No, that's not what's happened. I just don't have the time for dating right now. I've got two papers that need to be delivered in the next three months and I still have to correct the midterm papers for my students."

Bianca's laborious sigh travelled down the length of the telephone line and tugged a rueful smile from Harriet. Despite being best friends, they really couldn't have been more different if they tried. But then what was that old saying? Opposites attract and all that.

"How's Tilly getting on?" Harriet asked, changing the subject as quickly as possible.

Bianca took the bait without realising and Harriet sank into the familiar warmth of her friend's voice as she sang her daughter's praises.

"Sounds like you've got a budding prodigy on your hands there," Harriet said not unkindly as Bianca finished telling her about Tilly's latest piano recital.

"You're just jealous you haven't got one of your own." Bianca's laughter softened the sting in her words. "Anyway, there's something I didn't tell you." There was a sudden coyness to her friend's voice that piqued Harriet's curiosity.

"Give me a sec," Harriet said, pushing up from her seat at the counter. She crossed to the fridge and pulled a half full bottle of white wine from her fridge. Taking a glass from the cupboard above her microwave, she poured herself a hefty glass before retreating to the living room again.

"Let me guess, Australian Chardonnay?" Bianca said.

"Actually, it's a Pinot Grigio tonight," Harriet said. "Aldi had an offer on." She clicked the phone over to loudspeaker and Bianca's laughter filled the room. It was almost like having her here... almost.

"Go on, what's this big secret you want to tell me?"

"It's not a secret and it's not big."

"Could have fooled me with the way you've set this thing up. It better be good now or I've wasted this wine on nothing."

Bianca sighed. "I think I've met someone."

The words hung in the air and Harriet did her best to suppress her joy. Ever since Tom had died, Bianca had become the skittish type when it came to the idea of dating anyone else. On one drunken, tear-filled occasion she had confessed to Harriet that she felt the idea of starting a relationship with someone new was too much like cheating on Tom. No amount of persuasion on the matter had convinced her other-wise and Harriet had resigned herself to the idea that Bianca was perhaps the type to forever cut herself off from experiencing the happiness Tom would have wanted for her.

"I'm listening," Harriet said warily.

"Don't be like that, Harri," Bianca said, more than a little defensively.

"Like what?"

"Like you're talking to a fragile patient. For tonight I just need you to be my mate. Be normal, like it used to be."

Harriet took a gulp of the acidic wine and winced as she swallowed. Whether Bianca realised it or not, there were times when her words cut like a razor.

"So, who is he?"

"You don't know him. His name is Ryder and we met online."

Harriet sat up a little straighter as she folded her legs up beneath her so she was in semi-lotus. "But you have met him though, right?"

"We're going to meet this weekend and—"

"Wait, you've met some stranger online and you haven't even met him in person yet?"

"He's not some weirdo if that's what you're worried about. He's a business man from Notting-ham, he's single and—"

"I can come up this weekend if you want a bit of back-up."

"I don't need you to hold my hand, Harri. I'm an adult. I can go on a date by myself."

"That's not what I meant it's just—"

"Look, I know the kind of people you study but not everybody is out to hurt someone else. Some people are just good, normal types who are trying to make a connection."

Bianca had a point; not everyone was out to harm another human being—psychopaths only made up one percent of the population—but there was a huge difference in meeting someone face to face, getting a feel for them in person, versus getting to know the avatar of someone hiding behind a computer screen.

"And I'm not saying that this Ryder isn't one of those normal people," Harriet said, choosing her words carefully. "But I want you to be safe. Is that so terrible?"

Bianca sighed. "I guess not."

"When are you meeting him?"

"Saturday night."

"Then I'll drive up Saturday morning. If you want me to, that is..."

"Fine, Mom," Bianca moaned but there was an edge of laughter in her voice.

"Did he send you a picture?" Harriet asked, as some of the tension that had been building between her shoulder blades slowly loosened.

"I've sent it to your email."

Harriet reached over and set her wine glass down before she snagged her laptop from the coffee table. A couple of clicks later and she tapped her nails impatiently against the edge of the laptop as she waited for the picture to download.

When it did, she was confronted with a handsome man. If she had to guess she'd have said he was in his thirties although with the advancements in men's skincare regimes it was possible that he was older and just took care of his appearance.

"So, what do you think?" Bianca actually sounded nervous and Harriet felt a swell of empathy for her best friend.

The man in the photograph was the complete opposite of Tom. Where Bianca's late husband had been dark haired, and had a gentle kindness to his features, Ryder's hair was fair and cropped short and his expression was a little more severe. In the picture he sported a smattering of designer stubble across his sharp jawline. His aquiline nose was enough to prevent him from being model perfect.

But it was his eyes that truly caught Harriet's attention. They were so dark they looked almost navy blue and they lent themselves to an almost penetrating gaze. Harriet found herself wondering if perhaps it was just the poor quality of the camera which had taken the picture or if whether his eyes truly were so dark.

"He looks handsome," Harriet said, choosing to play it safe. It wasn't uncommon for those who were grieving to completely change their taste in partner and who was she to pass judgement on

Bianca's newfound taste for austere and cruel-looking men?

If she had been the superstitious type, she might have thought it was an ill omen but as it was, Harriet didn't hold much store in superstitions. To her they belonged to those whose anxiety made them paranoid about the world they lived in. A superstition at the end of the day was just a left-over emotion from a time when our ancestors still believed in magic, much like a vestigial tail or an appendix.

"You don't like him, do you?"

"I never said that." As much as she wanted to keep her resentment in check, Harriet found a little more of the emotion than she was entirely comfortable with slipping into her voice.

"Come on, Harri, how long have we been friends? I know you better than you know yourself and there's something about Ryder you don't like so why don't you do us both a favour and spit it out?"

Harriet sighed. Every alarm bell in her mind ringing she opted to buy herself a little more time. Reaching over the arm of the sofa she grabbed her glass and took a large mouthful. The wrong answer here and she would do untold damage to Bianca's fragile ego. If she tried to fabricate the truth, Bianca would know. It was a catch-22.

"I do think he's very handsome."

"But?"

"But I think you were right earlier when you said

that the work I do clouds my judgement on the world. It's not easy for someone like me to just let all that go."

"Well what can you possibly know about him just by looking at his photograph?"

Harriet shrugged and caught herself; Bianca couldn't see her gestures down a telephone line.

"Honestly, I can't tell anything from it." And it was the truth. Physiognomy had been pretty much debunked as little more than a pseudoscience a number of years ago. "I think my job has made me overly cautious and that's not a bad thing."

It was the other woman's turn to sigh. "I know you're right. Maybe I'm rushing into all of this. I mean Tom hasn't been gone that long..."

"Five years is not an insignificant amount of time."

"But it's longer than we were even together. If I'm honest I feel a little stupid. You hear about all of these couples who have been together for decades and then there's Tom and me and we only got five years."

"But they were five good years."

Bianca went silent on the other end of the line and Harriet glanced down at the screen of the phone to make sure the line was still active.

"You know it's not fair."

"I know it's not."

"We were supposed to be together forever. We

deserved more time."

"You did."

Bianca sniffed and Harriet found herself wishing that she wasn't separated from her friend by so many miles. At least if they were in the same room together, she would be able to wrap her arms around her friend's shoulders and give her the hug she needed right now.

"I'm sorry," Bianca said, her voice gruff with unshed tears.

"You've got nothing to be sorry for, you're grieving and there's nothing wrong with that. You're allowed to, whether you believe that or not."

"I do believe it," she said, although Harriet found herself wondering just how much she truly meant it.

"And if you think you're ready to move forward—not on—just forward. Then I'm behind you one hundred percent."

"Thanks," Bianca said. "I think I needed to hear that."

"You know I'm always here for whatever you might need, right?"

"I know that."

The silence stretched out between them and Harriet found herself wanting to say something more. Something more concrete. But she couldn't think of anything that would help her friend to come to terms with everything she was going through.

"I suppose I've taken up enough of your time,"

Bianca said, breaking the silence before Harriet could gather her thoughts together.

"You're not taking up my time, I—"

"It's fine, Harri, I need to go anyway. Got to be up early in the morning for Tilly's swimming lesson."

"Of course, give her my love."

"I will." There was another awkward beat. "You don't have to come up at the weekend you know."

"I know I don't have to," Harriet said. "I want to."

"Well if you're sure."

"I am."

"I'll see you then." Before Harriet could say goodbye Bianca ended the call, leaving her to sit there in silence.

Ever since Tom, Bianca hadn't been able to bring herself to actually say goodbye to anyone on the phone. Just another nod to the many phases of the grieving process she was going through.

Pulling her laptop back onto her knees, Harriet studied the photograph of Ryder a little longer. It was definitely just paranoia, she decided as she slammed the lid shut, cutting herself off from his austere glare. Saturday would come and Bianca would go out with him and everything would be totally fine. Really, she was worrying about nothing at all and come Sunday morning she would look back at all of this and smile.

Draining her glass of wine, Harriet found herself wishing Sunday morning would hurry up and arrive if only so she could feel like a complete fool.

CHAPTER FOUR

HE STARED down at the locket and turned it over in his hands. Sian hadn't wanted to part with it, he'd seen it in her eyes as he'd plucked the necklace from her throat. But she didn't need it anymore.

He closed his eyes and thought back to the moment she had succumbed. Such sweet bliss to watch her slip away. She hadn't fought as much as the other two and he found himself wondering if perhaps he'd given her too much sedative. It was important to get the dosage just right. Too much and they wouldn't know what was happening and then how would he know it was the right thing?

No. Perhaps it was time to changes things. The sedative had worked well on the others but for the next one he would use something else. She would know what was happening. She would consent in the end and he would watch as her light faded and she was free of this world.

After all, he wasn't a monster.

CHAPTER FIVE

BALANCING her notes in a precarious pile, Harriet pushed backwards through the swing doors that led to her office. From the corner of her eye, she spotted Mrs Martha Metcalf—her secretary—clicking out of the shared works calendar.

"Have I got an appointment this morning?"

"Actually, you've had a phone call."

"A phone call from whom?"

"The police actually."

The brisk tone of her secretary made Harriet jump and the pile of papers she'd so carefully managed to carry into the building scattered across the tile floor.

Swearing beneath her breath, she bent down to scoop them all into a heap as Martha stood and observed from the edge of her desk.

Harriet didn't bother glancing up at the older

woman; she already knew the censorious expression she wore. It was the same thing every morning. Harriet had asked her once if perhaps the reason she disliked working for her was because she resented her the position she'd managed to attain at the university. The question had gone down much as Harriet had suspected it would—in fact a lead balloon would have gone down easier—but it had confirmed at least some of her suspicions about the other woman.

Harriet tried to pull the notes together into some semblance of what they had been before she'd dumped them across the parquet flooring.

"Did they say what they wanted with me?" Harriet paused her rearranging of papers long enough to glance up in Martha's direction.

"No. Just that they wanted to speak to you as a matter of some urgency." There was an air of triumph in Martha's voice, as though she honestly believed the police had finally caught up to her for all her wrongdoing down through the years in the university. From what Harriet had seen of her reactions, the woman had a terrible tendency to equate misuse of a copier machine with murder.

As she spoke, Martha shifted back in behind her desk and proceeded to pick her coffee mug up from the almost empty workspace. "And now that you're here, I'm going to head out on my break."

Pursing her lips, Harriet kept her thoughts to

herself. It was easier not to make a fuss and anyway the older woman would only spend her time trying to eavesdrop on the conversation Harriet was about to have with the police. Definitely much easier to let her go on her break and have a little peace and quiet in the office.

Straightening up, she hurried into her small office space and dumped the papers down on her desk. The surface of which was the complete antithesis to Martha's. Harriet had often found herself wondering if perhaps the reason her desk was so messy was a small subconscious protest against her secretary. She certainly didn't remember being so untidy before Martha arrived.

She watched through the half open door as Martha slipped into her heavy outer coat. Was it her imagination or was the other woman deliberately taking her time?

"I'll be off then," Martha called out as she took a tentative step toward Harriet's office.

She didn't usually announce when she was going. Martha was definitely more the swan off without a word type.

"Fine."

Martha hesitated, shuffling from one foot to the other in the doorway. If she waited long enough, Martha would reveal her true intentions.

"Do you want me to call them back for you?"

Bingo!

Harriet sighed. Martha was never this helpful. She was definitely loitering in the hopes of hearing something she shouldn't.

"I can manage, thanks," Harriet said, meeting Martha in the doorway.

The older woman nodded briskly but made no immediate move to leave. "I've got the number here," she said, indicating her sparse desk.

Harriet glanced down at the desk and spotted the small yellow sticky note that rested on the edge of the computer screen.

"Enjoy your break," Harriet said, hoping her prompt would sink in.

"I could just call them up for you," Martha said, snatching the note up into her hand and holding it possessively against her chest as though it were a small child in need of protection and not a sticky note.

"It's fine, Martha, I'm more than capable of dialling a number myself. Thank you." Harriet held her hand out, palm up expectantly.

Martha startled and glanced guiltily at the floor as though she knew she'd been caught out.

"Oh, all right then," she said bitterly, dropping the note reluctantly into Harriet's hand before she finally moved toward the door.

Harriet waited until she was sure the other woman really had left. She certainly wouldn't have put it past her to sneak back in under the pretense of having forgotten something vital.

Satisfied, Harriet retreated to her inner sanctuary and shut the door, closing out the rest of the world.

Glancing down at Martha's spider-like scrawl, she drew in a deep soothing breath. The last time she'd had any interaction with the police it had ended in disaster. Her type weren't always the most welcome when it came to an investigation.

"This is completely different, Harriet. Stop fretting." Closing her eyes, she pressed her head back against the door. "Just get it over with."

Pushing away from the door, she crossed the floor quickly and snatched the phone up from its receiver before she had the chance to change her mind or find some excuse to put off the inevitable.

Dialling the number, she waited as the line buzzed and then began to ring.

After a couple of rings, the line clicked and she held her breath but instead of getting to talk to a human being, Harriet listened as the robotic voice of the voice mail kicked in and informed her the message box was full.

With a disgruntled sigh, she hung up and drummed her fingers against the wooden top of her office desk. At least whatever it was about, it couldn't have been important, if it had then she wouldn't have been met with a full voice mail box.

Relief washed over her as she turned and

dropped into the chair behind her desk. The old chair squeaked in protest but Harriet ignored it. She'd tried. There was nothing else she could do now. The excuse sounded feeble even to her. It would be very easy to keep trying the number but deep down she knew she wasn't going to do that. Not with everything that happened in the past.

No. If it were truly important, then they would call her back and until then she had more than enough work here to occupy her mind.

Firing up her computer, Harriet pulled up her weekly calendar and groaned as she realised she was already late for the quarterly review with Dr Baig. Just another fantastic start to a Monday morning.

Grabbing her bag from the floor, she pushed to her feet and hurried for the door.

She was already in the corridor when her phone began to ring. Glancing down at her watch, Harriet made a snap decision to ignore it. She was already late and whoever was on the other end of the line could wait.

CHAPTER SIX

"DI HASKELL, have we got a decision on the case yet?" Superintendent Burroughs paused next to the desk. From his position, Drew could see the wrinkled look of distaste on the other man's face as his gaze slid over Drew's desk. Some might consider it to be nothing but chaos but for Drew it was anything but. He knew exactly where everything was. Without glancing down, he snaked his hand out and scooped up the beige case file from beneath an empty, coffee-stained mug.

"Gods, man, the place looks like a dump. Can't you clean it up?" Burroughs asked, this time not bothering to hide his disgust as he eyed the grimy mug Drew set aside.

"That is tidy, sir," DS Arya said from the other side of the overcrowded office space.

"I don't need your help, Maz, cheers," Drew said

gruffly. He ignored the speculative look Burroughs gave him as he flipped open the file and presented the coroner's findings.

"As far as the autopsy is concerned, it's a suicide just like the other three."

"And you've informed the family of this?" Burroughs' clipped tone grated on Drew's last nerve.

"I have, sir. And I've shared the resources available to them but, sir—"

Burroughs nodded. "Good, good." He cut Drew off and began to move away.

"Sir, I'm really not happy with—"

"What was that?" Burroughs snapped turning back.

From the corner of his eye, Drew spotted Maz shaking his head but when Burroughs cast a cursory glance in the other DS's direction, Maz dropped his gaze, pretending to study the report in front of him as though it contained the secrets to the universe.

"I'm not really happy with declaring this a suicide. To be honest I'm not really happy to declare any of them suicides."

Burroughs folded his arms. "And why is that?" There was an edge to the older Superintendent's voice that set warning bells off in Drew's head but it was now or never. He'd already shared his discomfort with his DCI only to get shot down in flames there too. At this point--as far as Drew was concerned--he had nothing left to lose.

"Sir, three suicides in as many months is a little much for such a small area and—"

"And that's why it's such a tragedy, lad," Burroughs said, interrupting again.

Drew sighed and scrubbed his hands up over his face. He hadn't bothered to shave. In fact, he couldn't remember the last time he'd had a proper shower, never mind having the luxury of a shave too. Overworked and understaffed was the motto they seemed to labour under.

"With all due respect, Sir," Drew said, trying to keep the irritation in his voice to an absolute minimum. "I don't think you're hearing what I'm trying to say."

"Spit it out then, man. I don't have all day."

"I think these cases need investigating."

Superintendent Burroughs sighed. "These aren't cases that need looking into. They're tragedies, plain and simple, Detective. Don't you think the families of these youngsters have been through quite enough already without dragging them through the horror of a full-on enquiry?"

"Well, of course, but if it were me, I'd want to know."

"Lucky for them then, it's not your call. I won't authorise an investigation into a senseless tragedy, Detective, and that is final."

"But Sir—"

Burroughs fixed him with a glare and Drew fell

silent. He was already skating on thin ice after his last case went tits up. If he kept pushing now, he was only going to find himself in more shit than he could swim through.

"Of course, Sir," he said, balling his hands into fists at his sides.

Burroughs glanced down at his fisted hands and quirked an eyebrow in his direction before he moved off.

Letting out the breath he'd been holding onto, Drew dropped into his creaky office chair and closed his eyes.

"You were pushing it there, mate," Maz said.

"Don't see that I've got a choice. Anything less is just failing them." There was a heaviness in Drew's chest and he sucked down a deep breath in an attempt to dispel the uncomfortable sensation. Not that it did much good. It wasn't a feeling he could just shake off and even if he could, he wasn't entirely sure he would want to because that would mean he'd let go.

"Penny for your thoughts," Maz said, cutting through the sentimental track his thoughts had taken with the ease of a knife.

"They're not worth a penny," Drew said, pushing up onto his feet. The desire to move, to work, to do the one thing he was good at was almost overwhelming and he knew from past experience that if he stayed cooped up in the office for much longer, he would only end up causing some kind of clusterfuck.

"Haskell!" The shout went up from Detective Chief Inspector Gregson's office as he slipped his arms into the sleeves of his khaki overcoat.

"Shit! Tell him I've already gone," Drew said to Maz as he grabbed his car keys from the drawer in his battered desk.

"Too late for that, mate." Maz inclined his head in the direction of the DCI's office and Drew felt the telltale prickle of being watched slide down his spine. "The Monk has already spotted you."

The Monk was their own little pet name for DCI Gregson. No one really knew where it had come from as such, just that one day everyone seemed to refer to him with that moniker behind his back as though the name had suddenly crept into the zeitgeist and they'd all taken it up by osmosis or perhaps hypnotic suggestion. Drew had his own theories on where it had come from; the fact that the other man was rapidly going bald being one of the more obvious reasons for the name. And then there was his recent divorce. For a time, it had seemed that the DCI would live up to his new name. But that had been blown when one of the guys from the arts and antiquities squad had spotted the DCI out and about with a woman who appeared to be at least fifteen years his junior.

Of course, that knowledge had made the name

even funnier, not that Gregson would see the entertainment in it if he got wind of them using the name.

"In here, Haskell. Now." There was no arguing with the tone the Detective Chief Inspector was using.

Dumping the coat back onto his swivel chair, Drew headed in the direction of his superior's office. Sometimes it felt like he was nothing more than an errant and naughty schoolboy and not a senior member of Her Majesty's police force.

"Yes, sir?" It was an effort to keep his voice suitably level and neutral as the scent of the DCI's aftershave wafted toward him. Some sort of cheap musky scent that threatened to make his eyes water.

"Shut the door." The DCI's Baltic tone could have frozen the brass balls off a monkey. Christ, closing the door and trapping the lingering odour of the chemist's finest aftershave in here with them was going to make it feel like he was shut in with a teenage boy and not a middle-aged man.

Drew felt the tension in the air begin to climb as the door slid shut with a click. He hadn't even fully turned around when the DCI finally exploded.

"Just who the fuck do you think you are going behind my back and undermining me to a superior officer?"

"I didn't think I was undermining you, sir. I was just trying to get a second opinion is all." He was skating close to the wire and he knew it. And from the apoplectic expression on DCI Gregson's face he knew it too.

"A second opinion? The only opinion you should be concerned with around here is mine and I thought I made myself clear? These are suicides, Haskell. I know it. The families know it. The whole fucking world knows it. The only one who doesn't seem to know it yet is you."

"Sir, I just—"

"I don't know if it's your past is clouding your judgement on this one but I need you to move past it."

His words were a bucket of icy water to Drew and his body reacted as though he'd been submerged in that frozen lake all over again. His shoulders stiffened and he sucked an audible breath in through his nose as the memories of that night—memories he had carefully packed away into the deep recesses of his mind—flooded his mind much the same way the water had flooded the car after it had left the road and plunged into the inky darkness.

A couple of seconds passed during which Drew struggled to shove the memories back into the iron lock box he'd stuffed them into. But like the air from a punctured tyre, somethings couldn't be put back, no matter how hard you tried or even wished for it.

"Are you even listening to me, Haskell?"

"Yes, sir," Drew said, the words forming because his mind clicked into autopilot.

"So, you agree to close the cases and be done with it?"

"I'll file the paperwork now."

Drew noted the way his DCI narrowed his eyes at him in suspicion and for a moment he wondered if perhaps the Monk was more perceptive than he led them all to believe.

"Good, I'm glad we got that sorted," DCI Gregson said, relief etched on his face as he dropped back into his seat. The fluorescent light from overhead reflected in his bald pate. Did he get up every morning and deliberately polish it, or was it some naturally occurring joke the universe had played on him? Drew fought the urge to ask him which one it happened to be but bit back the question as it hovered on the tip of his tongue. The last thing he needed to be doing right now was pissing off his superior any more than he already had.

Gregson turned his attention to the pile of paperwork neatly arranged on his desk and sighed.

"You're dismissed," he said, without bothering to glance up at Drew.

Drew made it as far as the door before Gregson's voice brought him up short.

"I expect to see those files on my desk later today," he said, the warning in his voice implicit.

"You have my word, sir." Drew had to practically force the words out. It felt as though his tongue had thickened in his mouth, making the formation of words almost impossible.

"I know this is hard for you," Gregson said, his tone softening as pity began to creep in. Drew found himself beginning to despise the other man—or was it the other way around? Did he despise himself because he was someone worthy of pity?

It wasn't a question he was willing to answer. At least not right now anyway and he buried the thought as far down in his mind as he could.

"This isn't hard, sir," Drew said, silently berating himself for the telltale strain that coloured his voice. "It's my job. Nothing more and nothing less." He yanked the door open, a little more forcefully than intended—before Gregson could say anything else to him—and it slapped against the plaster wall with an audible thud, drawing the attention of everyone else in the room beyond.

Drew kept his gaze trained on the rough brown carpet as he crossed to his desk and snatched his coat up before anyone else could find a reason to detain him.

"What did the Monk want?" Maz leaned over the desk toward him.

"Nothing." Drew snapped and immediately regretted it. It wasn't Maz's fault. Hell, if he was honest about it this wasn't even the Monk's fault, they were all just doing their bloody jobs. So if that were true, then why did he feel like he was failing?

"Your phone rang while you were in with the DCI," Maz said, his voice several degrees cooler than it had been just a moment before.

"Thanks, mate," Drew said, sliding his phone out. The number was instantly recognisable. He'd dialled it less than an hour ago.

Glancing in the direction of Gregson's office he made the decision there and then. The DCI might want the case wrapped up nice and tight and Drew was willing to give it to them if it truly was just a spate of tragic suicides. But the voice in the back of his mind refused to give up. Something about the whole case stunk to high heaven. The last time he'd ignored his gut instinct had brought him three years' worth of heartache and sleepless nights and he wasn't willing to go through all of that again. Not now, not ever.

"If the Monk is looking for me, tell him I had to chase something down."

"And you're really not going to tell me what all of this is about?"

"Later, but right now I've got to go." Drew hit redial and pressed the phone to his ear, as he scooped his car keys from the desk drawer.

"You owe me a pint," Maz grumbled.

"Keep the Monk off my case and I'll owe you two."

Rather than answer, Maz rolled his eyes and

returned his attention to the computer screen in front of him.

By the time Drew had made it to the main door of the office the call had rang out and the clipped tone of a woman had cut in to inform him that he had reached Harriet Quinn's office and he could leave a message if he so pleased.

Drew killed the call and slipped the phone back into his pocket.

He would go one better than leaving a useless message; he would pay Dr. Quinn a visit in person and perhaps she would have a better understanding of how he could put the case to rest once and for all.

CHAPTER SEVEN

"TILLY, GRAB YOUR SCHOOL BAG," Bianca called up the stairs and waited to hear the tell-tale sound of her daughter moving around.

When there was nothing, she set her coffee down on the counter and started up the stairs. She made it almost to the top and peered across the landing into her daughter's room. Tilly sat on the side of the bed with Gruff, her favourite teddy clutched in her small hands. As Bianca watched, Tilly leaned in close and spoke to the bear in hushed tones.

From her position on the stairs, Bianca was too far away to hear what her daughter was saying but she could already imagine it.

It would be the same thing Tilly said every morning. Her little ritual had gone on undisturbed almost from the day she had started in pre-school right up to now.

Gruff had been Tom's last present to Tilly before he died and while Tilly's memory of her father was hazy to say the least and she definitely didn't remember him giving her the gift there was still a bond forged between the two of them nonetheless and Bianca felt a familiar lump form in the back of her throat.

It was strange to think of Tom not being here. No matter how much time passed, it never changed the oddness of the situation. How could you go from being so vibrant and alive to suddenly gone? It didn't make sense and not for the first time, Bianca felt like the universe had played some kind of terrible karmic joke on her.

It had given her Tilly, only to take Tom.

They could have been happy together, that much she was sure of.

"Tilly, I said get your school bag, please," Bianca said, unable to keep the smile from her face as Tilly turned her large expressive dark eyes toward her.

"I was just telling Gruff that he needs to keep you safe today," Tilly said sincerely as she clutched Gruff to her chest.

"I don't think you need to tell, Gruff that," Bianca said. "He already knows, and he's done a pretty good job of it so far, hasn't he?"

Tilly cocked her head to the side and seemed to consider her mother's words very seriously before she nodded. "I suppose so..."

"We're going to be late if you don't get a wriggle on," Bianca said, glancing down at her fit-bit.

"Ok!" Tilly jumped up from the bed and darted out of sight, only to reappear a moment later with her school bag clutched in one hand and Gruff in the other.

"You know Gruff doesn't come with us on the school run," Bianca said.

"But he could—"

"Tilly, Gruff stays on your bed until you come home. Or we'll have the same problem we had last summer when he nearly got lost."

Just thinking about Tilly's heartbreak when her bear had been left behind on the train was enough to bring Bianca out in a cold-sweat.

Tilly nodded and set Gruff back down on the bed. "Sorry, Gruffy, mommy's right." Bianca watched with love as her almost too serious daughter pressed a small kiss to the side of the bear's cheek before she darted for the stairs.

"Have you got your swimming gear?" Bianca asked.

"Yup!"

"And your notebook for Mrs Callan?"

"Yup! When am I going to Nana's?" Tilly asked, pausing on the stairs.

"Wednesday night," Bianca said. "They're picking you up after school."

Tilly looked very serious. "And when am I

coming home again?"

"Thursday after school." Bianca gave her daughter a reassuring hug. "You like going to Nana and Grandad's, don't you?"

Tilly nodded and chewed her lip. "I do..."

"But?"

"But I wish you would come too."

Bianca grinned at her daughter. "But just think how good it'll be to come home to me on Thursday afternoon. We can make cookies and watch a movie together."

Tilly's serious expression faltered and was replaced by a wide smile. "Extra chocolate chips!"

"All the chocolate chips you could possibly want," Bianca said, feeling her daughter's infectious excitement spread to her.

Tilly hopped up and down on the stairs and only Bianca's steadying hand kept her from falling.

"Be careful, Tills," she said, despite the chastisement, her voice was gentle. Tilly stopped jumping and her expression turned deeply thoughtful again.

"You don't want to slip."

"If I fell would I end up like Daddy?"

It took Bianca a moment to recover. Tilly was a pretty serious child but she wasn't usually prone to asking such deeply philosophical questions, at least not a ten to eight in the morning.

"You'd get hurt and I'd be very upset."

"But would I die like Daddy did?"

"You might," Bianca said. The counsellor had said that honesty, in Tilly's case was definitely the right policy and so she hadn't kept anything from her daughter. Even when it had seemed impossible to talk about Tom's passing, she had forced herself to do it. Part of her had wondered on more than one occasion if it was the right thing after all?

"Will you die like daddy?"

Bianca shook her head. "I'm not going anywhere, Tills, you don't need to worry."

"But—"

"Tilly, what's brought all this on?"

Tilly looked down at the floor and scuffed the stair carpet. "Nothing..."

"You can tell me."

"I know," she said before she raised her head. "Can we have white chocolate chips too?"

Bianca let go the breath she'd been holding onto and smiled as she took her daughter's hand. "I'll pick some up before Thursday."

Tilly started to jump and then changed her mind at the last second. "Sorry, Mommy," she said. "I won't do it again."

"That's good." Bianca led her daughter down the stairs by the hand.

"I won't do it because I don't want you to be sad." There was such sincerity in her little daughter's voice that Bianca felt her heart constrict painfully in her chest. Life definitely wasn't fair.

As Tilly, pulled her coat on, Bianca's phone dinged in her pocket. She slid it out quickly and stared down at the text message on the screen.

"Hey, babe! How are you this morning?" Ryder's message instantly brought a smile to her face and she hastily tapped out a reply.

"Fine. Just about to do the school run. How are you?"

She grabbed her keys from the kitchen as the phone dinged a reply.

"Damn, I was thinking maybe you were still in bed." The words were followed by a salacious winky emoji and Bianca felt heat spread up into her face.

"Ready!" Tilly said from the hall as she tugged the front door open.

Bianca slipped the phone into her pocket and dived after her daughter, sweeping her up into her arms before she could escape outside.

"Let me go!" Tilly giggled, squirming violently in Bianca's arms.

"No, one last hug!" Bianca buried her face in against her daughter's neck and inhaled her warm familiar scent. There was something so terribly comforting about it and a sliver of fear slid down her spine as she thought of all the possibilities that could befall her.

Her world had changed drastically after Tom. They were supposed to be together forever and look how that had worked out. What if something happened to Tilly too?

Tilly's giggles dragged her black thoughts back from the destructive route they'd taken, and she pushed them aside. With one last kiss to her daughter's face, she let Tilly down and took her small hand on the walk to the car.

The phone in her pocket buzzed against her leg and the urge to check it was overwhelming. Was she mad? Here she was thinking about Tom and everything she'd lost when he'd died and in the same breath, she was thinking about the man at the other end of the text message chain.

Perhaps she hadn't deserved Tom after all?

Cut that out right now. She could almost hear the words spoken in Harriet's voice. During it all, Harri had been a rock upon which Bianca had built what little stability she had in her life. Without her help and guidance, she dared not think what state she might be in now.

It had been Harri who had helped pull her back from the brink of destruction after Tom's untimely death. Harri, who had pointed out to her that it wasn't about her, that Tilly needed her. Not that she hadn't known it but that was the problem with grief wasn't it? When you slipped into that black hole it was very difficult to see a way out, never mind see the others around you who were suffering too.

But with Harri's help she'd begun the difficult

climb back to some semblance of a life and the result was the man on the other end of the phone.

It probably wouldn't even work out with Ryder anyway, but it was a nice distraction all the same.

Bianca strapped Tilly into the car seat in the back and shut the door, leaving her daughter to read one of her many books that littered the rear of the car.

Before climbing into the car, she slipped the phone out and read the message, her heart skipping in her chest as she scanned the words.

"I can't wait to see you. Saturday can't come fast enough. Do you want me to book a hotel room?"

God, what a question? Did she want him to book a hotel room? The thought of hooking up with him, while thrilling also terrified her.

She pushed the phone back into her pocket and pulled open the driver's door. The hair on the back of her neck prickled as the sensation of being watched slid over her. Turning she scanned the street but found it reassuringly empty.

Don't be so daft. The Fitbit on her wrist buzzed and she glanced down at the time before she swore violently under her breath. There was no doubt about it, they were definitely going to be late now.

Hopping into the car, Harriet started the engine and reversed out onto the street, her thoughts completely consumed by what she should reply to Ryder.

CHAPTER EIGHT

HARRIET SAT behind the steering wheel of her compact Mini and tapped her fingers against the soft black leather. Just who the hell did Dr Baig think he was? What right did he have to tell her she was falling behind on her duties as a lecturer in the university?

Harriet knew the man had every right. As the head of her department it fell to Dr Dennis Baig to ensure everything ran smoothly. But that didn't change the fact that in this instance he was wrong. She wasn't falling behind on her workload and she hadn't actually missed any of the lectures on her schedule—despite his protestations to the contrary.

Granted, she had been a little pre-occupied and her classes had lacked some of the imagination of last semester's lectures but surely everyone was allowed to be a little off their game?

The rain drummed against the windscreen and with a sigh, Harriet reached over to the passenger seat and grabbed her navy-coloured rain mac. It wouldn't provide much protection against the elements but it was better than nothing.

Scooping up her leather briefcase, she pushed open the car door and launched herself into the driving rain. Within seconds she was soaked to the skin as she dashed across the carpark toward the front door of The Hermitage Hospital. Harriet's first introduction to the place had been when it was still operating under the name North York Moors Mental Asylum.

It was an imposing building on a good day but with the pewter-coloured storm clouds gathered over head and the heavy fog of rain that blurred the cement walls—which some foolish do-gooder had decided to paint a crisp white causing it to stand out in the landscape like some huge white elephant—it looked more like a prison than a hospital. Of course, there were those within the harsh cement walls who would have agreed with calling it a prison. And in a way, Harriet could understand their perspective. Anywhere that deprived you of your civil liberties—which demanded you give up your personal free-doms—was nothing more than a prison.

But Harriet had to concede there were those whose personal freedoms needed to be curtailed, for their own safety as well as the safety of those around them. Sometimes humans were incapable of conducting themselves within the bounds of a society. And it was those humans who usually wound up in places like this. As cruel as she might consider it to be, unless those people could be rehabilitated, this was the safest place they could be.

Pushing into the main reception, Harriet was greeted by the familiar scent of bleach and chlorine, a combination that didn't exactly lend itself to a peaceful environment. It had a tendency to irritate the soft tissues of the nose and lungs if you were exposed to it too often. It lent an air of the clinical to the surroundings, a constant reminder to the patients and visitors alike that this was nothing more than a hospital.

Harriet had tried to persuade the hospital board to change the cleaning products to something a little more gentle but her suggestions had been met with stony silence. She'd been informed that it was necessary for the health of staff and everyone else and that the toxic combination was a necessity to keep the infections and bacteria to a minimum. Harriet doubted that. From what she had seen, it all came back down to money; bleach and chlorine tablets were cheap.

"I see it's started raining then," Clara said from behind the reception desk. Harriet set her briefcase down on the floor. Water dripped from her coat onto the floor, causing small puddles to form beneath her as she pushed down her hood and fluffed her dark, shoulder length curly hair out.

"What gave you that impression?" she said wryly as she slipped the rain mac off and placed it over one arm before she retrieved her briefcase from its place on the wet tiles.

"I haven't been out since eleven and it hadn't started raining then." Clara glanced over at the screen in front of her and frowned. "Monday isn't usually your day. Is there something up?"

Harriet shook her head, sending a light dusting of water droplets down onto her shoulders. "I had a little free time and I thought I'd drop in."

Clara nodded sympathetically. "Well, she's currently in painting but if you want to head into the visitors room I'll get them to bring her up to you as soon as she's done."

Harriet smiled gratefully. "Thanks." She turned in time to see Dr Jonathan Connor buzzing out through the side door into the main reception area. His hair had that natural salt and pepper look that so many men craved and yet never achieved. The white coat he wore emphasised the natural glow from his tan and his brown corduroy slacks and pale blue dress shirt lent him an air of sophistication many tried to imitate but he managed to achieve effortlessly.

"Harriet, I swear you can read my mind. I was just going to ask Clara to call you." His pale blue eyes crinkled up at the corners as a wide smile curved his full lips.

Her heart sank and she fought the urge to knit her fingers into the fabric of her wet jumper.

"Is she all right? Is there something wrong?"

"Your mother is fine," he said, and Harriet's heart rate returned to a more normal tempo. "I've got a new patient in. She has a fascinating history and considering your work on suicides in the past I thought you might be interested in meeting her."

Heat crept up onto her face and Harriet ducked her head. "I don't know. My work was more theoretical than anything else. I had no practical application and—"

"Nonsense," Dr Connor said kindly. "You had more practical experience than most do. And while you're not her attending physician it's within my power to consult outside expertise if I deem it necessary."

"I wouldn't see her without her consent," Harriet said, sliding her finger along the roughened edge of her briefcase handle.

Dr Connor pursed his lips. "Consent in this matter is a little tricky. The law has deemed her incapable of making decisions."

"And you, what do you think?"

"I think I'm asking you because so far she has refused to speak with me and I believe you might have a better chance at getting her to open up."

Harriet drew in a deep breath. There had been a time when all she had wanted to do was practice. To help those who couldn't help themselves. She'd believed it would bring her the peace she craved considering her turbulent past. And then in the blink of an eye it had changed and suddenly the idea of being alone in a room with another human being whose mind was utterly and completely sealed off from everyone else—either through choice or trauma —filled her with dread.

"I don't know. I—"

"Harriet, please..." Dr Connor wasn't the kind of man to beg and while him asking politely wasn't exactly begging it was as close to it as he was ever like to get.

"Fine. If you believe I can help her then I'll try but I'm a little rusty, it's been a while since I worked clinically."

His face lit up. "I knew I could count on you."

Harriet found herself wondering if perhaps she had been manoeuvered into the situation and the idea of it left a bitter taste in her mouth.

"Don't get your hopes up about this," she said, sounding a little sharper than she'd intended. "If she won't talk to you then I don't see why she would suddenly open up to me."

Dr Connor shot her an indulgent smile. "She might not but I still believe it is at least worth a try.

At this point, I can see that we have nothing to lose and potentially everything to gain."

"When do you want me to see her?" Harriet asked, choosing to ignore the optimism in his voice.

"Well I was rather hoping you might speak to her now?"

"I was hoping to visit Allison," Harriet said, glancing down at her watch. If she didn't get in to see her mother soon she would have no choice but to leave without speaking to her.

"Your mother is attending a session I believe," Dr Connor said, casting a quick glance in Clara's direction.

"You've got a little time," the receptionist said with a wide smile. "The sessions sometimes run a little over, especially if the patients are really into the experience."

Harriet smiled, more a barring of her teeth than an actual gesture of pleasure. She was definitely getting the feeling that she was being somehow out manoeuvered by everyone present.

"I haven't read any of the files," she said and even she was forced to recognise the futility in her argument. The chances of this woman speaking to her were slim to none and reading the background notes created by the other physician's she had seen over her time wasn't going to change it.

"I think that works to our advantage," Dr Connor said, he nodded in Clara's direction and the door he'd exited through a few moments previously buzzed loudly allowing him to push the heavy metal door open. "I'd rather you had a clean and unbiased reaction to her, uncoloured by another's opinion."

"What, even your own?"

Dr Connor laughed, a warm sound that sent a familiar thrill racing through Harriet's veins like the first blast of champagne bubbles over her tongue. There had been a time when she was younger where she had found herself attaching emotions to the good doctor. She'd never acted upon her feelings, at least she had managed to spare herself that embarrassment. And while time had tempered her attraction to the man directing her through the doors into a pristine and clinical hallway that led deeper into the hospital, Harriet still felt her heartbeat quicken as he placed his hand on the small of her back and guided her in the direction of the patient's rooms.

"If you'll leave your bag and coat here," he said, indicating the wire grated hatch that sat just inside the door they'd stepped through.

Harriet moved over to the grate and slid her belongings in through the small hatch to the guard standing on the other side. This was the high-security side of the hospital and there was nothing she could bring into the patient's wing.

The guard took her belongings and passed her a clipboard through the gap. Harriet quickly scrawled her name across the sheet before handing it back.

"All ready?" Dr Connor asked, giving her a broad smile.

Swallowing back her discomfort, Harriet nodded. She was here now and if she could help then she would. Not that she held much hope of doing anything. "I'm intrigued to know why you think my unbiased opinion is so important."

He smiled and shook his head. "You always were the impatient type. As soon as you've met Emily and you and she have had an opportunity to get to know one another, I'll explain everything to you." There was something so familiar about the name Emily and it caused something in the back of Harriet's mind to shift around a dim recollection of a past case but try as she might, she couldn't bring the memory to the forefront.

"I'm sure you two will hit it off."

Harriet picked up on the slight hitch in the doctor's voice and rather than make her second guess her agreement she found herself growing more intrigued. What could possibly be so fascinating about the case to make him be so secretive?

The deeper they moved into the hospital the more uncomfortable Harriet felt. The last time she had been in this particular wing she had been only fifteen. A young and impressionable age and the trauma associated with that visit had well and truly left its mark on her.

Dr Connor came to a halt next to a large metal

door painted a soft cream colour—the hospital's attempt at trying to make the place seem less like a prison Harriet supposed. He pulled a keycard from inside his pocket, the long zip-cord keyring allowed him to reach the card reader on the wall without having to unpin it from his belt. Before he could buzz the door open, Harriet touched his arm.

"A clean slate might be best," she said.

"I thought you wished me to ask if Emily consented to your presence?" He raised a quizzical eyebrow in her direction.

"I can ask her," she said. It wasn't strictly what they had agreed but she was here now. There was no point pretending that she was going to walk away not when her curiosity had been well and truly piqued.

Anyway, it wasn't a lie to suggest a clean break for the woman she was about to meet. First impressions were everything most especially so to those whose minds had been fractured by trauma. And the patients who found themselves on this wing had certainly suffered a trauma of some kind or other, Harriet was in no doubt about that.

If the patient's associations with Dr Connor were in anyways unpleasant—which seemed entirely possible considering the circumstances—then Harriet didn't want for those same emotions to become attached to her, at least not if it could be avoided.

Dr Connor stood back and unclipped the keycard from his belt before he presented it to her like it was the key to the city and not to a locked room.

Sucking in a deep breath, Harriet took it from him and waited for him to step back before she pressed the white plastic to the card reader mounted on the wall. There was a low click and a small buzz emitted from the speaker.

The woman inside would know she was coming.

Harriet knew she could just tug the door open and step inside. There were those who wouldn't have hesitated to do so but Harriet wasn't them. It had been ingrained into her—by Dr Connor and others like him—that to forget basic human decency in here was akin to dismissing the human rights of the patients.

Instead, she rapped her knuckles against the painted metal door, satisfied that the sharp sound would penetrate to the room beyond.

There was no response—not that she truly expected one anyway—and she pulled the door open gently. The room beyond was painted the same pristine white as the hall, so that if the outer wall had been removed they would blend into one another seamlessly.

There was a bed pushed back into the far corner, the bolts holding it to the floor a tell-tale sign that the room was made for containment rather than comfort. Harriet's gaze fell to the birdlike woman perched on the edge of the bare rubber mattress.

Harriet's throat constricted as she noted the distinct lack of sheets or blankets on the bed and she made a mental note to ask why they hadn't supplied her with the special bedding for those who were a suicide risk.

Harriet paused in the doorway and the woman on the bed stared unblinkingly at the wall, as though she could see straight through it to what lay beyond. Perhaps in her own way she could.

"Emily?" Harriet kept her voice level as hoovered at the threshold. "Emily, my name is Harriet. I was wondering if it would be all right for me to come in and have a short chat with you."

Emily didn't move and for a moment Harriet found herself studying the other woman to see if she was actually breathing. The slight rise and fall of her chest was the only indication that she was in fact alive and not the mannequin she appeared to be.

"May I come in?"

When Emily didn't move or look in her direction, Harriet decided to take it as a sign of her ascent. When a patient didn't want you in a room, they were usually pretty clear on the matter. She straightened her shoulders and resisting the urge to tuck her hair nervously behind one ear stepped into the room.

There wasn't a flicker of movement from Emily and Harriet longed to ask Dr Connor if she was cata-tonic or if her lack of response stemmed from the medication they'd inevitably given to her.

Harriet moved over to the small chair that sat in the corner of the room. Like the bed it too was bolted to the floor and as she sat down, Harriet did her best to ignore the scratch marks visible around the tops of the bolts keeping it in place. There was no accounting for the desperate measures some patients took, and Harriet had seen her fair share of suicide attempts in places just like this.

"I was asked to come and speak to you, Emily. Is it all right if I call you Emily?"

No response.

It would have been easy to sit there in the silence Emily seemed to favour. But Harriet's time was limited and building a rapport with the other woman was the only chance she had for reaching her. However, without having read her case file Harriet found herself floundering.

"I was actually here to see my mother," Harriet said and for one split second she was certain there was a hint of flickering movement at the corner of Emily's left eye.

Was it a flinch? Or was it an uncontrolled tic?

"She likes to paint," Harriet continued. "That's what she's doing right now. Is there something you like to do? Perhaps I could speak to someone and you could join one of the activities they have here."

Emily moved then and Harriet's heart stalled out in her chest as she found herself pinned in place by the other woman's arresting green-eyed gaze. There was no doubt in her mind as she stared into Emily's bloodshot unfocussed eyes that Dr. O'Conner had her heavily medicated.

"Want to—" Emily's words were slurred, as though her tongue was too dry and was stuck to the roof of her mouth. It was a nasty side-effect of some of the medications that Harriet had seen before.

"I can get you something to drink, Emily, if that would make you more comfortable?"

Emily's eyes rolled in her head as her tongue darted out to moisten her lips before she attempted to speak again.

"Only want to die..." Despite the medication she was obviously on, there was no concealing the emotion her words were loaded with.

"Why do you want to die, Emily?" Harriet did her best to keep her voice neutral but there was a small sliver of ice that slid down her spine.

"I wanted to make it better—" Emily's voice cracked as she started to rock slowly, backwards and forwards.

Harriet knew that if the woman was capable of crying she would have but just like dry mouth, drying of the tear-ducts was another common but painful symptom. She was on dangerous territory here but what other choice did she have but to ask the next logical question?

"Was there something you needed to make better?"

Emily shook her head. The sudden violence of her movements sent a jolt through Harriet but she steeled herself and remained seated.

"I didn't want him to suffer..."

The pieces of the puzzle Harriet's brain had been frantically trying to put together suddenly clicked into place. Shock and horror kept her silent as she watched Emily rock back and forth, her arms wrapped protectively around her body.

"Couldn't bear for him to suffer. I couldn't bear it. I couldn't bear it. I couldn't bear it—" Emily's words broke down until the noises leaving her mouth no longer resembled words but more primal sounds.

The sounds only a grieving, heartbroken mother could make.

Emily's hands shot to her face and she began to claw and gouge at herself as though attempting to dig the thoughts from her own brain.

Harriet was out of the chair faster than she thought herself capable of but not before Emily managed to rip a chunk of limp blonde hair from her own scalp. Harriet hit the alarm on the wall and crossed the floor to Emily's side, only registering in the far recesses of her mind that she was only a visitor here and as such shouldn't lay hands on the patients. But the sheer level of anguish shown by Emily wasn't something she could ignore.

Despite the time that had passed since she'd last worked clinically, her body remembered the movements with a kind of muscle memory borne of practice.

In a matter of seconds, the room was full. Emily screamed, a long ragged guttural sound that tore at Harriet's heart as well as her ears as the other woman kicked and lashed in the grip of those who had come to her aid. Dr Connor was there and from the corner of her eye, Harriet watched as he administered a shot to Emily's exposed arm.

It took only seconds for the drugs to take effect.

Adrenaline buzzed in Harriet's veins as she felt the woman quieten. The noises she was making softened as her limbs grew heavy and the light Harriet had witnessed in her eyes dulled.

Harriet stepped away and allowed the hospital staff to do their job as she smoothed down the front of her cream blouse and navy trousers. There was no point in getting in the way, not when they were the professionals.

"You got her talking," Dr Connor said animatedly.

Harriet rounded on him. Her hands shook as she brushed her tousled hair back out of her eyes and tucked several stray strands behind her ears. It was a comforting gesture—one she'd developed from childhood and she hadn't been able to shake free of it. She knew it only happened when she was particularly stressed or upset and as she'd stood in Emily Hawthorne's room and watched her fall apart

Harriet knew now was as good a time as any to be upset.

"You sent me in there blind," she said and was pleasantly surprised to find her voice remained steady despite the adrenaline still pumping through her body. "You sent me in there and look what happened."

"Yes, you got her talking. Nobody else has managed to do that yet."

"She tried to gouge her own eyes out, Jonathan." Harriet hardly ever used the doctor's first name. Ignoring the looks of surprise from the orderlies that her outburst had garnered, Harriet ploughed on. "You and I both know she's not capable of talking about what happened. At least not yet, maybe not ever."

"I wouldn't say that," Dr Connor said, sounding more than a little irritated.

"We don't know what's she's yet capable of. And anyway, what else are we supposed to do? I can't just leave her in here to rot like the courts have."

Harriet sucked in a deep breath. He meant well. But the road to Hell was paved with the best of intentions and sending her into the room with Emily Hawthorne without first tipping her off about potential landmines had been dangerous. As it was, Harriet could only hope her short conversation with the fragile woman hadn't damaged her further.

"And I'm not saying you should leave her in here

to rot. But you and I both know just how delicate her mind is right now. Anything that pushes her too far could mean the end to ever leading her back onto the path to recovery."

"No one is ever too far gone, Harriet," he said and she flinched under the severity in his voice.

"Some people don't want to come back," she said softly. "Sometimes it's too painful to force them to remember and recovery—true recovery—demands that you remember."

He sighed and pushed his hand back through his greying hair. His gaze looked past Harriet to the woman on the bed, his expression unreadable.

It wasn't the first time she'd seen the look on his face, but it didn't matter how often she was exposed to it, she had not yet mastered the art of reading him. At least not the way he could read her.

"Perhaps you are right," he said. "But unlike you I find it too hard to just walk away and pretend that those who need my help are beyond it."

Harriet took a step back, the sting of his words too much like a slap to the face. He'd asked her for her opinion and when she'd given it he'd tossed it back in her face.

"I'm going to go and see my mother now," Harriet said, turning on her heel.

She made it as far as the doors that led to the next wing before Dr. O' Conner caught up to her.

"I'm sorry, Harriet." There was no doubting the

contrition in his voice and on his face. But she'd learned a long time ago that his apologies didn't actually weigh all that much in the grand scheme of things. The next opportunity he got, the next time they disagreed he would do it all over again, consequences be damned.

"No, you're not." She buried her face in her hands. "You were right. I have walked away from all of this." Taking her hands from her face, she gestured to the space around them. "But I did it so I wouldn't end up in here like my mother."

Dr Connor managed to look suitably shocked and if it had been any other time—perhaps during any other conversation that wasn't quite so serious—Harriet might have found the look on his face funny.

"That would never happen."

"You and I both know you can't say that. We don't know what the human mind is truly capable of handling—or in my mother's case—not handling. For all we know I have inherited her illness and it's right now festering inside me, just waiting for the right moment to drag me under. Just like it did with her."

Simply talking about her mother was enough to bring Harriet out in a cold sweat. It was a time she'd tried to forget but no matter how hard she attempted to wipe that memory from her mind it crept through, like a stain that refused to budge.

Dr Connor placed his hand on her arm. "You are not like her."

"But how can I really know?" They both knew the answer to that question.

He sighed and let his hand fall away from her arm. "I'm sorry for bringing up uncomfortable memories for you. I didn't think and that was selfish of me."

Harriet smiled and shook her head. "You're just trying to help your patient. I can understand that."

"Do you think you could come back and speak to Emily again?"

"Considering her violent reaction to me I'm not sure it would be such a good idea."

"I think because of her violent reaction to you, seeing you again is just what she needs." Seeing the look of discomfort on Harriet's face he added. "Not yet of course. She needs time and I will continue to work with her but perhaps if I can get her to a more settled place you would consider it?"

Harriet nodded. "I'll consider it but if and only if you can get her to a place where she is more able to face her demons. I won't be your hammer, Jonathon. You used me like that once before, I won't do it a second time."

Before he could say another word, Harriet used the keycard he had given to her and left him behind as she pushed out through the heavy double doors.

CHAPTER NINE

IT TOOK ONLY a few minutes to get back to the main reception area. Clara stared at her as she entered but if she noticed her dishevelled appearance, she was too polite to say anything. That was a miracle in itself.

"Your mother is waiting for you in the day room," she said instead as Harriet handed her Dr Connor's key card.

"I think the good doctor will be looking for this."

Clara nodded and buzzed a door to the left that led to the day rooms and counselling centres.

Harriet slipped through to the other side of the hospital and nipped into the first bathroom she spotted on the corridor. She clicked the lock home and turned to face the small basin and the mirror positioned over it.

Her face was drawn and pale, her hair an unruly

mess. Leaning on the edge of the porcelain sink, Harriet closed her eyes and was instantly treated to an image of Emily Hawthorne's face. Distress etched into every line and the downward curve of her lips.

Her case had been one of those that captured the public's attention. Headlines splashed across every newspaper and online news outlet had painted her as the Medea for the modern day.

But the woman Harriet had spoken to bore no resemblance to the vengeful granddaughter of a bloodthirsty Greek god hellbent on making the man who had wronged her pay for his crimes. However, despite being the complete antithesis of this her story was no less tragic.

On the heels of her husband leaving her, Emily's newborn son had been diagnosed with Cystic Fibrosis. Many had wanted to believe that she had acted selfishly, that her inability to cope with the diagnosis had led to her actions.

But Harriet had witnessed the devastation in her face. Would she ever recover? There was a time when she'd worked clinically that she had believed everyone was capable of recovery. In fact, that mindset was tantamount to successfully treating patients. However, a run in with one particular patient had caused Harriet to doubt her own ability to be the catalyst for recovery.

After splashing water up onto her face, Harriet grabbed a fistful of paper towels from the dispenser and pressed them to her mouth. Dwelling on the encounter wasn't going to make her visit with her mother run any more smoothly.

She balled the papers up and tossed them into the trash before heading out of the bathroom.

"HOW ARE YOU FEELING TODAY?" Harriet sat opposite the woman she called mother and resisted the urge to fold her arms defensively over her chest.

"This place isn't doing me any favours, Harri. The air in here is making me sick. Couldn't I come and spend some time with you. Just for a little while at least?"

"You and I both know that's not possible," she said as kindly as possible.

"Any why not? You don't want me, is that it? Too good for your own mother now?"

"That's not what I'm saying. You know why you have to stay here, why you can't come home with me."

"Home." Her mother's voice was wistful as she glanced out through the large picturesque window that looked out over the moors. "You know I barely remember what it was like to have a home."

Harriet sighed. "Why did you attack the care assistant?"

"Twenty years doesn't sound like a long time but

when you're in here." Her mother turned to stare at her. "When you're trapped in here for something you know you didn't do it's an awfully long time. Don't you think?"

"We've been over it before, Mom," Harriet said, keeping her voice as level as she could. "You told the Doctors that you did drive us off the pier that day. You told them it wasn't an accident."

"Lies!" The word was hissed. Her mother leaned over the table toward Harriet, her voice dropping to a conspiratorial whisper. "I only said that because that was what they wanted to hear. You and I know it never happened."

"I was there, Mom, I remember."

"You were too young to remember anything."

"I was ten. I remember you telling me to take my seatbelt off. I remember refusing and you unclipping it anyway. And I remember you ordering Kyle to do the same thing."

As she spoke, Harriet watched the glint that formed in her mother's eye, the steely determination in the set of her jaw as she folded her arms over her chest and leaned back in her chair.

"That wasn't me."

Harriet sighed and sat back. Her mother wasn't entirely wrong. It had been a part of her that had tried to kill her children. The untreated psychosis that had poisoned her mind and forced her to press her foot down on the accelerator.

"Kyle is such a good boy."

A headache was beginning to form in the centre of Harriet's forehead. It was only just after lunch and the day was already too long.

"Why did you attack the care assistant, Mom?"

"He was stealing things from my room. He thought I didn't know but I know everything I have in there. They let you keep so little, everything I own is precious. But that bastard was taking it so he could sell it."

"What did he take?"

"My jewellery. Do you remember the butterfly necklace your father gave to me?"

Harriet nodded. She remembered the butterfly necklace but she also knew her mother didn't have it anymore.

"He gave that to me on our fifth wedding anniversary and that bastard Grant tried to take it from me."

"I have the necklace," Harriet said.

"Why would you have it?"

"I've had it this whole time you've been in here. I told you I would keep your jewellery safe when they took it from you."

Harriet watched as her mother shook her head. "No. You're wrong. Dr Connor said I could keep that necklace. I have it here and Grant stole it."

"Mom..." Harriet leaned over the table and stretched her hands out toward her mother. "I'm telling you. I've got the necklace. I promised I would keep them safe, remember?"

Tears crowded her mother's eyes and Harriet's stomach lurched.

"I don't want to be in here anymore, Harri. I don't like it. It scares me."

"Why does it scare you?"

"Everyone is so ill and I'm afraid I'm going to die in here. I don't want to die in hospital, please..."

When she got like this, Harriet found it difficult to refuse her. As much as she knew she had to, it still tore at her heart to see her mother—a woman who had one time been as loving as any mother could be—reduced to such a pitiful state.

Harriet took her mother's hands in hers and chaffed the cold flesh between her fingers—something her mother had done for her when she was small.

"You know this is the safest place for you to be. In here you don't have to—"

Her mother jerked her hands back from Harriet's grip and stared at her with distrust and disgust.

"You don't care, do you?"

"That's not true, I—"

"You've got your own life now and you don't care what happens to me in here. You always were the selfish one. Well, just you wait and see when they kill me in here, you'll be sorry then, Harriet. You'll be sorry then."

With a sigh, Harriet straightened up and met her mother's stormy eyed gaze head on.

"I should go," she said. "I'm just upsetting you."

"I think it would be best."

Harriet nodded and pushed up onto her feet.

"Tell your brother to come and see me when he can." Her mother's expression softened as she spoke of Kyle.

"You know he can't do that."

"He comes to see me more than you do," her mother spat the words at her. "At least he doesn't blame me for everything that happened."

Rather than argue with her further, Harriet nodded. "I'll tell him."

Satisfied, her mother sat back in her chair and folded her arms over her chest.

Harriet turned to leave.

"I didn't think he would bleed so much..."

"Who?"

"Grant." Harriet watched her mother stare out through the large picture window again. It was typical of her avoidance of a situation. "I was covered in it and he was screaming. It sounded strange though, wetter."

Harriet said nothing, her fingers digging into the back of the chair she had vacated.

Despite seeing her mother over the years, it never ceased to amaze her the sudden mood changes she displayed. Not to mention, the cold and calculating way she could recount some of her more vicious attacks.

"Grant said you told him to be quiet, that he was making a fuss over nothing."

"Well he was. He's a grown man and he'd done wrong. He needed to be punished."

"When did you stop taking your medication?"

Her mother turned then, and the glint was back in her eye. The same calculating look she had given earlier, and it was the same expression that Harriet recognised from the day when she had driven them off the pier and into the freezing waters of the North Sea.

"I don't know what you're talking about, Harriet. I'm under constant supervision here. They make sure I take my medication."

It should have been true. She was under constant supervision, although not as much supervision as she had once been under. As she'd progressed through her treatment, she'd been entitled to receive certain benefits that other patients like Emily would not yet enjoy. But even then, ensuring the patients took their medication should have been a top priority. However, Harriet couldn't shake the feeling that her mother had somehow managed to slip the net.

It was something she would have to discuss with Dr Connor the moment she got the chance. Perhaps, if she was lucky, she would get to see him before she left.

"I hope that's true," she said, feeling utterly impotent as her mother smiled beatifically up at her.

"Don't forget to tell, Kyle," she reminded as Harriet pushed away from the table and started across the parquet floor of the day room. "Tell him, mommy loves him."

A shiver raced down Harriet's spine as she was buzzed out through the doors into the main corridor.

Dr Connor stood in the hall and Harriet knew he'd been waiting for her.

"How do you think she is?" Although he tried to hide it, Harriet noted the curiosity in his voice as he asked the question. Despite being the primary physician in charge of her mother's care, he couldn't help but look to others for their thoughts. It was definitely a professional hazard Harriet had noticed occurring in other doctors besides Dr Connor. As though there was a part of them that sought out reassurance that they were doing a good job, that their efforts were noted and appreciated. She knew it ran deeper than that but as she stood in the hall after meeting with her mother that was how it felt to her.

"Has she been taking her meds?"

Dr Connor's eyes widened and he dropped his gaze to the charts gripped in his hands. "As far as I'm aware there hasn't been any issues with her refusing to take her medication."

"That's not what I'm asking."

He glanced up at her. "Then what are you

asking?" There was no denying the thread of steel in his voice.

"I'm asking if you know for certain she has been taking her pills."

A look of horror mixed with consternation crossed his handsome features. "I don't think I appreciate the direction you're taking this, Harriet. You know—"

"I'm not saying you're not doing your best. I just want to know if you're certain she is getting her meds."

"You clearly think she isn't," he said, side-stepping the question neatly.

"There's something off about her. The attack on the care-assistant for starters."

"It wouldn't be your mother's first attack on a member of staff," he said not unkindly. "I've still got the scars from our first meeting."

Harriet gave him a tight smile. "But she wasn't on medication then, or at least she was refusing most of it. She's been more stable since you got her into a routine with her tablets. Until now at least..."

"What did she say to you that has you so worked up?"

"It's not just what she said to me." Harriet sighed and covered her face with her hands. Visiting her mother tended to take the wind out of her sails but today had been particularly brutal. "It's the look on her face. I recognise it."

Dr Connor smiled and placed a gentle hand on Harriet's shoulder. "I'm telling you, Harriet, she is taking her medication. If it makes you happy, I'll stop by this afternoon when they're handing out the meds and watch her take them myself."

"Really?" She hated the note of needy relief that made up that one word.

"Of course. I can give you a buzz after, let you know how it went if that'll help take a load off your mind?"

"I'd really appreciate that," she said, feeling the knot of tension that had formed below her sternum since she'd spoken to her mother loosen.

"And about earlier," she said.

Dr Connor shook his head. "Forget about it," he said. "That was my fault. You were right. I shouldn't have dumped you in the deep end like that."

"Well, I was thinking I would like to visit with Emily again. If you'd still like me too?"

Despite her misgivings about the entire situation, Harriet couldn't deny the thrill of excitement that raced through her at Dr Connor's expression of joy.

"I would very much appreciate it," he said, a broad smile lighting up his features.

Glancing down at her watch, Harriet felt her stomach plummet. What was supposed to have been a short visit to see her mother had eaten into the afternoon. As it was, she was going to be late to her last meeting of the day if she didn't leave immediately.

"I must go," she said, smiling up at the man opposite her.

"So soon?"

"I've got a meeting this evening."

Dr Connor nodded his understanding. "You know, perhaps we could get together some time for a drink?"

Harriet's heart flip-flopped in her chest. A few years ago, she would have jumped at the chance. But now...

"I—"

"We could discuss your mother's case and treatment. I'd be interested to get your perspective on her progress."

Heat slid up her neck and into her face as she realised her mistake. He wasn't asking her out like she'd initially thought. He was asking in a professional capacity and her mind had instantly taken a turn towards something less innocent.

"Well, I suppose... yeah," she said, her words tumbling over one another as he led her back to the reception desk where Clara sat with her bag and jacket awaiting her.

"Great," he said. "Shall I call you to arrange a date and time?"

Harriet nodded, feeling Clara's attention settle on her as she gathered up her belongings.

"Sounds good. I'll speak to you then, Doctor."

He opened his mouth to say something else but seemed to catch himself at the last second and simply nodded instead. Harriet, started for the door, rather than wait for him to say anymore. After everything, all she wanted to do was escape out into the rain. Perhaps if she was lucky, the cool raindrops would take some of the shame heating her cheeks away.

Pushing out into the rain, she glanced back up at the imposing building and caught sight of her mother in the picturesque window that took up one wall of the day room.

If her mother saw her, she didn't make any indication of the fact. Her gaze was pinned on the landscape of the moors beyond the glass.

The rain had become a mist. It clung to Harriet's eyelashes as she stared up at her mother inside the window.

The older woman leaned forward, her forehead almost pressed to the glass and for a moment Harriet's heart stalled in her chest as she half expected her to force her face into the glass. It certainly wouldn't have been the first time she'd self-harmed since her illness had been diagnosed. But her mother didn't collide with the glass. Instead, her face became obscured by mist as she breathed out onto the glass. Raising her finger, she quickly drew a circle, it was followed by three dots inside and a quick half-moon shape to make up the mouth of the smiley face.

Beneath the drawing, with hands that shook, Harriet watched as her mother wrote the word ELYK.

It took a moment for it to sink in and when it did Harriet's heart sank. She was viewing the word backwards. It seemed Kyle was never far from her mother's thoughts.

Her mother caught her eye then and raised a hand to the glass as Harriet waved up to her.

Her mother's expression was blank, devoid of any feeling. It was an expression Harriet had grown used to seeing on her face. She turned away and started down the steps.

As much as she was used to seeing the blank incomprehensive mask her mother often wore it still hurt. And no amount of professional understanding would ever take that away.

CHAPTER TEN

THE WORLD WAS in so much pain. Every day of the week there was a new horror to deal with. And right in the middle of it all, people kept trying to battle against that pain instead of just giving in. There was something to be said for the acceptance of not being able to carry on. There was a strength in that and it was beautiful to behold.

But it took a special person to admit defeat like that. It took the kind of strength that only came along once in a lifetime.

Sliding down in the car seat, he watched as she pulled open the front door and strode out. The little girl in her arms laughed and wriggled to get down.

She would never give up. That much he knew with the kind of conviction that came to those who watched people suffer every day of the week. She would keep struggling, fighting to keep her head above water and for what?

Who would thank her for it?

Nobody, that's who. Nobody would see the struggle. Nobody cared.

Except for him.

He loved her for her struggle. Admired it. But the time was drawing to a close and soon it would be all over.

It was so close he could practically taste it.

"Soon my love. So soon. Then all of this will be over and your pain will just float away."

The tune he hummed under his breath—a lullaby—brought a tear to his eye. He dashed it away with the back of his hand as he started up the car and pulled away from the curb.

CHAPTER ELEVEN

"WHAT TIME DID you say she'd be back?" Drew asked the severe looking woman—who'd introduced herself as Mrs M. Metcalf—perched behind the desk opposite him.

"She was supposed to be back an hour ago."

Drew nodded and ducked his head in an attempt to keep his smile to himself.

"I don't know why you find all of this so funny, Detective Haskell," Mrs Metcalf said. "This institution is one of the finest in the country and this blatant disregard for—"

"Blatant disregard for what?"

Drew jerked in his seat as Mrs Metcalf's tirade was interrupted by the cool tone of another woman who'd slipped silently in the door next to him. He turned and glanced up at her, noting the way her still damp cream blouse clung to her frame in spite of the raincoat she carried. Her dark hair curled around the collar of her shirt and seemed to emphasise her large, expressive blue eyes.

If Maz was here he'd probably declare they were the kind of eyes a man could lose himself in, or some other such nonsense. Not that he'd be wrong but Drew preferred to keep things simple and a lot less poetic.

There was something so terribly familiar about her but as much as he tried to grab onto the elusive memory it slipped out of reach.

He leaned back in his chair and adopted and air of mild interest as Mrs Metcalf flushed.

"I was merely stating that your continued disregard for your office hours—office hours I might add that you set yourself—reflects poorly on you and everyone around you."

The woman in the doorway opened her mouth but caught Drew's eye and turned to him instead.

"You're not James," she said, as though his presence instead of the elusive James was somehow an affront to her.

"I am not." Drew pushed to his feet and held his hand out to the woman in front of him. "My name is Detective Inspector Drew Haskell. If I could have a few moments of your time and—"

Her eyes widened. "Martha mentioned that the police had tried to contact me earlier today. Is this visit pertaining to the same matter?"

He nodded and tried to give her a reassuring smile. Not that he was very adept at the whole reassurance thing. That was for other people. He was much more a go out and attack the problem head on kind of guy. He'd never found platitudes or reassurances to be particularly useful during his life as a police officer. People tended to look to him for action as opposed to empty promises too easily broken.

"I did try to get you on the phone earlier," he said. "I was hoping I might pick your brain over a case I'm currently working on?"

Drew watched as her expression became guarded and her eyes shuttered. She took a tiny step backward and only the doorjamb at her back prevented her from leaving the room entirely.

"My assistance?" She repeated the question as though trying to familiarise herself with the concept.

"Yes. I had heard you have a particular area of expertise and I was rather hoping you would take a look at the case files for—"

Before he could even finish, she shook her head. The smile on her full lips was polite but she gave him an air of disinterest.

"I'm sorry, Detective Haskell, I don't think I would be of any use to you. I—"

"Detective Inspector," he corrected. It was a stupid pedantic thing to do and the moment the correction left his mouth, he could tell he'd made a mistake. But he just couldn't help it. His inability to keep his mouth shut when he was supposed to had gotten him into trouble more times than he could count and her seeming disinterest rubbed him up the wrong way. Not that he believed it for a second. Behind the polite façade, there was another side to her; one that was more than interested in looking over the case files. But there was something holding her back.

Of course, if he couldn't find a way around whatever it was that was holding her back then he'd just wasted an entire afternoon coming over here to see her. The DCI would have his arse in a sling if he got back with nothing to show for the day and no files to hand him come the end of shift.

"Look," he said, deciding that starting over was definitely the right thing to do. "I'm sorry we've gotten off on the wrong foot here. I need your expertise on this and—" He held his hand up to ward off her protests before continuing. "I know you've got it in your head that you can't help but that's where I think you're wrong."

"And you would know what I'm qualified to help you with, how?" She arched an eyebrow at him but Drew knew her interest was piqued.

"I've read some of your papers on suicides," he said, going straight for the kill. "Or at least your exploration of why suicides appear in clusters."

She looked surprised and Drew straightened his

shoulders, a small kernel of pride igniting within his core.

"You've read my papers on the Werther effect?" She didn't bother to keep her surprise to herself, and Drew found himself wondering if she knew all of her emotions played out across her face for anyone to see.

"I have," he said. "And I'm man enough to admit I first thought it had something to do with a Werther's Original."

She stared at him for a moment longer before she threw her head back and began to laugh. It was a rich sound and the smile that curled her lips brightened her face, making her appear younger, almost vulnerable.

"I take it you haven't heard that one before?"

She shook her head and placed a hand over her mouth as though she was suddenly self-conscious about her laughter. He caught her casting a surreptitious glance in the direction of her disapproving secretary before she beckoned for him to follow her into the office.

"I suppose you better come in."

She held the door for him before she poked her head back into the main room.

"Martha, hold my calls until I'm through with Detective Inspector Haskell."

"But you have a four o' clock—"

"I said, hold my calls. Please."

"Fine."

Not for the first time, Drew tried to stifle his smile with his hand as he took the seat directly opposite Dr Quinn's desk.

She settled into the swivel chair and peered at him over the large pile of folders that dominated her tiny desk.

"I'm sorry about the mess." Her tone was contrite as she cast a baleful eye over the items in front of her.

Drew shook his head. "Don't be sorry. You should see my desk."

She smiled at him again but it wasn't a patch on the one she had shared with him in the hall and he found himself wishing he could make her laugh like he had before.

Get a grip man. One pretty woman and suddenly your head is turned.

"You have the files with you?"

Drew jerked in his seat. "Pardon?"

"The files, from the case you're working. You brought them with you, yes?"

Nodding, he withdrew a small packet from inside his khaki overcoat and reached across the desk. She took them and this time he was certain that what he saw in her eyes was a kind of eagerness.

"We've had three suicides in the village of Tollby," he said. "Three teenagers actually."

"And you want to know why?"

And this was where it all got a little complicated. Was he supposed to tell her the truth about his suspicions, or was he supposed to let her do her thing and make up her own mind?

Drew leaned forward, placing his elbows on his knees as he steepled his fingers. "Well you see that's just it."

"You don't think they are suicides, do you?"

He smiled ruefully at her. "Am I that transparent?"

"Well, you wouldn't be here if it were that easy, now would you?"

He sighed. "No. If these were just open and shut cases then I wouldn't have bothered you at all."

She glanced down at the file in front of her but made no attempt to open it. "Why did you really seek me out?"

Drew opened his mouth to answer but she smiled indulgently at him. "The truth now, Detective Inspector."

Leaning back in his chair, Drew stretched his long legs out in front of him and closed his eyes. He knew how it looked to others. He was the picture of ease. It was a calculated move on his behalf though, one that gave him the time he needed to formulate an answer in his head.

Hadn't he spent the entire drive over here asking himself the exact same question. He hadn't come up with an answer then so why should he have one now?

"Because I'm stuck between a rock and a hard place if I'm being perfectly honest with you."

"Go on."

In for a penny, in for a pound mate. "My boss wants me to file these as suicides and if I was a smart man that's just what I'd have done."

"But you're not a smart man, is that it?"

Was she just teasing him now?

"I suppose not." Drew closed his eyes again and this time he was treated to the image of Sian Jones', her body laid out on the still dew damp grass, the discolouration of her face and protruding tongue. It was an image that would haunt him for the rest of his days.

"Are you all right, Detective Inspector?" There was no denying the concern in her voice and it was sufficient to pull Drew out of the dark direction his thoughts had taken.

"I've been to these kid's houses. Yesterday, I watched them cart the body of another teenage girl out of her back garden where she'd allegedly hung herself and then I had to question her parents." He didn't dare meet Dr Quinn's eagle eyed gaze as he spoke, choosing instead to plough ahead. "I had to sit there in front of the poor bastard who cut his step-daughter down and watch him fall apart as the realisation struck that his daughter—his baby girl—was really gone. I can't in all good conscience just pass these kids off as suicides when I know deep down that it's not."

Dr Quinn remained silent, obviously giving him

a few moments to compose himself after his emotional outburst. It wasn't like him, he was normally so in control of his emotions but there was just something about the case that slipped under his skin and got to him.

Deep down he knew why but he wasn't fully prepared to face it just yet. Maybe he never would.

"I will look at the files," Dr Quinn said, her tone decisive.

Drew let go a long sigh and felt some of the tension he'd been carrying in his shoulders slip away. He'd known he was uptight about the meeting but it wasn't until she'd agreed to take a look at things that he truly began to comprehend just how affected he was by the entire situation.

"Thank you," he said and he meant it.

She sat there and stared at him a moment longer, he could practically see the questions hovering on the tip of her tongue. Instead of asking them, she pushed onto her feet and held her hand out toward him.

"It was good to meet you, Detective Inspector."

Startled by the suddenness of her dismissal, Drew climbed to his feet and took her hand.

"I thought you said you were going to review the case files."

"And I am," she said, glancing down at the stack on her desk. "But I can't very well do it justice with you hovering at my elbow?"

"Oh, right, of course."

What a stupid mistake to make. She was busy, judging by the mountain of yet to be filed paperwork cluttering her desk it would take her quite a while to get around to reviewing his case. Shit.

Dr Quinn pumped his hand firmly before releasing her hold on him.

"I'll be in touch as soon as I've had the chance to review it."

Drew nodded and couldn't help but feel like he was being dismissed. How he was supposed to face his boss when he had nothing at all to show for it. The Monk was going to have his guts for garters.

It definitely wasn't like the television shows liked to make it out to be. There would be no understanding nod as he explained to the Monk about his gut feeling and the case. And there definitely wouldn't be an opportunity to pursue things further. Once it was closed, the case would remain that way and not even God himself—if he appeared in the office—would make the Monk re-open the files.

"I don't mean to sound like I'm pushing here," he said. He was grasping at straws but what else was he supposed to do?

"But I really need your opinion on this."

"Sooner rather than later," she said with a broad smile.

Despite her openness earlier, Drew found himself at a loss and unable to read her expression now. The knowledge that she wasn't as transparent as he'd first thought wasn't exactly comforting.

"My boss thinks these cases should be closed," he said, as she manoeuvered him toward the door.

"I understand," she said. "Like I said, as soon as I have anything useable, I'll be in touch."

Drew's heart sank in his chest as he watched his last chance to get justice for the kids whose lives had been so cruelly stolen from them slipped through his fingers. If he was better at this then he could make her understand the urgency.

But this wasn't his forte, never had been. As it was the idea of schmoozing and charming those he needed favours from brought him out in hives.

Before he knew it, he was outside the door and Dr Quinn had shut it in his face. Either her social skills were sorely lacking or he'd just allowed himself to get the brush off.

"Sent you packing?" Mrs Metcalf asked as he paused in front of the door.

Turning on his heel he gave her his best hundred-watt smile but his heart wasn't really in it.

"No," he said. "I got everything I came here for."

Mrs Metcalf snorted derisively and turned her attention back to the computer screen she sat behind. Just why Dr Quinn had a woman who clearly didn't think a whole lot of her was beyond him. If Maz behaved in the same way, it wouldn't be long before Drew's temper got the better of him.

With one last lingering look over his shoulder at the closed office door, he made his way back toward the corridor. There was no point in hanging around in the hopes that things changed. The sooner he got back to the office now and began the necessary paperwork for the Monk the better.

The elevator doors dinged open and Drew stepped inside.

"Well, shit," he muttered beneath his breath as the doors slid shut, cutting him off from his last chance at serving justice.

CHAPTER TWELVE

HARRIET BURIED her face in her hands and sucked in a deep breath. He didn't remember her. That, at least, was a blessing in disguise.

But then why should he?

When they'd last met, his entire world had just been ripped apart. It stood to reason that his ability to recall the faces of everyone he met during that period would be compromised.

When she'd first seen him sitting there in the waiting area, her heart had stalled in her chest and her mind had started to race over all the possibilities for his appearance. Ever since that fateful day, DI Haskell hadn't been far from her mind. Although he hadn't been a DI then, clearly his career path hadn't been overly affected by the death of his fiancée.

It was an unkind thought and Harriet regretted it the moment it popped into her head.

People had lots of different ways of dealing with the deaths of those they cared for. Some collapsed beneath the weight of their grief, their lives spiralling down into a black pit of misery, guilt and depression. Others still threw themselves headlong into their work, choosing to bury their grief in something they could control. Neither path was better than the other and in the end the outcome was nearly always the same.

Grief wasn't something you just got over, no matter how much you might wish you could. The one you had lost was still gone, the hole they'd created in the fabric of your life still gaped like an open wound and no amount of papering over the cracks could repair it.

Harriet found herself wishing she kept a bottle of whiskey in the lower drawer of her desk. After all, she was no stranger to throwing herself headlong into her work to escape the pain grief caused.

With hands that shook, she picked up the small case file and flicked it open. She was immediately assaulted by the visual images that made up the bulk of the file. Closing her eyes, she tried to clear her mind before returning her attention to the photographs.

Some mistakenly believed that hanging was a quick and easy way to die. And for those who committed the act and got it just right, it was both quick and relatively painless. However, the odds of getting the knot in just the right place for the drop to dislocate or even fracture the cervical vertebrae and cause vasovagal shock was uncommon.

Death wasn't something that came easily. Conscious and subconscious reflexes worked to keep us alive and to fight against them was no mean feat.

Harriet swallowed back the welling emotion that threatened to see her lose the meagre contents of her stomach.

Turning over the images of the bodies, Harriet picked up the coroner's report that lay at the bottom of the packet. She scanned the results, unsurprised to discover his findings were in keeping with the general thought that these were in fact tragic suicides.

Sitting back in the chair, Harriet closed her eyes and her mind instantly conjured the image of DI Haskell.

Why was it that everyone around him believed the three deaths were nothing more than a tragedy but he was determined to believe they were something more?

It was possible that his previous brush with suicide had clouded his judgement.

He hadn't wanted to believe it then either. Being forced to concede to something so terrible would undoubtably have taken its toll on him.

But this, this was something different.

She caught sight of the small white card—his

contact details scrawled across the front—clipped to inside of the file.

Harriet straightened up in the chair and tugged her phone from the inside pocket of her handbag.

As she waited for the call to connect, her gaze fell to the top image in the file. A close up of the last girl's hand, twisted around her fist was what appeared to be a golden chain.

The fact that she was holding it at all was a little strange but not entirely uncommon. However, something niggled in the back of Harriet's mind.

Sifting through the other pictures, she was only vaguely aware of Drew Haskell's voice on the other end of the line as he answered.

"Hello?"

"Just a moment," she said, her mind straining to put the pieces of the puzzle she'd just discovered together.

Why was it so familiar?

"Is this Dr Quinn? You called me." He sounded incredulous but Harriet was too far down the rabbit hole to fully appreciate the irony in his statement.

"The chain wrapped around the last girl's hand," she said. "Is there another picture of it?"

"The chain?"

"Yes. I can see a chain wrapped around her fist. I want to know if you have a close up of it?"

"Well, I think so. Why?"

Was the suspicion in his voice simply there

because of his job? Had it been foisted upon him—a by-product of the kind of work he did—or had his naturally suspicious nature led him to choose a career in law enforcement?

It wasn't a question she was going to get an answer to now and Harriet dismissed the thought as quickly as it had arrived.

"I'd like to see it."

"I've gathered that," he said. "I want to know why."

She sighed, her patience rapidly wearing thin as she pushed her hand back through her hair.

"I cannot finish making my assessment until I am in possession of all of the facts."

"So, you think there's something in all of this?" His words ran into each other.

He wasn't even trying to conceal the excitement in his voice and it was that fact that caught Harriet's attention. She needed to be cautious. There was no point in allowing her curiosity to destroy a man's career.

"I didn't say that."

"But you're thinking it, aren't you?"

"Look, do you have it or not?"

Drew's laughter on the other end of the line took her by surprise and Harriet flopped back against her chair.

"You do think it's suspicious." There was a loud whoop of joy and Harriet pulled the phone from her ear. "I knew it wasn't straightforward. I knew there was something off about every one of these and—"

"Let's not get ahead of ourselves here," Harriet said, in attempt to rein the conversation back in. While looking over the file had raised certain questions in her mind, there was still the small matter of the coroner ruling all three deaths as suicide.

"What you've given me raises certain questions but I can't in all good conscience say whether there was another person involved."

"What kinds of questions?"

"Give me the photograph I've requested, if you have it, and we can discuss this further."

"I don't have it on me," he said. "I didn't think you'd need something like that."

"I need everything you've got so far," Harriet said. The thought of trawling through more photographs like the ones already spread out across her desk left her cold but this was the evidence she had to go on.

"Wait, is there any way I could get in to see their bedrooms and the place where they died?"

Drew fell silent and Harriet found herself checking to see if the call was in fact still connected. "Hello?"

"Yeah, sorry," he said. "I was miles away. I think I could get you in to see Sian Jones' room and the back garden. The SOCOs only finished there this morning and the parents haven't returned to the property."

Harriet's stomach churned uncomfortably. *What if you're wrong about this?* The voice in the back of her mind didn't hesitate to go straight for the point of her greatest insecurity. She'd been wrong before and look how that had turned out?

"How soon?" Her voice sounded oddly choked to her own ears but if DI Haskell noticed the sudden hoarseness, he was too polite to say anything.

"I'm still outside," he said. "We could go now."

Harriet glanced over at the wall clock. "What, now?" Three thirty. The day was crawling by but it would soon be dark outside and the thought of poking around in the room of a girl who had more than likely taken her own life seemed wrong somehow.

"We won't get many more opportunities like this," he said. "Like I said, my boss wants this all wrapped up and—"

"Fine. I'll be down in five minutes." She started to end the call but not before she heard Drew voice again. "What did you say?"

"I said, thanks." He cleared his throat awkwardly. "There's not many out there who would take a chance like this."

The line went dead and Harriet was left to stare at the phone. Just what had he meant by that?

She set the phone back down on the desk and glanced over the photographs of Sian one last time.

"What happened to you?" Harriet asked the question to the empty air of her office before she pushed the photographs back into the file and stood.

Sian wasn't going to answer her, at least not here like this. If she was going to figure out what kind of mental state the teen had been in before she died, then she needed to go where she had felt safest.

And for a teenager, that place was usually behind the safety of their bedroom door.

CHAPTER THIRTEEN

"I THOUGHT YOU SAID FIVE MINUTES," Drew said to her as she tugged open the passenger door of his car.

"I lost track of time."

He sighed and didn't bother waiting for her to slip her seatbelt into place before he gunned the engine.

He handled the car easily, as though it was an extension of him rather than just a means of getting from point A to point B.

"Why are you so interested in the necklace?"

Harriet found it interesting that despite his apparent ease behind the wheel, he gripped the steering wheel tighter as he cast a sideways glance in her direction. Had he always been this way or was it a more recent habit he'd developed?

She pulled the file open on her lap and withdrew the photograph that sat on the top.

"For starters, the clasp is broken," she said, examining the image closely.

"Broken. Are you sure?"

Harriet suppressed her irritation. "I'm very sure, DI Haskell. I know what a broken clasp on a necklace looks like."

"I didn't mean it like that—" he started but then seemed to change his mind. "What does it mean? That it's broken?"

"Well it could be something and it could be nothing."

"If it means something, tell me," he said, exasperation colouring his voice.

"It's impossible to tell if she was wearing the chain before she died. The bruising and swelling around her neck is extensive, making it difficult to say with any real certainty whether it was ripped off her."

Drew said nothing but Harriet could see the cogs whirring inside his head as his concentration on the road increased.

"Couldn't she have just ripped it off herself?"

Harriet nodded. "It's entirely possible. What's more plausible is that the clasp was already broken on the chain but that she held a sentimental attachment to it and wanted it close by as she ended her own life. What's less plausible is the manner in which she's holding it."

She raised the picture closer to her face, scrutinising every inch of the close up shot of Sian's hand and the chain wound around her fingers.

"I don't understand," Drew said, taking a right turn abruptly much to the irritation of the other road users who shared their displeasure with him in the form of their car horns.

"The chain has been wrapped around her wrist and is wedged up between her index and middle finger. Now I don't know about you but that's not how I would hold something so dear to me."

Silence filled the car.

"Maybe she was afraid of dropping it?"

Harriet shrugged. "It's possible. At this point, anything is possible. I don't know enough about Sian to make any particular pronouncements about her."

"Anything else?"

"I would have expected a note."

"On her phone she had written the words, 'I'm sorry', but that was it."

"It doesn't say that in the file," Harriet said, shifting through the papers in her lap.

"Sorry," he said. "I didn't think."

Harriet turned to stare out the window as they left the city behind and headed out into the countryside. "Even so, 'I'm sorry', isn't a whole lot to go on.

Some teens—when they do take the time to leave notes—leave extensive, well considered missives behind. There's usually something in there about what they want their parents to do with their personal belongings. Some describe how life will be better for those left behind without them there. Not to mention teens are much more clued in to technology so they tend to video record themselves, or use social media."

"Maybe this was spontaneous?"

Harriet shook her head and turned her attention to the image of the girl in the photograph.

"They make plans. For most successful suicides, there are at least twenty-five attempts. It's not an exact science, and the number of studies completed aren't extensive, but what information we do have paints a certain picture."

Harriet chewed her lip. "Of course, there is something else that we haven't mentioned yet."

Drew's shoulder's tightened and he flexed his fingers against the leather of the wheel. "Oh yeah, what's that?"

"Teenagers are more prone to clusterings of suicides. What we're seeing here isn't entirely uncommon."

"You mean like a suicide pact?"

Harriet nodded. "It could be. Or there are indications that some do it as a means to feel as though they are a part of something."

"Now that's ridiculous."

"It could be but you've read about the Werther effect. We see it at play in all areas of our lives— advertising is one prominent area—not just in something like this."

Drew glanced over at her quickly. "I didn't really get it, if I'm honest. All that psycho-babble bullshit tends to go over my head."

"Look at it this way. Why do companies pay celebrities to endorse their products?"

Drew shrugged. "I don't know."

"Because we're conditioned as humans to look up to those who are greater than we are. Back when we were still all living in caves it was the strongest warrior in our tribe who was given the choice pieces of meat. People looked up to them because of the value they added to the group."

Harriet sighed. "Nowadays instead of the strongest, or the fastest, we have the richest, or prettiest, or most popular to admire and emulate. Companies know all of this. They understand our desire to be just like those we admire most and so they pay celebrities to say they wear this perfume, or these kinds of trainers all so we in turn will run out and part with our hard earned cash just so we too can feel special. So that we can feel like we're not so far removed from the person at the top of the pyramid."

"Jaded, Doc?" There was a lightness to his tone that belied the serious expression he wore.

"Why contact me if you think all of this is just psycho-babble bullshit?"

"Because you're my only shot to get the DCI on board with the case. If he hears from an expert that this isn't just a bunch of suicidal teens, he'll let me take a closer look."

"You know I'm going to be completely honest in my findings. If I don't agree with you, I'm going to say it."

Drew shrugged. "Wouldn't be the first time I got shafted by one of your lot," he muttered beneath his breath.

"I take it you don't hold 'my lot,' as you so fondly referred to us, in high-esteem."

"No offence," he said. "But like I said before it all feels too much like psycho-babble to me. Nobody really knows what someone else is thinking, not if they're honest anyway."

"I never claimed I did."

"No but that's what it's really all about isn't it? Your ability to peel back the layers in someone's head so you can see how they tick. I just don't think it sounds like a good idea."

"But that still doesn't answer why you think all of this is nonsense."

Drew fell silent, his attention riveted to the road ahead.

"You don't have to tell me if you'd prefer not to,"

Harriet said finally, turning her attention back to her own window and the fields that flashed by.

"Someone close to me," he said, clearing his throat awkwardly. "She was seeing someone like you. Had been since she was a teen actually—not the same one obviously—different ones down through the years. They'd diagnosed her with all sorts but when I met her she was so normal. And we were happy, content even. And then they changed her meds and it was like something switched in her."

Harriet's mouth felt dry and she gripped the folder in her lap a little tighter. He obviously didn't remember her because if he had, Harriet had the sinking feeling that he wouldn't have been sitting next to her so calmly.

"She started to go downhill. She was even admitted for a week and when she came out, I thought things were improving." He fell silent again.

"But they weren't."

Drew shook his head. "She killed herself four days after she got out of the hospital."

Harriet bit her tongue and dug her fingers into her knee. It was wrong to keep what she knew back from him. But would mentioning it to him cause more damage?

"You think they should have done more for her?"

Drew parked the car in front of a compact two-storey house. From the corner of her eye, Harriet spotted the fluttering yellow tape that declared to the world that something terrible had occurred there.

She met his haunted gaze as he turned to face her in the car. In the fading light he looked exhausted, the lines on his face exposing the raw unbridled emotion he had until that moment kept hidden.

"I think they killed her. She was doing just fine and they went messing with her. They couldn't leave well enough alone and because of all of that she's gone."

"But you said it yourself that she'd had difficulties, issues that were there long before you two met. How can you say that what happened wasn't something that would have happened anyway?"

"No." There was a rough edge to Drew's voice and Harriet knew that to push him further would only end with him breaking down.

"I am sorry for your loss," she said, feeling the inadequacy in her words keenly. But what else was she supposed to say? There was nothing she could do for him, nothing that would take away his pain. All she could offer him was the knowledge that she empathised with his pain. In this world it was all anyone could offer someone else.

"No need," he said abruptly. "It wasn't your fault. You didn't kill her. Anyway, we're here. I suppose we should head in before we lose all the light."

Drew pushed open the car door, letting a swirl of

cold air slip inside. Gripping the case file to her chest, Harriet watched as he climbed out and headed up the path toward the front door and the guilt she felt inside gnawed at her.

He wasn't entirely wrong. She hadn't killed his fiancée, the troubled young woman had done that all on her own. But he was wrong if he thought her hands were clean in all of this.

It was at that moment that Harriet wondered if she'd made a mistake in agreeing to look at the files. When all was said and done, the likelihood of this being anything more than a tragedy was tiny. Which meant that DI Haskell was fighting shadows that weren't really there.

He beckoned to her and Harriet drew in a deep breath. If that's all this was then she would disengage at the first available opportunity. But she had to look into it, if only to put her own mind at ease. If there was even the remotest possibility that he was right, then it meant someone had so far gotten away with murder.

Three deaths in three months. If it were true, then others would die.

And that wasn't something she could have on her conscience.

CHAPTER FOURTEEN

"I THOUGHT you were going to stay in the car all evening," he said. "Is there something wrong?"

Harriet shook her head. "No. I was lost in thought is all."

Drew nodded and turned away from her but not before she glimpsed something akin to understanding flash in his eyes.

"I do that sometimes," he said quietly. "Especially with the cases that involve kids. They're harder to deal with somehow. I don't know why but they slide under my skin easier."

"Do you dream of them?"

He pushed open the front door and the stale air swirled out, engulfing Harriet in its dry warmth.

"Sometimes," he said. "I don't get much sleep."

"Because of the nightmares," she surmised, more to herself than to him.

"That would be a better description," he said grimly, directing her to move ahead of him. "I'll follow your lead."

"Forensics have been through here?"

"Yeah, it's safe. Just don't break anything or I'll have to log it and then explain the extra paperwork to the Monk."

Harriet glanced over her shoulder. "The Monk?"

Drew's face went police detective blank, nothing more than a mask behind which he could hide his true emotions from her.

"It's just something we call DCI Gregson. We don't mean any harm by it. I guess it's our way of blowing off steam."

She said nothing as she stepped into the hall. It wasn't unusual for those in the lesser ranks to chafe beneath the authority of their superior officers. And it certainly wasn't her place to draw any kinds of inferences or conclusions on the working relationship between Drew and his boss.

"Her bedroom, it's on the first floor?" Harriet paused at the bottom of the stairs and peered up into the gloom.

Drew answered her question by flicking on the downstairs lights. The staircase was suddenly illuminated in a warm yellow glow that seemed to highlight the pictures hanging along the walls.

"Is this the rest of the family?" Harriet pointed to a framed picture of four people huddled together on a beige sofa. Their bright smiling faces reflected warmth and happiness.

"That's Janet and her first husband Roy. He died six years ago when Sian was just eight and her brother was five. Cancer."

"I didn't know," Harriet said softly. She stared at the image, her mind conjuring the scene as it must have been. They'd been happy, there was no doubt about it. Pictures could sometimes hide a multitude of sins but the open, innocent smiles that all four of them wore weren't something that could be faked.

"That must have been hard for her," she said. "The death of a parent isn't easy for any child."

"She'd have been too young to fully grasp it," Drew said from behind her.

Harriet shook her head. "Her brother maybe. But not Sian. She would have memories of her father. They might not be solid but the feelings he evoked in her—safety, joy, love—" Harriet ticked them off on her fingers. "—They would all be there. Eight is old enough to recognise the trauma something like cancer causes. And, well, it's certainly old enough to realise that death is something permanent."

"Maybe they didn't tell her when he was sick?"

Harriet shook her head and glanced back at the picture. "It would be difficult to keep something as traumatic as cancer hidden from an inquisitive eight-year-old."

"You sound like you speak from experience."

Harriet shook her head. "Not exactly."

She moved up the stairs, noting the progression of photographs. The family pictures stopped, replaced instead by photographs of Sian smiling in her school uniform. Her brother's image was much the same although he appeared in more pictures with his mother, their familial relationship as plain as the noses on their faces.

Sian's smile faded in the images, replaced instead by a teenager who looked a little sullen, but it was the eyes Harriet found herself most interested in. There was a profound sadness that lurked in the pictures. But just like many things, where teenagers were concerned, it wasn't uncommon.

"This one here," Harriet said as she paused next to another family photograph. The set-up for this image was so far removed from the last family picture that it stood out in stark contrast.

"Who is that?"

"Sian's mother remarried. Nigel Thompson, forty-eight, previously unmarried with no children."

"Was there friction between the children and Nigel?" She glanced over her shoulder at Drew who stood just below her on the stairs.

"Well, not according to Sian's mother Janet but I find it hard to believe."

"And Mr Thompson what did he have to say?"

"Not a whole lot," Drew said with a shrug. "The

bloke seemed pretty cut up about the whole situation."

"What do you mean?"

"He could barely form words he was crying that much. It's not uncommon to see a father break down over the loss of his child."

"But you thought it was odd," she finished for him.

For a moment he seemed to consider her words before he finally nodded. "It was odd. Janet was in shock, you could see that, and it's what I would expect. She helped to cut her daughter down and Sian, when they found her, was not in a good way. It's not something I would wish on anyone."

Harriet nodded. She'd seen enough suicide in her life to know just what he meant. When she'd worked with patients in a clinical capacity, suicide was the sword of Damocles that hung over all of their heads.

"I'm sorry that they had to see that."

"So am I."

"In spite of this you still think Mr Thompson's reaction was unusual?"

"Look, I don't know the bloke but after what happened, I'd have expected shock. Not the watering can he turned out to be. He went through four packs of tissues and Officer Crandell in the end had to take him out of the room so I could finish speaking to Mrs Thompson and make sense of things."

Harriet's lips twisted into a rueful smile and she

turned away on the stairs to hide it from the detective. It had been a long time since she'd heard anyone describe an emotional person as a watering can but it was certainly descriptive and it instantly conjured an image in her mind.

"And how did Mrs Thompson respond?"

"She didn't say much. Everything she did say had to be prompted but I can deal with that," Drew said gruffly. "If I'm perfectly honest with you, she looked to me like a broken woman."

"What about Sian's brother; Paul isn't it?"

"The grandparents were there and they kept him and the little baby sister, Clare, out of the worst of it."

"We should go up," Harriet said as she started back up the stairs. Reaching the landing, she paused outside Sian's bedroom made obvious by the teenager's name written across the door with faded multicoloured letters that wouldn't have looked out of place on a child's bedroom.

"I thought that was strange too," Drew said, noting her observation of the name.

"It probably holds some sentimental value to her," Harriet said, raising her hand so that her fingers hovered over the worn lettering. "Perhaps her father put them up for her."

Drew said nothing but she could feel him at her back, a warm comforting presence as she stood outside the dead teenager's room.

Harriet took a step forward and the floorboard

creaked ominously beneath her foot. Why not ask to have it fixed? The question popped into her mind alongside a thousand others and she pushed it aside. Questions could come later, for now she needed to soak in as much information as possible, only then would she be able to form a picture in her mind of who Sian was.

Her hands closed around the handle and she pushed the door inwards.

The room was much as she imagined most teenagers' rooms to be; clothes strewn around on most surfaces except for where they belonged. The wardrobe stood opposite the bed, despite the doors being ajar the light from overhead didn't penetrate the gloaming filled cavernous space. The bed reflected in the mirror on the dresser and Harriet turned to stare at it.

The sheets were pulled up and tucked in, the corners folded so neatly that Harriet was instantly reminded of the hospital corners she saw used on the beds in the institution where she'd worked.

"Who made the bed?"

"Excuse me?" Drew leaned against the doorjamb as though he didn't want to cross into this sacred space.

"The bed," Harriet said gesturing to it. "Who made it?"

"Sian I suppose," he said.

Harriet shook her head and took a step back from the bed. "I don't think Sian made it."

"What makes you say that?" He sounded genuinely confused.

"How many teenage girls do you know who make their beds this neatly? I know that when I was a teenager, I wasn't doing this. It was a good day if I pulled the duvet up, never mind actually going to the effort of creating such tight, pristine corners."

Drew craned his neck around the door.

"You can come in," Harriet said softly.

He shot her a guilty look. "I know that."

"You just don't like to?"

He nodded. "Yeah, you could say that. I was in here the day we got the call about her. I always feel like I'm snooping. I mean if she was still here, she wouldn't want me pawing through her stuff."

Harriet turned and looked about the room. "No, she wouldn't. But the problem is that she's not here anymore. And if you're right and someone is responsible for that, then I think that even Sian would agree to you searching her room for clues."

Drew nodded and stepped into the room. "I suppose when you put it like that."

He moved around the bed and peered down at the perfectly neat sheets. "One of her parents must have done this."

Harriet nodded. "It's possible. Although it's more

common for the parent to do things like this when children go missing. They prepare the space as though by doing it they expect their child to return at any moment."

"And when a child dies?"

"Most parents leave the rooms exactly as their loved one left it. Many treat the bedrooms of their children as if they're sacred. You've got to remember that for some people, something like this is their last connection with their deceased loved one."

Drew's lips thinned as he turned and examined the room. "You still think she committed suicide?"

Harriet hesitated. There was nothing so far to suggest otherwise, at least nothing overtly obvious.

"It says in the file that Sian knew and was friends with the second teenager to commit suicide. Aidan Wilson."

"They were boyfriend and girlfriend," Drew said. "According to her mother, Sian was pretty cut up about his death."

"You see, that makes it sound like this was a Romeo and Juliet tragedy," Harriet said. "Two teenagers in love with each other, one kills themselves and the other can't live without them and so follows them."

"So, you're saying you think this is just a cluster of suicides then?"

"I'm saying I need more information. There are a lot of unanswered questions but so far most of them point in one direction."

"The one direction I don't want them to point," Drew said. "Shit."

"I'm sorry."

"It's not your fault," he said. "You're not the one looking for crimes where there aren't any. I'm the one who should be sorry for dragging you out here for nothing."

Harriet chewed her lip nervously as he paced back and forth in the small space.

"I really believed this was more, you know?"

Harriet nodded but she didn't answer him. She didn't need to; his questions weren't really the kind that required an answer.

From the corner of her eye, Harriet spotted the empty place where she imagined Sian's laptop would have sat. "Have they found anything on her laptop?"

"Her what?"

"Sian's laptop. Have they found anything of interest on it?"

Drew shook his head. "Nothing outside the ordinary stuff you'd expect to find on a teen's laptop."

"What about research for suicide? Had she looked up any sites that might have told her how best to tie the knot?"

His forehead creased. "I don't think so. Why should they have?"

"Maybe she wiped the history..."

"I can have my people do a more thorough search if you'd like."

Harriet nodded. "It wouldn't hurt. And do you have any statements from her friends?"

"What we do have I can send over to you."

Harriet paused her perusal of the room. "Why do I get the feeling you're holding something back from me?"

Drew raised his hands in mock offence. "I've got nothing to hide."

"But I can't help but have the feeling that there is something. I told you before Detective that everything and anything could be important here. You holding out on me isn't going to help me make an accurate assessment."

Drew sighed. "Fine, there is something."

Harriet bit her tongue to keep from interrupting him. If there was one thing that really frustrated her when working with a detective like Drew Haskell it was their inability to trust her with all the information. It was almost as though they believed if they told her everything it would somehow influence her in the wrong way. A preconceived bias that ultimately hindered her understanding instead of focusing it.

"When we looked through her phone, we found a lot of troubling text messages."

"And you're worried that I'll take that into account and just dismiss everything out of hand?"

He glanced sheepishly down at the ground. "You wouldn't be the first. I mean, even the Monk said it confirmed suspicions that this was nothing more than a troubled teen who had her heart broken."

"But I'm not him." Harriet said trying and failing to keep the anger from her voice. It was all too easy to dismiss the thoughts and feelings of the young as though once you turned a certain age your mind caused you to forget just how painful it was to grow up.

Harriet sighed and turned away. Getting angry at Drew's boss wasn't going to help anyone, least of all Sian.

She pushed her hand back through her hair and studied the room with a critical eye.

What are you trying to tell me?

The back of the door caught her attention and she moved toward it as though drawn there by an invisible cord that tugged her closer.

"What is it?"

"I don't know," she said, pausing next to the door. Dropping down into a crouch, Harriet eyed the lock. Tiny screw holes dotted the surface above the handle and the paint was discoloured as though there had been something there once but it had since been removed.

"What does this look like to you?"

Drew moved over and crouched alongside her. He reached up and brushed a gloved finger against the wood. "Maybe there was a lock or something here?"

Harriet nodded. "It makes sense, most teenagers are fiercely protective of their privacy. But why remove the lock?"

"Maybe she got a key for the door and didn't need the lock anymore?"

"If she did, then where is the key now?"

Drew climbed onto his feet and felt along the frame that ran over the top of the door. "I don't know," he said finally admitting defeat. "What do you think it means?"

Harriet shrugged. There were too many variables and possibilities as to why the lock had been removed.

"I don't know," she said finally. "It could be something and nothing. Without talking to her parents as to their reasons I couldn't possibly say."

"Why couldn't Sian have taken off the lock?"

Harriet shot him a withering look. "You don't have many dealings with teenagers, do you?"

"Nah," he said. "My sister's kid is only four and a half and likes Paw-Patrol. I'm pretty lucky."

"A teenager isn't going to willingly remove a lock. Especially when it adds an extra layer of security to their safe haven."

Drew stared down at the blank place where the lock had sat.

"But you think it's important?"

"I really don't know. If I had the answer don't you think I'd have said it?"

"We should go then," Drew said, his tone icy as he strode from the room.

With a bemused shake of her head, Harriet did another turn of the room. If he thought he could just growl at her and she would jump to attention then he could dream on. She would leave when she was good and ready and there was something about the room that nagged at her.

Dropping down onto the mattress, Harriet stared up at the landscape pictures that were framed on the walls. It wasn't entirely a typical teenager's room.

Climbing onto the bed, she peered at the wallpaper noting the slight discolourations and variations in the paper itself in various sizes and shapes that to her eye at least looked rectangular. If she had to guess she'd have said there were posters on the wall at some point in the not so distant past. But someone had removed them all and replaced them with the bland framed images that now adorned the space.

She'd been wrong to assume when she'd first entered that the room belonged entirely to Sian. There was something underlying it all but she couldn't quite put her finger on just what it might be, yet.

Leaning over she pressed her fingers in along the edges of the mattress, finding a gap, she pushed her hand into the space; fingers scrabbling for purchase.

When she found nothing, she straightened up again and moved over to the bedside locker.

Dropping to her knees in front of the small cabinet, she tugged open the top drawer—careful not to disturb the contents too much—she searched it from top to bottom before moving on to the next one. When she'd completed her search of the second one, she started to close it but the drawer caught on its runner. Harriet jiggled it and the drawer slid shut with an audible click.

Narrowing her eyes, she pulled the drawer open again and slid her fingers into the gaps along the side of the wood. It wasn't until she felt across the underside of the wood panel that she found the reason it had refused to shut in the first place.

Bending down, she peered up at the crisscross of silver duct-tape that made up a kind of pocket shape, the inside of which held a pink sparkly notebook.

"Bingo!" Harriet said, tugging it free. She flipped open the hard cover and traced her fingers over the stickers that adorned the curling pages.

Scrawled across the front were the words: *This diary belongs to Sian Jones! Keep out! Or ELSE!!!*

With a smile, Harriet settled back against the bed and flipped quickly through the pages. She'd been hoping Sian was the kind of teenager who religiously kept a diary and what she found on the pages certainly seemed to suggest it. However, there was something else. Harriet turned the diary on its side and peered at the top of the book, noting the missing pages by the fraying of the spine.

"Who else knew about your diary, Sian?" Harriet whispered to herself as she flipped open the diary again and started to read. "Did you tear the pages out yourself, or did somebody not like what you had to say?"

"Are you talking to yourself?" Drew asked, popping his head around the door.

"Not exactly," Harriet said, holding the diary up triumphantly. "This might help shed some light on her state of mind on the run up to her death."

"What is it?"

"Sian's diary."

Hope dawned in Drew's eyes. "Anything in there about her planning to kill herself?"

"I've only just found it," Harriet said. "And anyway, someone beat us to it. There are some pages missing."

A crease appeared between Drew's brows as they snapped together. "Missing?"

"Someone tore them out." Harriet ran her finger along the ripped edges of the missing pages. "They weren't exactly careful about it either."

"Could Sian have done it herself?"

"Of course she could. But why bother keeping the diary if you're just going to rip the pages out? Most teenagers try to cover up their mistakes by scribbling over the top of them, hoping to see them disappear beneath a sea of black ink."

"I should take it into evidence," he said, fishing a clear plastic bag out of the inside of his jacket.

"Can I have a copy of the pages when you're done with them?"

He nodded and Harriet glanced back down at the open page in front of her.

"You asked me earlier if I thought this was a suicide."

The air stilled and she fought the urge to meet Drew's gaze head on.

"I'd be remiss to say it wasn't a possibility that there was foul play involved."

"I need more than that to take to the Monk," Drew said. "He'll say I'm grasping at straws and wasting resources."

"Then I'll talk to him," Harriet said, making up her mind. She wasn't sure that it was anything more than a tragedy, but the coincidences were beginning to mount and if there was one thing she didn't believe in, it was coincidences. At least not the kind that ended with three dead teenagers.

"I can make him understand that we need to look at this closer." A word in the diary caught Harriet's attention and she paused. "And if it's not too much to ask, I'd like to meet Nigel Thompson."

This time she did look up at Drew.

"You don't think he's responsible for this."

"Who knows? But I'd like to know why his name appears over and over in Sian's diary."

"What do you mean?"

Harriet held the notebook up to the light so Drew could read Sian's angry words.

"Aidan told me today he'd kill Nigel for me if I wanted him to and there was a part of me that wanted to say yes!"

"Christ," Drew said, crossing the carpet to pause next to the bed. "It's not exactly a motive for murder. But it's not good either."

Harriet let him take the diary and watched as he slipped it into the plastic evidence bag. He dated it quickly before offering a hand to help her to her feet. She hesitated for just a moment before taking his gloved hand and letting him pull her back onto her feet.

"Good catch," he said. "It might be something."

"And it might be nothing," Harriet warned. "But I'd feel better knowing we had at least looked into all three deaths. I can't put my finger on it but something doesn't feel right and I'd like to know what it is."

"You and me both," Drew said with a sigh. "You and me both."

CHAPTER FIFTEEN

"IF IT'S ALL RIGHT, I'd like to take a look at the place where she died." Harriet addressed the back of Drew's head as he moved down the stairs ahead of her.

"Why?" He paused and she pulled herself up short to keep herself from running into him.

Harriet shrugged. It was hard to explain to someone who didn't spend half of their life living inside the heads of others.

"Let me guess," he said. "It could be important?"

Harriet smiled as he turned from her with a sigh and started off down the last three steps.

"Fine. We'll go out around the front and into the back garden that way."

"What route did Sian take?"

"I don't know," Drew said. "Forensics didn't

decide on a particular path, just the most likely route."

"And that is?"

"Out through the back door."

Harriet chewed her lip and paused on the stairs. "Do you have a key for the backdoor?"

Drew rolled his eyes and held aloft a set of keys. "I've got a set here. What does it matter what route she took?"

"Retracing her steps tells me what she saw before she died."

"And what does that prove?"

"Something and maybe nothing. Look, I don't tell you how to do your job. The moment I do, feel free to tell me how to do mine." She stared pointedly at him and he sighed but handed the keys over to her.

"Let's just get this over and done with."

Harriet nodded and took the keys. He stepped aside to let her pass on the stairs. There wasn't a whole lot of space and Harriet was acutely aware of the heat of his body as she slipped by.

Reaching the hallway, she peered into the darkened room that waited for her at the end of the illuminated corridor. Taking her time, so as not to miss anything, she moved into the kitchen.

Typically, kitchens were considered the heart of the home. It was usually where a family spent the most amount of their time together. After all there was something communal in the act of eating together. Food brought people together. Without it, without nourishment, we would die.

There was a part of us, deep down, that remembered that ancient drive. The primitive inside us all. Some scientists called it the reptile brain. It understood that food was life and that having it was the difference between living and dying.

The first humans were hardwired to not share their life-giving food.

However, our basic instincts evolved and the animals that we are learned quickly that the act of sharing meant survival for the tribe. If we hunted together—if we sacrificed together—then our chances of eating multiplied exponentially and all those thousands of years ago we understood this fundamental truth.

The sharing of food was sacred. Sitting down to break bread with your brother was an act of community, a coming together. Religions traded on this knowledge and Christianity had certainly gotten it right when they used the iconography of Christ breaking bread with his disciples as a means to bring their flock together.

Whether we admitted it or not the sharing of food was vitally important and so without realising it our kitchens became the hub for this sacred act.

As she stepped into the kitchen, Harriet could almost imagine it as the warm and welcoming room Sian would have known it to be.

A WICKED MERCY

Three of the walls were painted a warm latté. The largest of the four was painted in what could only be described as raspberry. It was this wall that was dominated by the large family table which was piled high with papers and books.

As she stood there in the fading evening light, Harriet could picture the family sitting together; talking over one another in an attempt to be heard. And in the middle of it all was Sian.

"Did you feel they weren't listening to you?"

Harriet moved further into the kitchen and noted the large calendar near the back door. There were all kinds of notes and dates circled. Letters dotted the surface and it took Harriet a moment to work out this special code that the family had shared.

PJ stood for Paul Jones, Sian's younger brother. CT was her baby sister. JT was obviously Janet, her mother. NT was Nigel. Harriet scanned the letters and found only one instance of SJ.

There was so much going on with the rest of the family but Sian was the only odd duck in the group.

"Were you alone amongst them, Sian? Did you feel neglected? Ignored, perhaps?"

"Do you always talk to yourself like this?" Drew's voice broke through Harriet's concentration making her jump. "I'm sorry. I didn't mean to startle you."

"You didn't," she said, sounding flustered. "I was just miles away."

"I can see that." He paused and Harriet could

143

almost see the wheels inside his head ticking over. "So, do you always talk to yourself out loud like that?"

"Sometimes," she said. "It depends. I'm so used to having someone to ask the questions too. But in this case, I can't ask Sian. It still helps to say it aloud."

He looked unconvinced. Obviously, he hadn't exaggerated when he described the work she did as psycho-babble bullshit.

"Are you learning anything?"

Harriet indicated the calendar with a tilt of her head. "Everyone else is on here multiple times," she said. "Everyone else's life is busy and full. After school activities, doctor's appointments, hairdressers, dentists. You name it, they're doing it."

"But that's typical for a busy family, isn't it?"

Harriet nodded. "Yeah, except Sian is only on there once."

"So maybe she didn't need to go to the doctor, or dentist?"

Harriet could tell that Drew wasn't understanding the importance of what she was trying to say.

"According to the list that was the one thing Sian was going to do this month. She had an appointment to see the family GP on Wednesday afternoon at half-four. Aside from that, there was nothing else."

Harriet sighed and let her fingers trace over Sian's initials.

"As though she wasn't really a part of the family at all."

Realisation dawned on Drew's face and he moved over to look at the calendar a little more closely.

"Everything in this house set her apart from the others. She was an outsider in her own home."

"Are you saying they deliberately isolated their own daughter?"

Harriet shook her head. "I'm not saying that at all. There's a certain amount of isolation bound to happen with all teenagers. In most cases it's cause is combined; the teenager pulls away and the family adjusts without them."

"And here?"

"It feels a little more extreme here. And if this isn't a suicide then whoever murdered Sian knew she was an outsider in her own home. They knew it and took advantage of it."

Drew sucked a deep breath in through his teeth. "Do you think the same is possible for the others?"

Harriet nodded. "If it's the same person involved in all three cases then I would look for tell-tale signs that they were isolated from their loved ones too."

Drew nodded, pursing his lips. Harriet took the opportunity to jiggle the back door handle and it popped open easily.

"I thought you said the family hadn't been back

since Sian's death?" Harriet said, as she paused with her hand on the door.

"They haven't. Why?"

"Then one of your people must have left the door unlocked when they closed up. Not exactly the smartest thing to do if we're thinking this is a murder and not a—," Harriet cut off as she noticed the pinched expression on Drew's face. "What is it?"

"I locked up," he said. "That's why I have the keys. And that door was definitely locked when I left here."

"Maybe you were mistaken. I mean it must have been a shock—,"

"And what?" He snapped, his face contorting in rage. "You think I left the door open on purpose?"

"That's not what I was about to say." Harriet tried to keep her voice level.

"Well that's what it sounds like to me. You're accusing me of incompetence."

"I'm saying it's easy enough to make a mistake in such an emotional case, DI Haskell. I'm not accusing you of incompetence at all."

"The door was locked. I checked and double checked."

"Well then how do you explain the door being open?"

"Perhaps the family did come back?"

"Well before you decide to snap at anyone else,

I'd suggest you check with the family. Otherwise we've got a situation on our hands here."

"What do you mean?"

Harriet sighed and pushed her hand back through her hair. "It's not uncommon for murderers to return to the scene of their crime to—" She gestured to the air as though for inspiration. "—re-live it."

"They'd need to have a key," Drew said, his face turning white. "Shit. We've been through here. If the killer did return, they might have left prints or some other forensic traces."

"I don't think so." Harriet stepped out through the backdoor and surveyed the garden. The trees that lined the bottom fence swayed rhythmically in the sharp breeze.

"What makes you so sure?"

"If they were going to leave traces, they'd have done so when they murdered Sian. With their adrenaline pumping they were most at risk for making a critical mistake. If you didn't find anything unusual then, you're definitely not going to find it now."

Drew swore under his breath as Harriet made her way onto the deck that sat outside the backdoor.

Was this the last thing Sian saw? Had she planned her end out here; staring up at the tall trees that protected the house? Was she lulled by the rhythmic creak of the limbs as they reached toward the sky and danced in the wind?

Or had someone else stood here and, mesmerised by the sheer force of nature, decided to act? Had they watched Sian? Stalked her, even? And seeing her unhappiness, had they pounced?

"Was it mercy, or just your own perverse desire to inflict your power and control over others that drove you to this?"

"It was the third from the left," Drew said from close behind her. This time Harriet had heard him approach and so she only flinched inwardly.

Her gaze snagged on the tree he'd pointed to and she turned to stare back at the house.

"That's Sian's window up there, isn't it?" Harriet pointed to the dormer style window above their heads.

"Yeah. Looks like it."

"Did they watch her from there and that's why they chose that window?" Harriet's breath caught in the back of her throat as she let her gaze drop to the kitchen window.

"Wait, who found Sian's body first?"

Drew tugged a notebook from his pocket and flicked through pages upon pages of illegible handwriting. "According to the interview Nigel said he was the first to find her."

"Did he say how he found her?"

Drew cocked an eyebrow in Harriet's direction. "I don't understand?"

"Well did he check her room, or did he come down to the kitchen and spot her from the window?"

"I never asked him."

Harriet nodded and moved back toward the house. She pressed her back to the wall, imaging the glass between her and the outside wall.

"I think he saw her through the window." Harriet lowered her voice and crossed the garden to the spot directly in front of the tree. She turned and gazed back up at the house. "They placed her here deliberately, in full view of anyone in the kitchen."

"They wanted her found."

Harriet shrugged. "I think they wanted to shock. To wound. Perhaps Sian wasn't the only victim in all of this. Who was usually the first one up in the mornings?"

"Nigel," Drew said without hesitation. "That's how I know he was the first to find her. I asked him who was usually first up."

Harriet nodded. "Then the person we're looking for knew all of this. They took their time, planning their crime. Observing and watching the family."

"The coroner found no defensive wounds on Sian, did he?"

Drew shook his head. "Nothing."

"So, she didn't put up a fight and that's unusual."

"I'm just going to play devil's advocate here for a moment," Drew said. "If someone has made up their mind to end it, why would you expect to find defensive wounds on them?"

"Because people fight. It's instinctual. Even those who plan to commit suicide fight back. Their bodies don't know any better. Long after they pass out, their bodies writhe and fight until the bitter end. We're programmed for survival and Sian was a young healthy teenage girl. Finding nothing on her tells me she wasn't the one in control."

Drew let out a long breath. "That's proof then?"

"It's going to take a little convincing and we'd need to talk to the coroner about it all but, yeah. I'd say you've got your smoking gun with this."

CHAPTER SIXTEEN

DREW SAT in the stiff-backed chair and waited for DCI Gregson to explode. If the colour of the man's face was anything to go by, he wouldn't have very long to wait.

"You're telling me you went behind my back and contacted an outsider so you could bring them onto a case? A case I said was closed?"

Drew contemplated all the different answers he could give to his boss. Of course, not one of those answers would save him facing the DCI's wrath.

"I followed my intuition sir, and it paid off. Dr Quinn is in agreement with me about what we're dealing with."

"And just what is it that Dr Quinn thinks we're dealing with?"

"It's her expert opinion that Sian Jones was murdered."

The silence in the room was heavy and Drew had to force himself to take a breath.

Gregson leaned forward and pressed his thumb and index finger against the bridge of his nose, pinching down hard enough that Drew could see the outline of the man's fingers in his ruddy complexion.

"I thought you understood," DCI Gregson said. "I thought we were on the same page here, Drew. And then you go and create a shit-storm like this."

"Sir, I wouldn't have done this if I didn't think it was important."

Gregson let his hand drop down to the desk and met Drew's gaze head on. "Well get her in here, let's see if we can't make sense of this mess."

Drew kept his expression deliberately blank as he stood and moved to the door. Pulling it open, he beckoned to Harriet who sat waiting at his desk.

She stood; every male eye in the room surreptitiously followed her movements as she smoothed down her unruly hair and picked her way through the desks to the office.

"DCI Gregson, I'd like to introduce Dr Harriet Quinn."

Gregson stood behind the desk and held his hand out toward Harriet. She took it and shook the other man's hand firmly before taking the offered chair next to Drew's.

From the corner of his eye, Drew watched as she

leaned back; a picture of ease despite the obvious hostility in the room.

"I'd like to thank you for agreeing to speak with me," She started to speak and Drew winced as Gregson dismissed her with a wave of his hand, effectively cutting her off.

"Let's cut to the chase here, shall we?" Gregson said, there was no mistaking the authority in his voice. It was something Drew had always admired in the other man. When the DCI was firmly on your side there was nobody capable of standing against him. Fights were easily won, or at least that was how it appeared. For all Drew knew, the toll it took on his boss was a heavy one.

It was certainly that way in his case.

"You don't really believe that we're dealing with a murder here. At least not deep down you don't. We both know it's a tragic suicide and the last thing either of us wants is to drag the family through anymore hurt by scrutinising every little detail of their life and their daughters'."

"DCI Gregson, I think—"

He raised his hand. "If you'll let me finish please, Dr Quinn. I'll give you your chance to respond in a moment.

"I've reviewed the case files myself. I'm familiar with the evidence presented and it's my opinion on this matter that the case is closed. DI Haskell here made a mistake by getting you involved and—"

"DCI Gregson," Harriet said, cutting the older man off before he could continue.

Drew didn't know her but the few hours he'd spent in her company had given him the impression that Harriet was not a woman to be so easily dismissed.

"I'm not here to tell you how to do your job. What I am going to tell you is that these cases deserve more than just a cursory glance."

DCI Gregson straightened up in his chair, his face taking on an unbecoming shade of crimson.

"Just who do you—"

"Who do I think I am? I think I'm the only person in this room who has spent years researching and studying the human mind. I think I'm the only one in this room who has published several papers on suicide, particularly that among young teenagers and the clustering that can occur in particular age groups. I think out of everyone here, I am best qualified to tell you that no matter how much you want this case to be an open and shut tragedy. The likelihood of it being just that is infinitesimally small."

Drew held his breath as Harriet sighed. It was an opportunity for the DCI to cut her off and Drew expected his boss to order her out of the office for such disrespect. The fact that he didn't and instead sat back in his chair as though he were actually listening to what she had to say gave Drew the kind of hope he'd been dreaming of.

"Go on," DCI Gregson said finally.

"There are several inconsistencies in this case. I can't speak to the other two yet because I haven't fully reviewed their files. But in the case of Sian Jones it's my expert opinion that it should be—for the time being at least—considered suspicious."

"You still haven't told me why you think that."

"The necklace she was wearing," Harriet said. "I have a few questions that I'd like answered regarding it. From my cursory examination of some of the evidence DI Haskell here provided me with, it's not clear how it came to be in her hand and not around her neck. Not to mention today's discovery of her diary, which I feel should be reviewed with an eye to her state of mind directly leading up to her death."

"Her diary?" The DCI quirked an inquisitive eyebrow in Drew's direction. "And just where did you discover this diary?"

"At Sian Jones' house," Harriet said.

Drew swallowed past the lump in his throat. "Dr Quinn felt she would get a better feel for the victim if she had access to the girl's bedroom and the place where she died."

"Oh, did she now?" The warning in Gregson's voice was implicit but if Harriet picked up on it, she made no acknowledgement of it.

"There are questions that need answers, DCI Gregson. Important questions. And I think Sian deserves our respect in following up on them."

"You still haven't told me anything that as yet would make me believe that these are anything other than they appear."

"Sir, Dr Quinn mentioned to me when we were attending the crime scene that she would expect to find defensive wounds on the victim's body. The coroner doesn't mention any such injuries in his report. Shouldn't that at least warrant a closer look?"

DCI Gregson gave Drew a frosty glare and any other detective sitting in the chair might have withered beneath such a look. Drew held his nerve.

Why was it so important to him that these not turn out to be so straight forward? Perhaps the others were correct to question his motives and mindset regarding the case. It wasn't impossible that he was jumping at shadows and searching for a bad guy when there was nothing there.

"Fine. You can speak to the coroner and if he agrees with yours and Dr Quinn's assessment on this then I will allow an inquiry."

"And the other two cases?" Harriet asked, her voice steely in her determination.

"You can review the case files for those as well," Gregson conceded. "However, if Jackson says these are open and shut suicides then I'm going to take his expert opinion over yours Dr Quinn, no offence."

"None taken," she said. Drew found himself wanting to leap out of the chair and swing her around the small cramped office space but thought better of it.

"I'll set up an appointment with Dr Jackson," Drew said instead, pushing onto his feet.

He left the office in a daze and made a beeline for his desk.

"DI Haskell?" Harriet's voice pulled him up short and he turned to find her hovering at his elbow.

"Sorry," he said. "I was miles away."

She nodded and gave him a tight smile that never touched her eyes. She was definitely an enigma and Drew found himself wanting to get to know her better. Just what was she hiding and holding back from him? What secrets lurked in the depths of her blue eyes?

"I was just wondering if you could get me set up with a copies of the other files and the images I requested earlier?"

Drew found himself nodding as he scooped up the telephone from its cradle. "Of course," he said. "I can get them all sorted for you in the morning and—"

Before he could finish speaking, Harriet was already shaking her head. "No, I was rather hoping I could get them now. That way I can have a jumpstart on them for when we meet with the coroner."

Drew stared at her in surprise. What in the world had given her the impression that she would be meeting with the coroner?

"I don't think that's going to be possible," he said.

"Which part?"

"All of it really," he said, scrubbing his hand over his face, his stubble rasping against the palm of his hand. Christ he must look like some sort of mountain man. It was a wonder the Monk hadn't pulled him up on his appearance yet.

Harriet pursed her lips and folded her arms over her chest. "I'm afraid I'm not following you. I thought my request seemed perfectly straight forward and given the time constraints, under-standable."

"It is, except I'm just one bloke. The files are more than extensive and going through them to—"

"You mean picking and choosing the elements of the files you're willing to share with me? The bits and pieces you think I need to see?"

Drew felt the weight of Maz's eyes on the back of his neck. He wasn't the only one staring either, just the most blatant.

Reaching out, he took Harriet by the elbow and steered her toward the empty briefing room at the opposite end of the office. With the door closed, he turned to face her.

"I'm not going to cut you out of the loop, not when you've helped me keep the case open."

"Then what's the problem?"

"The files are huge," he said. "Do you know how much goes into an investigation, even one like this? Every item from forensics catalogued. Each witness statement. Every report I've had to file on each dead kid."

"I should hope it's extensive not to mention thorough," Harriet said icily. "What's your point?"

"My point is, it's going to take me some time to put it all together for you. To make copies of everything and—"

She laughed, a high tinkling sound that caused the hairs on his arms to stand to attention. It was the kind of laugh you could get used to hearing and he found himself suddenly wishing he'd caused it.

"I can stay here this evening and go through the originals myself and help you copy them. That way I can get a head start on it all."

Drew nodded. In a way it made sense. He wasn't entirely comfortable with it but it would at least free him up to pursue other things. Not to mention he owed her. Without Harriet's help he would be sitting here having Gregson put his rubber stamp of approval on closing the case down. As it was, she had bought him some precious time.

"Fine. We can do that."

"Great," she said, before she paused. "Was there something else you had to say?"

"I can't take you with me to meet with the coroner."

"Why not?"

"Because it's not professional. At the most you're a consultant and even that's tenuous."

"I'd have thought that described this relationship perfectly."

Drew sighed, a knot beginning to form between his eyes. "DCI Gregson hasn't signed off on it. Without his consent—"

Harriet shook her head. "That's nonsense. I don't need his consent to visit the coroner."

"No, but Jackson doesn't like outsiders and unless the order has come down from on high he won't want anything to do with you. In fact, he'll probably dig his heels in and insist they were all suicides without doing one ounce of extra probing."

"I don't understand, why would he do that?"

Drew shrugged. "Your guess is as good as mine. All I know for certain is that Jackson is a stone cold bastard when he wants to be and—" Drew cut off. "Shit, I'm sorry. I shouldn't have said that."

Harriet shot him an incredulous look. "Don't apologise on my account. I've heard much worse."

"It's unprofessional of me," he said.

"It shows you care," Harriet said. Was she just saying that to be kind or did she really mean it?

She was almost impossible to read which frustrated the hell out of him. He'd never met anyone like her, at least not since—

He killed the line of thought his brain was meandering down and pulled his attention back to the task at hand.

"If you write everything down for me, I promise I won't screw it up."

A mutinous expression flitted across her face but it was there and gone in the blink of an eye making Drew doubt he'd ever seen it at all.

"Fine. But if you can't get all the answers from him to my satisfaction then I'm going to see him myself. It's his job to at the end of the day. He'll do it, if I have to make him do it."

Drew stifled his laughter and hoped his expression remained suitably serious.

Harriet pulled her jacket off. "Right, so where are these files then?"

CHAPTER SEVENTEEN

WALKING down the corridor after DI Haskell, Harriet couldn't help but feel a thrill move through her. How had she gotten tangled up in all of this? Only a few hours ago, she'd been settling in behind her desk in preparation for an afternoon of mind-numbing tutorials. It wasn't that she disliked teaching the students, it was just that many of them had no interest in their chosen topic; a situation which Harriet struggled to understand. And the irony wasn't lost on her.

Why bother doing a degree in behavioural psychology if you had no interest in how the people around you ticked?

Watching Drew attempt to navigate the choppy waters in his bosses' office hadn't been pleasant. She'd gotten the impression that DCI Gregson was a fair man but he'd been beaten down by the system he'd been sucked into. There was only so much you could take at the end of the day and as far as Harriet was concerned, he'd passed that line a long time ago.

It was something she'd feared herself when she had worked clinically. The risk of getting jaded towards those you were treating was extremely high. At the end of the day you were only human and there was only so many times you could sit there and listen to a woman coldly and calmly discuss how she wasn't the one responsible for her children's deaths; or a man explain how his feelings about the filthy whores he'd killed were justified, before you started to grow somewhat numb towards the horror.

The moment that happened you were done.

It would eventually happen to everyone who worked in that kind of environment. It was the reason police officers working violent crimes or child pornography could only do so long in the trenches before a change was necessary to maintain their equilibrium and sanity.

Harriet had never reached the point of no return in her clinical work and for that she was grateful. The idea of it happening to her had frightened her. Would she have recognised the symptoms and signs before they happened, or would it have insidiously crept over her?

Drew pushed open the door to the records room and ushered her inside. The place was piled floor to ceiling with shelving units that housed boxes, filled with files Harriet presumed.

"Take a seat over there and I'll bring over the first box."

Harriet pulled out the plastic chair he'd indicated and laid her coat across the dusty seat before she lowered herself gently onto it. The room looked like it had seen better days and she found herself studying the boxes of case files stacked on the shelves nearest to her.

"Are all of these open cases?"

Drew tugged a box down off a shelf near the door and carried it back to the table before he answered her.

"Some are. Most are closed. They get shipped out of here pretty regularly to the main storage unit."

Harriet nodded and watched as he pulled the lid off the box. Despite the relative newness of the cases, the boxes were loaded with dust and as Drew disrupted the contents, it puffed into the air, causing Harriet to sneeze violently.

"Sorry," he said. "It can get pretty bad in here."

Harriet nodded and took the proffered case file. "Is this the first one?"

"Yeah, Jack Whitly, aged seventeen. He lived on the other side of Tollby and didn't attend the same secondary school as the other two victims."

Harriet flipped open the file and stared down at the photograph of Jack. He smiled broadly at the camera, his brown eyes were crinkled at the corners, his smile wide, dark hair tousled over his fore-head giving the impression that it was a windy day when the picture had been taken.

Harriet took in the image and Jack's black T-shirt.

"Where was this taken?"

"Over in Whitby," Drew said. "The Goth Weekend last April, I think his parents said."

"And was he a goth?"

Drew shrugged. "I couldn't tell you. It didn't really come up. Why, would it have made a difference?"

Harriet shook her head. "Probably not."

"You don't think him being a goth would have meant he was depressed after all? You hear a lot of stories about them dabbling in things they shouldn't."

Harriet smiled and lifted her head to meet Drew's gaze head on. "I think you're confusing Goths with emo," she said. "Typically, people inter-ested in the goth lifestyle are happier than the general public."

"How do you figure that out? They spend all their time dressed in black and hanging out in cemeteries."

"They're accustomed to people looking at them like they're outsiders. To them it's nothing new but what makes them happier is the fact that they've embraced what makes them unique. They're not so much concerned with fitting in and so it removes some inhibitions that the rest of us struggle against."

Drew rolled his eyes. "I'd like to be happier, doesn't mean I'm going to embrace my inner goth."

Harriet returned her attention to the image in front of her. "It's not unusual for teens to embrace being different. Generally, those who are already considered outsiders find it easier to slip into that role."

"But does this look like a kid who was an outsider to you?" Harriet lifted the picture and held it aloft so Drew could look at it.

"Not to mention Sian. According to the file you supplied me with she had lots of friends, did well in school, although in more recent months her grades had started to slip."

"Her boyfriend Aidan Wilson moved in the same social circle as Sian. They were both pretty popular in school according to the teachers we spoke to."

"Did you speak to Sian after Aidan's death?" Harriet asked, glancing up hopefully in Drew's direction.

"We wanted to, but her parents said she was in no fit state and the DCI agreed. Gregson said we were just upsetting an already broken community."

Harriet sighed; it would have been helpful to read through a statement written in Sian's own words, it would have at least given some insight into her mindset.

She returned her attention to the papers, sorting through the statements she scanned the documents as quickly as possible. Once she had the copies, she needed she could review it all in her own time.

Although, if she was correct, then whoever had killed Sian and the other two boys would be at that moment hunting for another victim.

"How long between each death?"

"Pardon?"

"How much time passed between each death?"

"Eight weeks between Jack and Aidan and three weeks from Aidan's death to Sian's," Drew said. "He's escalating."

"It certainly looks that way."

"Well why would he do that?"

"Killing Jack gave him a thrill. The initial rush would have been intoxicating. He probably re-lived the crime over and over." Harriet paused and closed her eyes, imagining the person responsible. He would take trophies. It wouldn't be enough to just re-live the memory. The killer would need something tangible. "Do you know if anything was taken?"

Drew shook his head. "Not that we're aware of but then again once the coroner decided it was a suicide in Jack's case, it kind of shut everything down."

"Well what about Aidan, was there anything missing there?"

Again, Drew shook his head and Harriet tried to

keep her frustration in check. She couldn't blame him, not when he had tried so hard to keep the cases open and going.

"Well, I'll go over the case files for the first two and any discrepancies I find we should follow them up with the families. We might get lucky. We should probably follow up with the families anyway. Some time has passed and if there was anything missing then they're bound to have noticed it by now."

"So he's escalating because he's looking for bigger thrills?"

"He probably tried to recreate the initial thrill again with Aidan but it's never as good the second go around."

"Why not?"

"You can never recreate your first time. Those emotions and experiences are a one and done deal." Noting the look of consternation on Drew's face caused Harriet to continue. "When you taste chocolate for the first time, that experience is catalogued by your brain and you spend the rest of your time trying to recreate the experience with every subsequent bar. It's the same when you read a book for the first time. When you go back for a re-read you already know the thrills and twists before you get to them. You're anticipating it before it ever happens and that dampens your excitement whether you want it to or not."

"Killing another human being is more complicated than just reading a book twice, though," Drew said, dropping into the seat opposite her.

"Of course, but not everyone is capable of planning and carrying out a cold-blooded killing of another human being. I merely used the analogy of reading an exciting book for the first time as something you could relate to."

"And with Sian what did our guy get by killing her?"

"Probably much the same. The killer will keep trying to recreate that one perfect moment he experienced when he took Jack's life; like an addict chasing his next high. He won't stop until someone puts a stop to him."

"A serial killer then," Drew said, his expression unreadable.

"He exerts the ultimate control over his victims. Takes the most vulnerable and for lack of a better term in Sian's case he put her out of her misery. Or at least that's how the killer perceives his actions."

"He doesn't think what he's doing is wrong?"

"No more than you think the job you do every day is wrong," Harriet said. "In his mind, he's providing a service to them. Giving them something they can't or won't give to themselves."

"And what's that?"

"Peace."

Drew scoffed and turned his attention to the file in front of him. "What kind of sick bastard thinks he's bringing peace to a bunch of kids he murders?"

"The kind that will kill again, Detective. In these files, in the lives of his victims is the missing key to figuring out just who is responsible for these crimes."

"People don't even want to admit there is a crime, how can we catch him when everyone is burying their heads in the sand?"

"Or her," Harriet corrected.

"What?"

"We've been referring to our killer as a he, it could just as easily be a woman."

Drew started to smile but cut off when Harriet frowned at him.

"More often than not it's women who fill the role in society of caregiver. It conjures all kinds of connotations in the mind not least of which is someone who is merciful. Our killer, man or woman, sees themselves as a mercy killer."

"But the way they killed them, there's a brutality there that I just don't see a woman carrying out."

Harriet smiled thinly at him. "You would be surprised, Detective Inspector, the levels of brutality a woman is capable of. Don't underestimate the opposite sex just because you believe them to be fairer."

Drew dropped his attention to the case files in front of him.

"It's a bloody needle in a haystack."

"Not necessarily. I'm telling you to keep an open mind. However, it is more than likely our killer is a male in his early thirties to mid-forties who has suffered a recent tragic loss."

"What makes you say that?"

"Something triggered our killer a little over three months ago," Harriet said. "If we can figure out what that is then we'll be one step closer to finding our man."

Drew climbed to his feet. "Well I need a coffee," he said. "Do you want one?"

Harriet nodded "A coffee would be great, thanks."

She watched as he moved toward the door, noting the slump in his shoulders and the weary expression in his eyes as he pulled the door open.

"We will catch him, Drew," she said. "I can promise you that."

It was a foolish promise to make. She couldn't truly promise him anything, at least nothing concrete anyway. But seeing the look of despair in his eyes made her want to reassure him.

He glanced back at her and for a moment Harriet was certain she saw a flicker of recognition in his eyes as he looked at her. It was gone in an instant and she found herself wondering if perhaps she had imagined the emotion.

"Of course we will," he said, his voice tight. "What choice do we have?"

He was gone before she could answer him. As she sat there surrounded by the files of so many whose lives had come to an untimely end, she couldn't shake the feeling that something had passed between them.

Did he remember her after all? And if that were true then what was he going to do about it?

Pushing the questions that swirled in her mind aside, Harriet turned her attention to the file of the seventeen-year-old boy whose life had ended so abruptly.

"Why him? What did you see in him that made him your perfect first victim? Does he remind you of yourself? Or is it just what he represents to you?"

They were questions she didn't have the answers to but as she flipped over the statements of Jack's family, Harriet knew the key to cracking the case lay in finding out the truth.

CHAPTER EIGHTEEN

BIANCA PUSHED the trolley around the super-market, only half paying attention to the shelves.

Ryder's most recent picture was the only thought on her mind. She wasn't entirely put off by his forward nature. After all, it was practically blasé these days to receive a dick pic or two, right?

No, it was him asking her for 'something to help him get by until Saturday night', that had thrown her for a loop. The idea of sending a stranger on the internet a picture that most would consider compromising sent a prickle of discomfort racing over her skin.

Or was it excitement?

There was something exciting about the whole situation. Risqué and dangerous. What if he turned out to be nothing like his pictures or his profile? What if everything he'd told her was a complete lie?

It wasn't implausible, she'd watched enough television programs about women and men getting catfished on the internet.

What if he took one look at her and decided she was nothing like her profile, or pictures?

The more she thought about it all, the more her mind spiralled into panic.

"Just breathe, Bianca." If Harri were here she'd tell her she was just overreacting.

No, Ryder wasn't cat-fishing her. It just wasn't likely, not when they spent most nights on the phone, talking into the wee hours. If he was pretending to be someone he wasn't, then he was the most practiced liar to ever walk the earth.

Bianca prided herself on not being easily taken in by those around her. Having a forensic psychologist for a friend made her more suspicious than most. Plus she had Tilly to think about, being a single parent to a child wasn't exactly a cake walk and so more often than not she found herself airing on the side of caution when it came to most situations.

But this was different. This was all about her and her desires and wants. Tilly wasn't involved and she certainly wasn't going to get hurt if something went wrong with Ryder. No, Bianca had been careful to keep her daughter distanced from it all. If Ryder turned out to be an asshole the only one who would get hurt in it all would be her and her fragile ego.

As she passed down through the baking aisle, she

recalled the conversation with Tilly from Monday morning and paused to grab the ingredients for cookies. There was only milk-chocolate chips on the shelf and she grabbed three packets and dumped them into the shopping cart before making her way toward the milk.

As she rounded the corner, the same feeling of being watched slid down her spine. It was happening more often now. Was it just her imagination?

Pausing, she scanned her surroundings but everyone around her was going about their business. Nobody stood out as suspicious and nothing seemed out of the ordinary.

Her pocket buzzed and she jumped, startling the woman next to her who had at that moment reached into the fridge for a pint of milk.

"Sorry," Bianca said, smiling apologetically as the woman shot her a dirty look.

She moved away from the milk and tugged her phone from her pocket.

"Hey, Baby! I'm just in a meeting and bored out of my box. If I hear one more time about shareholders percentage, I might just jump out the window. The only thing getting me through is the picture you're going to send me."

"You're very presumptuous," Bianca typed quickly, her fingers flying over the touchscreen. "I'm in the supermarket, I can't just drop everything to cater to your needs." She added a tongue faced

175

emoji at the end to make it a little more light-hearted.

Ryder's response was almost immediate. "You're killing me here. If you're not comfortable sending me a nude, maybe just a preview before Saturday?"

Bianca grinned and slid the phone into her purse as she directed the trolley toward the tills. It took only a few minutes to check out all the items she had and within ten minutes she was back behind the wheel of her Ford.

"Do you mind if I kiss you when we meet?" Ryder's message sent a thrill racing through her.

Did she mind? He seemed to be pretty clear about what was going to happen when they met. He'd gone ahead and made a booking for a hotel nearby even though she'd been hesitant to agree and when he'd texted her the reservation number, Bianca had gotten butterflies in her stomach. She hadn't felt like that in what felt like so long and experiencing it now seemed so strange, especially when she was experiencing it because of another man and not the one she'd originally pledged to spend the rest of her life with.

Was this her being unfaithful? Scooping her phone from her handbag she dialled Harriet's number and listened as the call rang and rang without an answer.

"This is Harriet's house number. If this is important, please feel free to call me on my mobile number. If not, then leave a message after the beep."

"Oh, Harri," Bianca sighed as the beep echoed in her ear. "Hey, it's just me. I was just checking to see if you were still coming up this weekend. You know you don't have to if you don't want to..." She trailed off. It wasn't the real reason for her call but trying to explain the sudden emotional surge she'd experienced to an answer machine seemed a bridge too far. So instead she resorted to tried and tested conversations. When Harriet got back to her, she could tell her then. Maybe at that point she would have figured it out and wouldn't need to burden her friend.

Ending the call, she let her head drop back against the back of her seat. She was definitely making a mountain out of a mole hill. She was an adult and Tom was dead, she could either live in the past or... Her eyes filled with tears and she blinked them away. He wouldn't want her to live like this. He'd want her to move on and build a new life for her and Tilly.

But knowing it and believing it were definitely two different things.

Scrubbing her hands over her eyes, she started the engine and pulled out of the car park. Maybe when Harriet called, she could help her navigate the murky waters she was sliding into.

CHAPTER NINETEEN

DUMPING her coat and bag onto the kitchen counter, Harriet tipped the precarious pile of papers and files next to them.

The time had passed faster than she'd imagined possible. How long had it been since she'd been so engrossed by something that she hadn't even noticed time passing at all?

She'd always prided herself on her ability to focus so intensely that the rest of the world fell away from her. But since the incident in the clinic that had caused her to leave her beloved clinical work behind, she'd found it difficult to lose herself in the work as she had once done.

Moving over to the phone, she clicked a button on the answering machine and listened to the familiar beep following her instructions to leave a message.

The first call went dead without anyone bothering to say anything and Harriet had the sneaking suspicion that it was probably just a robot call offering her insurance she didn't need or some other such nonsense. The next message was from Bianca who wanted to know if Harriet still planned to come up at the weekend and would she mind looking after Tilly because the babysitter had fallen through. As she listened to her friend's enthusiastic voice, Harriet smiled and moved over to the fridge.

She rummaged through the contents before emerging a moment later with a half-eaten block of cheese and a bunch of grapes that had definitely seen better days.

Grabbing a packet of crackers from the cupboard, she carried her meagre meal into the living room and kicked off her shoes before she settled onto the sofa. Bianca's bubbly 'bye!' left Harriet alone in the silence.

The phone next to her rang and without thinking about it, she reached over and scooped the phone off the cradle and pressed it to her ear.

"I'm only just in from work, Bianca, give me a minute to—" Harriet started to speak and cut off abruptly as the sound of rich male laughter curled down the line and into her ear.

"Harriet, it's me, Jonathan."

She ran the name over in her mind and came up blank.

"Dr Connor." There was no denying the disappointment in the doctor's voice at her lack of recognition or enthusiasm.

"I'm so sorry," Harriet said, instantly feeling guilty for not recognising him sooner. "I thought you were somebody else."

"Evidently," he said wryly. "I hope you're not too disappointed that it's just me?"

It was a loaded question and Harriet instantly recognised it for what it was. Others might enjoy those sorts of games but she wasn't the kind of person to enter into pointless flirtations to soothe the ego of a colleague.

"What can I do for you, doctor?" Harriet kept her voice cordial without losing the professional tone she'd perfected over her time in psychology.

"If you remember, I said I'd call to see when we could arrange for that drink."

"Of course I remember," Harriet lied. She'd gotten so caught up with Drew and his case that she'd forgotten Dr Connor ever mentioning that he would call her. "You wanted to discuss my mother's care."

"That and other things," Jonathan said smoothly. "I was hoping I could entice you to meet tomorrow evening?"

"Well, I—"

"I think it would be particularly beneficial to your mother's care if we were to review her care plan together. I'm sure you've got some thoughts on how we could move forward with her therapy."

Was he laying a guilt trip on her in order to ensure she agreed to the drink with him? After all, when he put it like that, how was she supposed to turn him down?

"What time did you have in mind?"

"Does eight suit you? I can pick you up and—"

"No, I'll meet you," Harriet said. "I don't know what time I'll be finished in the office so this way I can go straight from there."

"It sounds like they're working you too hard up in the university," Jonathan said. "All the more reason I think you should come back to clinical practice. I'm sure we could find a place for you—"

"As enticing as that sounds, we both know it's impossible. You know my personal relationship prohibits me from working in the same hospital with her."

"It always seemed like such a pointless rule to me," Jonathan said. "I mean why make our hospital suffer just because you happen to be related to a current patient?"

They'd had the same conversation a number of years before when Harriet had said she was searching for a position in clinical practice. As far as she was concerned even discussing the matter was an exercise in futility.

"Oh well, I don't suppose my hoping and wishing

it were different is going to change anything."

"If wishes were horses," Harriet said automatically. It was something her mother used to say when she was a child. Why had she thought of it now?

"Well if you won't let me pick you up. How about we meet at Daphne's at eight?"

Harriet's stomach lurched uncomfortably.

"I thought it was just a drink?"

"We've all got to eat too," he said amicably. "Why not discuss your mother's case with a good meal?"

"Eight o' clock is fine," Harriet said, suddenly wishing she had let the answering machine pick up the call, that way she could have pretended ignorance about it all. "I'll see you there."

"I look forward to it." Jonathan said before the line went dead.

Harriet settled the phone back on the cradle before dropping back against the cushions.

"Well, shit," she swore aloud.

She stared down at the pile of grapes and cheese she'd placed on a plate, her appetite now dead. Was she reading too much into Dr Connor offer? It was a professional risk to do just that and it wouldn't have been the first time she'd foolishly thought there was more going on than there really was.

But as much as she wanted to believe that it was all in her mind, she couldn't help but feel like Dr Connor was slowly manoeuvering her into a position she didn't want to find herself in. She might have enjoyed the idea of finding him attractive when she was younger. Maybe even indulged her thoughts of letting him sweep in and protect her from all the terrible things her mother had done but that was a long time ago. And she was certainly no longer the impressionable teenager she had been then.

No, she had moved on since then and now she only regarded the good doctor in terms of the care he could provide for her mother or the potential mentorship he offered her.

There was nothing more between them.

Or at least that was how she hoped he saw it too. If he didn't it was going to make for a very awkward situation between them and Harriet couldn't bear the thought of that kind of friction. Visiting her mother was already painful enough as it was, without adding another layer of salt to rub in the wound.

As she sat on the couch, she allowed her eyes to slide shut. The room was warm and for the first time in a long time Harriet actually found herself somewhat exhausted.

Sleep hadn't been her friend in so long that she didn't expect it to creep up on her now and when it did it took her completely by surprise.

Her last thought as she let herself drift off into the oblivion that sleep provided was of the trees that swayed outside Sian Jones' house, the limbs reaching toward the sky like skeletal fingers that threatened to choke the life out of anyone who got too close.

CHAPTER TWENTY

"I KNOW you told me this already," Drew said, trying to keep his temper in check as he faced Dr Jackson, the coroner, in his tiny office. "But I'm revisiting the evidence and I've got a couple of questions I'd like to ask you."

"Do you think I enjoy writing reports, detective?"

"I don't think anybody enjoys writing reports," Drew said, flexing his fingers.

"So what makes you think I wrote that one for the sheer hell of it?"

Drew shook his head. "That's not what I'm saying here. I just have a couple of follow-up questions."

"Well you can ask but everything I've got to say on the matter is in the report I sent over to your department."

"The necklace wrapped in Sian's hand—"

"The body is my area of expertise," Dr Jackson interrupted him with an exasperated tone. "Anything pertaining to physical evidence such as jewellery is up to the SOCOs and forensic officers to catalogue and index."

Drew did his best to ignore the interruption and plowed on with his question. "I noticed the clasp was broken on the necklace. Is there any evidence to suggest it was ripped off her?"

Dr Jackson dropped back in his high-backed leather chair and propped his hands behind his head. "It could have been."

"Could she have done it herself?"

"She could have."

Drew sighed. "Would there be anything on the body to support this?"

Dr Jackson grimaced. "The bruising and contusions around the neck and throat area due to the nature of her death was significant that any injury caused by the forceful removal of the necklace wouldn't show up."

Drew shook his head and stared down at the list of questions.

"What about defensive wounds?"

"She had none."

"I know that," Drew said. "I meant—"

"Good to know you actually read the report. I

thought for a moment there that you were here to waste my time."

"Look. I get it. You don't like me but I've got three dead kids and three grieving families. If I could answer these questions without your help then I would do it in a heartbeat but as it is you're the expert and I'm asking for your help."

Dr Jackson peered down his hawkish nose reminding Drew of a large buzzard he'd once seen.

"No. There were no defensive wounds on any of the bodies."

"And in your opinion, is that unusual?"

Dr Jackson sat forward as he drew his hands together and leaned his elbows on the desk in front of him.

"It is a little unusual, yes. Not entirely uncommon. Some people lose consciousness very quickly when their vagus nerve is compressed which often happens during hanging. However, I would still have expected some injury due to reflexive convulsions." He smiled thinly. "Many people tear at their throats once the process begins."

"What could account for this?"

Dr Jackson closed his eyes. "I can see where you're going with this, Detective, and I can't say I agree with you."

"But you couldn't rule it out?"

Dr Jackson shook his head. "No. I couldn't categorically rule it out if you had evidence to back up your theory because that's all it is. A theory." Dr Jackson uttered the last word as though it were something truly abhorrent to him.

"Why are you so determined to believe that this is a straight-forward suicide?"

"Because that's what I do, I follow the evidence presented to me and I make an assessment based on that. I do not allow my feelings to colour the process because to do so would be a disservice to the body in front of me."

"But by being so rigid isn't it a disservice to the victim all the same? What if I'm right in this instance and someone murdered all three and your determination to look at this with tunnel vision allows a killer to do it all again?"

"Why would anyone commit a murder but make it appear as a suicide?"

"I can think of several reasons," Drew said. "But the most obvious is to avoid detection which from where I'm standing, they're doing a damn good job of it." Drew cut off in frustration and jammed his hand into his short hair.

Dr Jackson nodded. "Touché, detective."

"Does that mean you'll review the bodies again?"

"The first two bodies have already been released back to their families and I would imagine they have been buried."

"And Sian Jones?" Drew said, no longer caring that his voice was sharp. As far as he was concerned if he could have arrested the asshole sitting in front of him for obstruction of justice he'd have done just that. But that wasn't how the system worked and unless he got Dr Jackson on side then no amount of pleading with the Monk would see him keep this case.

"I'll take a second look," Dr Jackson said, and Drew let go of the breath he'd been holding onto. "But what exactly am I looking for?"

Drew glanced down at the notes made by Harriet and decided to discard them. He'd been a detective long enough that he didn't need to follow a script.

"Supposing this is a murder and not a suicide."

"Hypothetically speaking?"

Drew nodded. "Yeah, hypothetically. At least until my theory has some concrete evidence to back it up."

Dr Jackson shot him a predatory smile. "You've got three teenagers. Two of them strapping, fit blokes."

Dr Jackson nodded. "They were indeed fit and healthy," he said. "Both of them quite athletic judging by the muscle tone and lack of fat."

Drew pushed the image the coroner's words had conjured from his mind. Despite not eating anything for breakfast, he'd downed enough coffee to sink a battleship and he didn't fancy losing it all over the good doctor's immaculate desk.

"And Sian was no slouch either. She was on the hockey team according to her mother."

"Where are you going with all of this?"

"Three fit teenagers and you're going to hang them without them fighting back. How do you do that?"

Dr Jackson shook his head. "You don't. Human nature would force them to fight for their lives. They would not go gentle into that good night."

"But our killer manages it. How would he do it?"

Again, the coroner shook his head. "Like I said—"

"Hypothetically speaking?" Drew's question brought the coroner up short. He pursed his lips and dragged his keyboard toward him. A couple of clicks of the mouse and his fingers flew over the keys, his eyes rapidly darting back and forth as he read whatever had popped up on the screen.

"There was a toxicology panel taken and nothing turned up, if that's what you're asking."

"But there are plenty of drugs out there nowadays that can slip under the wire. We both know not everything shows up in bloods."

Dr Jackson nodded. "It's possible they were drugged before they were murdered. It would account somewhat for the lack of defensive and self-inflicted injuries I would have expected to see in cases such as these."

"Is there any other tests you could run on Sian to see if there was anything given to her?"

The coroner sighed and slipped his glasses off his hooked nose. Drew sat impatiently and watched as the other man scrubbed at his eyes before replacing the glasses.

"I will take another look detective. Not that I expect to find anything but you've managed to insert enough doubt into my solid conclusions that I feel it's my duty to take a second look."

Drew pushed onto his feet and held his hand out. "That's all I ask."

The other man stared at Drew's hand as though it were a foreign specimen that needed intense scrutiny. He let his hand fall back to his side and turned toward the door.

"Detective, why is this so important to you?"

The question brought Drew up short. It was the same question he'd asked himself often enough since all of this had started and he was no closer now to an answer than he had been then. There was no definite answer. At least not one he wanted to admit to himself, never mind to someone like Dr Jackson who would rather see him on the moon than anywhere near his office.

"It's my job, I suppose," Drew said. "If I don't ask the right questions and ensure every stone is turned over then how can I call myself a detective?"

It was a non-answer and Drew knew it but he didn't care. Without waiting for a reply, he tugged the door open and stepped out into the hall, leaving the coroner behind at his desk.

Once he was outside in the fresh air, Drew pulled a packet of cigarettes from inside his coat and tugged open the top. The packet was empty, just like it always was.

Crumpling the plastic-coated cardboard in his fist he contemplated tossing the box and buying a new one. It would be so easy to do it and in his current state there was nothing he wanted more than to jam a nicotine-fuelled stick into his mouth and inhale the richness of its flavour.

Just thinking about it was enough to make him clench his jaw. If he gave in it would be just like everything else in his life that he gave up on. And it would too much like letting go.

Instead of tossing the packet the way he wanted to, he smoothed it out, forcing the box back into some semblance of the shape it had before he'd taken his frustration out on it. Satisfied that it was as perfect as he could make it after initially destroying it, he slipped the empty packet back into his inside pocket.

Sucking in a deep breath, he closed his eyes. "That's as good as it's going to get," he said to no one in particular.

With his eyes shut he expected to see Tasha, she was never far from his thoughts especially since he'd picked this case up. The constant reminder of suicide had opened old wounds he'd thought long closed.

Clearly, he wasn't as good at figuring out his own mental state as he'd initially thought.

But this time it wasn't Tasha that came to mind but Harriet. When she'd sat at the desk the night before, there had been something so terribly familiar about it all. As though he'd been there before. It was impossible of course and deja-vu was just the brains way of sending the same message twice. It was after all just a computer and like all machines it could get screwed up.

But as much as he tried to shake the feeling he couldn't. It had unnerved him the night before, not that he would admit it aloud.

Shaking his head, he pushed the thoughts aside. He needed to concentrate, especially if he was going to get to the bottom of the mystery he found himself embroiled in.

"Get a grip," he said. "Or you'll be talking to yourself just like the good doc."

Fishing his keys from his pocket he headed for the car with a grin on his face.

CHAPTER TWENTY-ONE

HARRIET STOOD OUTSIDE THE STATION, waiting for Drew. Glancing down at the watch on her wrist, she tried to keep her frustration to a minimum. He was only running a little late but Harriet was impatient due to her desire to know what the coroner had said in answer to her questions.

A flash of silvery light caught her eye and she glanced up in time to see Drew's car draw into the car park.

Before he could get out of the car, she was halfway across the path to him.

"Well?"

"Jeez," he said. "Let a man get his bearings before you accost him."

"Sorry. It's just I've been here for thirty minutes and I'm not very good with the whole 'patience' thing."

"Clearly," he said, but there was no malice in his voice. "I don't suppose you want to let me grab a coffee before we go badgering these poor families again?"

Harriet knew her emotions showed in her face and he sighed. "Fine, hop in. I'll get something later."

She moved around to the passenger side and slid in. The inside of the car was warm. Heat blasted out through the vents and she pressed her frozen fingers against them in an attempt to get some of the feeling back. From the corner of her eye she caught Drew watching her and she paused.

"The coroner doesn't agree with us, then?"

"What?"

"Your expression says it all. The coroner is not on our side in all of this."

Drew shook his head and stared down at his hands. "He doesn't agree with us, no. However, he's willing to take another look at Sian's body."

Harriet felt a clench of excitement and joy thrill in her veins. It was an emotion she hadn't felt in quite some time and it took her by surprise to experience it over something as simple as this.

"So, your boss will let you keep the case open now?"

Drew grimaced. "It's not a sure thing. Until we get something concrete, we're still on rocky ground. I mean Dr Jackson only agreed to have another look at the body because I created enough doubt in his mind. He could just as easily call me up and tell me he's standing by his initial assessment."

Harriet's happiness was short lived. Drew was right; it would be all too easy to dismiss everything they'd come up with so far. They needed proof that what they were saying was right and she had a feeling that they only way they would find it was by talking to the families.

"I guess we should get going then."

Drew nodded. "Fine. But I can promise you this, it won't be pleasant."

Harriet turned her head away and stared out the window. "I've dealt with grieving families before, Detective Inspector. There is nothing about death that's easy."

If he thought she was afraid to face the grief of Jack's and Aidan's families, then he was in for a bitter disappointment. While it was true that most of her time had been spent working with those whose minds functioned differently to what was considered, 'normal'—whatever that was—she'd done enough time in the trenches with their loved ones too.

She'd broken the terrible truth about a loved one's passing before; watched the shock and denial as it registered in their eyes. And as for the hospital's directions to cut ties with them once the deed was done, Harriet had always found it impossible to just walk away. Her desire to heal was just as strong as those who worked in a more general practice setting.

Sometimes maybe even more so.

CHAPTER TWENTY-TWO

THEY PULLED up outside the first house and Drew's palms were so slick with sweat he found it difficult to keep a firm grip on the steering wheel.

She said she wasn't afraid to face the grief—perhaps if she kept telling herself that lie it would eventually become truth—but he was.

Well, fear was the wrong word. But he couldn't figure out a better way to describe it, especially when it came to what they were about to do. It was no mean feat to take all the grief and pain of the families left behind and compound it.

Enough time had passed that the families in question, while not accepting of their children's passing, had begun to live with it. That was all you could hope for when it came to the slippery evil that was grief. Necessary, yes, but evil all the same. It had the power to rob even the strongest of those of their joy.

Memories became grenades lurking in your mind that at any moment could detonate and rip your already broken heart into further shreds.

Anyone who told you that time was a healer was either a well-meaning liar or they hadn't suffered a loss themselves. Time didn't heal jack-shit. All it allowed you to do was to learn to live in the new world. A world without your loved one in it.

"If we sit out here for much longer, they'll wonder what's going on." Harriet's words cut through his thoughts, jerking him back to the moment. "This will be difficult enough for them without making them worry unnecessarily."

How could she be so calm about it all?

"Yeah." Drew shoved the car door open with a little more force than he'd meant and the hinges creaked ominously.

He slammed the door behind him and paused, resting his hands on the roof of the car as he waited for Harriet to climb out. The last time he'd been here—

He closed his eyes in an attempt to block the memory out but it only served to make it stronger.

"Are you all right?" He felt her hand tentatively touch his arm and he jumped, pulling back out of reach.

"I'm fine," he lied, swallowing back the bile in his throat. He would get through this. This was his job and he would get through it. The families deserved to know the truth. They needed to know the truth.

"We're doing the right thing here," Harriet said softly as though she'd peeled back his skull and peered into the soft mush that made up his brain.

"So why does it feel like I'm causing more pain; doing more harm than good?"

"Because you are," she said simply.

"Thanks, doc, I feel really reassured now."

Harriet smiled at him, a warm affectionate expression that brought a rush of heat through his body.

"I don't mean to sound so flippant," she said. "But we will cause pain here today. Unfortunately for the people in that house it's a pain that will help them heal."

Drew gave her a confused look. "I don't understand. How can pain help you heal?"

"Think of it like a wound. It's already scabbed over but the wound itself is infected. Beneath the surface, it's festering inside and if you do nothing, the poison will eventually spread to the rest of the body. A slow painful death. But if you open the wound again, expose it to the air and clean out the infection it will eventually heal."

"Losing a child isn't like healing a wound," Drew said sharply. "Losing someone you love isn't something you just get over."

"I know," she said, and for the first time since

they'd met, she actually sounded like she meant it. "Nothing we say or do here today will make their loss greater than it is. They've suffered the worst thing imaginable in the loss of a child." She sighed.

"What I'm trying to say here, is that letting them believe a lie about the people they've lost is a poison. They need to know the truth. It's not going to make it better or even take the pain away for them but they need to hear it just the same."

There was a kind of perverse truth to what she was saying as far as Drew could see. When Freya had decided to remove herself from the board completely he'd spent days, weeks—hell he was still thinking it now—wondering if there was something he should have done, could have done differently. The answer was always the same; nothing he thought or felt would change what had happened. But deep down in the darkest recesses of his mind there was a cruel voice that whispered to him that he hadn't been enough for her. That it was his fault she was gone, if only he'd been better, more loving, more empathetic of her suffering then she would have stayed.

And as he stood there outside Jack Whitly's family home, Drew understood that the woman up in the house was probably thinking and feeling the same as he did; wrongly or rightly. No amount of someone telling you that you weren't to blame would take that guilt away.

"What are we waiting for then?" He strode

toward the path but Harriet caught his arm, drawing him up short.

"It was never your fault."

He glanced down at her hand and then raised his gaze to her face. There was a sincerity there that he hadn't seen in the faces of any of the counsellors he'd been forced to visit after Freya's death.

"So why does it still feel like it was?"

She shrugged and let him go. "Human nature," she said. "We blame ourselves for the impossible believing if only we were better, more godlike, then we could have saved them. It's a universal flaw but it proves one thing."

"And what's that?"

"It's proof of the love you had for them; have for them still."

He swallowed around the lump in his throat and inclined his head. "Now we really should go in," he said. "Or they're going to assume the worst."

Harriet let him go with a sad shake of her head. "I'm afraid for them, that already happened."

He remained silent but he agreed with her. For the families of those left behind their world had come to a grinding halt the day they discovered their child dead. There was no coming back from it, no return to the happiness that had once been. There could only be forward progression and a grim determination to carry on.

CHAPTER TWENTY-THREE

HARRIET LET Drew knock on the door and when it was answered by a woman with wide expressive eyes, she stood aside to let him do the introductions.

Despite his initial uncertainty, he handled himself with care and precision. There was a softness to his voice as he dealt with Jack's mother, a warmth and compassion to his manner. Harriet found herself wondering just how many facets the detective truly had.

Within a few moments, Harriet found herself ensconced in a comfortable cream leather armchair. accepting an offered cup of tea from Jack Whitly's grieving mother.

The room was modern, the walls painted and wallpapered in silvers and whites lending it an air of cold detachment that to Harriet felt too much like a treatment room in a hospital. She'd never really understood the desire to decorate a room in nothing but a monochrome colour scheme. Not that she could really have an opinion on interior design. Her walls were still the plain white they had been since the day she'd moved into her house.

"Mrs Whitly, I think you already know that we're here today to discuss Jack with you," Drew said, his voice and manner gentle as though he were afraid Mrs Whitly would startle and bolt like a prize racehorse.

"I figured as much," the woman said, her York-shire accent suggesting she'd lived her whole life in the area. She closed her fingers around the handle of her tea cup so tightly that her knuckles turned white and Harriet found herself worrying she would snap the handle off entirely.

"We only buried him ten-days ago," she said. Her voice hitched. "He seemed smaller than I remembered."

"I am so very sorry for your loss, Mrs Whitly," Harriet said, leaning forward in her chair. It was a pointless statement but a necessary one all the same. Being sorry for someone didn't make it better but it was more what the words represented that truly mattered. By telling someone you were sorry for their loss you were showing them you empathised with them, a show of solidarity over something that was usually so deeply personal.

"Thank you," Mrs Whitly said, keeping her eyes

trained on the cup in her shaking hands. "Call me Kate, everybody does. What was it you wanted to know?"

"Your son was very handsome," Harriet said. "He had a very open smile. That's so rare to find in people these days."

Kate raised her gaze and shot Harriet a watery smile. "He was, wasn't he?" Kate's eyes flickered to the side and up toward the mantle where a solitary framed photograph of Jack sat beaming down on them all.

"He was kind, too. Jack took after his dad in looks and personality. I always joked that it was lucky I wasn't sensitive, or I might feel left out because he didn't take after me at all."

Harriet smiled and took a sip of her tea. "I was sorry to read about your husband's passing," she said. "That must have been quite a blow to both of you."

"It was. Jack took it hard." Kate said. "He was only eleven and I worried that he was getting a bit too introverted. You see Jack's dad was a teacher in the local school Kirkbridge Academy so I got some advice and moved Jack out of there. He did better." She paused and stared down into her cup. "I think he needed a fresh start. At least I hoped it was the right thing, you can never really tell with kids, can you?"

"Of course, you were doing what you thought was right and that's what mattered. It's difficult for anyone to come to terms with loss and I suppose for

Jack having so many of his memories tied up with his dad and the school made it particularly painful. I think a fresh start was just what he needed."

Kate set her cup down on the small glass coffee table in the centre of the room and tugged a worn tissue from inside her pocket. "Sorry. It's just—"

Harriet shook her head. "No need to apologise."

When Kate seemed to have herself under control again, she lifted her head and stared at both Drew and Harriet. "You're not really here to discuss Jack's depression over his dad dying, unless..." She trailed off as her voice grew more choked. "I thought he was doing better. I thought we were passed it and then—"

"You said you took some advice on moving Jack out of Kirkbridge, does that mean you took him to see a counsellor?"

Kate nodded and sniffed loudly, dabbing at her tear-filled eyes with the shredded tissue. "I didn't know what else to do and it seemed like such a good idea at the time."

"Do you remember the name of the counsellor?" Drew interjected.

"What has this got to do with my son's death?"

Harriet shot a look in Drew's direction.

"You're aware that since Jack's death there has been two other teenagers who have died."

"The said on the radio that it was suicide. I hear about it everywhere now. Before Jack it never even occurred to me to pay attention to something like that but now it's all I hear about on the news and the radio. I stopped having the papers delivered because it's just every day, a new death."

"Well we're investigating the possibility that there's a link between the deaths of these teens and your son."

"Like a suicide pact?"

Drew shook his head. "Not exactly."

"I don't understand," Kate said, and Harriet's heart constricted in her chest.

"We're pursuing the possibility that there was another person involved. That perhaps Jack's death wasn't voluntary on his behalf."

"You mean someone murdered him?"

The colour drained from Kate's face and the shake in her hands became so pronounced Harriet was glad she'd set her cup down earlier.

"It's a possible line of enquiry, yes." Drew's tone of voice was brisk and professional, and Harriet cast him a sideways glance in an attempt to get a read on his state of mind.

"Why would anyone want to harm him? He was a good boy. He was so kind and—" Kate's voice broke off into a sob and Harriet tugged a packet of tissues from inside her own handbag and handed a fresh one to the grieving woman sitting opposite her.

"It's possible your son was targeted for all those reasons," Harriet said. "Some people are drawn to the bright stars among us because they crave what it is they have. They want to be just like them, possess them even because they know they can never hope to be what they are."

"So, you're saying my son was too nice and that's why he was murdered?" There was a harshness to Kate's voice that hadn't been there a moment before.

"I'm saying, Kate, that your son was special. He loved and was loved in return and there was nothing you could have done to stop the person responsible for his death. You did everything right."

"But how can I have? Jack's dead. I'm his mother and I was supposed to protect him and I failed."

"You didn't fail," Drew interrupted. "What Dr Quinn is trying to say is that you were the best mother Jack could have hoped for. It was your love for him that turned him into the man he was growing up to be. Kind, generous, and loyal. But you couldn't have known that the monsters of this world would see all that and want to take it. You couldn't have known because that wasn't your job."

"But we need your help now," Harriet said, drawing Kate's attention back in her direction. "Is there anyone you can think of that would have wanted to harm your son?"

Kate shook her head, her tears flowing more freely now. "Everybody loved him."

"Did anyone new come into his life in more recent months, perhaps? Someone new at the school, or down the rugby club?"

"I don't know," she said. "He didn't talk to me about things like that."

"What about online, did he spend more time on his computer or did you notice him becoming more secretive or withdrawn?"

Her face brightened then." He was always on his laptop, clicking away at it and when I'd ask him what he was doing he'd just brush it off."

"Where is the laptop now?"

"I've got it here. When your lot finished with it, they sent it back to me." Kate sounded stronger than she had before, and Harriet detected the vaguest hint of accusation in her tone as she addressed Drew.

"Has anyone else had access to the laptop?" Drew asked, seemingly oblivious to the danger that awaited him.

"Shouldn't you know all of this?" Kate quipped back, tightening her fingers around the tissue so that it ripped in half. "You came in here and searched this place from top to toe or at least that was what you told me."

"We did."

"But it's taken you this long to figure out that my son was murdered. What kind of detective are you anyway if you can't even investigate properly?"

"I'm sorry," Drew said. "It's a little bit more complicated than that—"

"Complicated?" Kate pushed onto her feet, two spots of colour riding high on her cheeks as she stood over Drew. "My son is dead, Detective. Don't you stand there and talk to me about complicated."

"I'm sorry, I just meant—"

"Maybe we should go," Harriet interjected. It wasn't as though they would get any new information from Kate Whitly now anyway, at least not now that she was so upset. The best thing they could do was leave her in peace and maybe call back in the next couple of days to try again.

Drew opened his mouth as though he was about to protest but whatever he saw reflected in her eyes caused him to keep silent.

"Thank you for your time," Harriet said, climbing to her feet alongside Drew. "You've been a big help, Kate." She held her hand out to the other woman who stared at her with barely concealed anger.

"What you're going to both scurry back underneath your rocks now that you've brought all this upset to my door?"

"We will find the person responsible," Drew said, hesitating in the doorway.

"It's a little late for that," Kate spat back at him. There was a moment where Harriet wondered if the other woman would give into the rage coursing through her body. Instead, the moment passed and Kate's face crumpled, tears spilled over her lashes and tracked down her cheeks as she dropped back into the chair she had stood up from.

"He was still my baby," she said. "He was all I had left and they took him from me."

"Kate," Harriet said, crouching down next to the arm of the chair. "Is there someone I can call to come and sit with you? A friend or a relative perhaps?"

Kate shook her head. "He was all I had and now he's gone."

Harriet shot Drew a concerned look. They couldn't just walk out and leave the woman like this. As it was, she was barely clinging on and it would be all too easy now for her to tip over the edge.

"Get out," she said.

"Let me call someone and—"

"I said, get out!" Kate' voice rose and in her eyes, Harriet saw a confused mixture of rage and grief both of which were clamouring for control.

Harriet hurried to the door alongside Drew and out onto the steps leading up to the house.

"This is a murder enquiry now," Harriet said. "Isn't there some kind of family liaison officer you could call to come over and be with her?"

"You saw her, even if I did get Gregson to sign off on having a FLO call here she'd probably slam the door in their face."

Harriet shook her head. "I don't think so. She needs a sympathetic ear right now. Someone who can sit there with no judgement and who has no negative connections to the case."

"You don't think she'd do anything stupid, do you?"

Harriet glanced back at the door. "I can't say with any kind of real certainty but I'd feel better knowing she has someone with her just in case. It's not worth the risk. You heard her in there, he was her world and now he's gone."

Drew nodded as he pulled his phone from inside his jacket. Harriet sat on the small wall outside the door as he paced along the edge of the road. Snatches of conversation drifted back to her and more than once she heard Drew's voice rise in anger. In the end he moved over to her and nodded.

"Gregson's agreed to a FLO considering the situation and your opinion on Mrs Whitly's state of mind."

Harriet inclined her head and gazed back up at the house. "I hope I'm wrong."

"You and me both," Drew said, following her line of sight.

"Should we try and go back in there?"

Harriet shook her head. "I don't think so. If she's going to do anything, she'll wait for us to leave in case we might raise the alarm."

It had started to rain and Harriet's jacket was no match for the British weather.

"I can stay here if you want to wait back in the car."

"I'm fine," she lied as a particularly cold droplet

of water slid down the back of her shirt and trailed down over her spine like an icy finger.

"Will it be like this for all of them?" Drew tilted his head back so that his face was upturned toward the sky. He rocked back on his heels and Harriet could almost have imagined how he must have been before his life fell apart.

"Probably."

"When Freya died," he paused, and Harriet's heart stalled out in her chest. Was this it, was this the moment when he remembered? "I woke up in that hospital bed and I asked for her."

Harriet bit her lip to keep from interrupting. He needed someone to listen to him, no judgements, no opinions.

"And when they told me what had happened, I broke down. I sobbed like a baby and they had to sedate me. In that moment I wanted so badly to go to her." He turned his attention to Harriet.

"Have you ever felt like that?"

"No. Or at least not as you described it."

"What then?"

The memory of her mother's frantic fingers fumbling with her seat belt filled her head and Harriet pushed it aside.

"When I was ten my mother drove my brother and I off a pier into the sea. She was sick and wanted to end it all but she couldn't bear the thought of leaving us behind."

"Jesus Christ, I'm sorry," Drew said.

Harriet met his concerned gaze and shook her head. "Don't be. You didn't cause it."

"No but—" He cut off. "You both got out all right thought?"

Harriet tipped her head down and gazed at her hands clasped in her lap.

"I did," she said. "Mom managed to get my seat belt off before we went over, I think she thought it would be over faster that way. My brother, Kyle was in the front seat and he fought back against her." Harriet coughed and cleared the lump that had formed in the back of her throat.

"How did you get out?"

"When we hit the water, Mom changed her mind and bailed. Kyle helped me out to the front but his seat belt had jammed after the impact. He told me he'd be fine but that I needed to go and get help." Harriet blinked back the tears that filled her eyes. "I was ten and I believed him because he was my big brother. He was sixteen and when I look back at it now, he knew if he didn't tell me to go we'd both have died."

Drew's expression of horror said it all. It was a typical reaction to the memory of her childhood and despite part of her being used to it, it still surprised her to see him so affected by it.

"What happened to your mother?"

"She was taken into custody but deemed incapable of standing trial so they sent her to an institution. I saw her yesterday. That's why I was late coming back to the office."

"You still visit her?"

Harriet nodded and clasped her hands tightly together. "Despite everything she has done, Detective Inspector, she's still my mother. There's a part of me who will always love her. I can still remember her when she was well, when things were good. And for the most part my childhood was good."

Drew turned and paced down the side of the road alongside his car.

"I don't know how you could forgive her for something like that."

"It's amazing the things we can forgive those we love for the terrible things they do to us, isn't that what love is all about?"

Drew opened his mouth but Harriet cut him off with a shake of her head. "You asked if I'd ever felt as you described. I was too young to fully grasp the idea of suicide as a viable option but in the months following Kyle's death I searched for an answer as to why I got out and he didn't. They call it survivor's guilt."

"Is this your roundabout way of telling me that what I was feeling then was perfectly normal?"

It was Harriet's turn to smile. "I suppose you could say that, yes. We all suffer from these things in our own way."

It was at that moment that another car pulled up alongside the road.

"Saved by the bell," Harriet muttered more to herself as Drew went to speak to the two FLO's who climbed from the small silver Fiat.

Harriet returned to the car and slid inside. What had behooved her to share with him like that? What had happened in her past was just that, a past event. The last thing she ever tried to do was allow it to encroach on her present in any real way. It was enough that she went to see her mother on a regular basis without letting the shared memories of that tragedy infect other aspects of her life too.

IT TOOK ONLY a couple of minutes for Drew to get the FLO's up to speed but when he returned to the car, he started the engine up without saying a word, something Harriet was more than grateful for. She'd made enough of a fool of herself by sharing so much.

They sat in silence as the FLO's approached the front door and knocked. It took a few minutes— Harriet's heart seemed to beat louder with every second that passed—for Kate Whitly to answer the door and when she finally did, Harriet felt the tension in the back of her neck loosen.

"Were you as nervous as I was?" Drew asked as

he pulled away from the curb, leaving the FLO's to their job.

Harriet laughed, a release of the unspent tension that still gripped her body and Drew glanced over at her.

"You all right?"

She nodded. "Yeah, I'm fine. But yeah, I was nervous."

He grinned and turned his attention back to the road. "Sian's parents are staying with a relative nearest to here, maybe we should hit there before we go on to Aidan's?"

Harriet nodded. The last thing she wanted at that precise moment was to submerge herself in the misery and trauma of such fresh grief. It had been hard enough with Kate Whitly and she at least had moved past the initial stages of shock. But it needed to be done.

"The file is there if you want to review it," Drew said, indicating a pile of beige folders at her feet.

She scooped it up and was once again greeted with the teenagers smiling picture. It was so unfair.

Why them? Why these teenagers in particular? Harriet let the questions mull over in her mind and the germ of an idea began to form.

What commonalities did these three teens share?

She glanced down at the files again and grabbed Aidan's file off the top. Flicking through the pages, she pulled the sheet with a list of his family out from among the others and scanned quickly down over the list.

"Damn."

"What is it?" Drew glanced over at her.

"I thought I'd found something is all," she said. "But it's nothing."

"Well what was it anyway?"

Harriet sighed and slid the sheet back into the file.

"Sian's father is dead. Cancer, right?"

Drew nodded.

"Well, Jack Whitly's father is also deceased. Car accident."

Drew shot her an incredulous look. "And Aidan's parents?"

"Both alive," Harriet said and bit back the inappropriate giggle that threatened to erupt from her. "I never thought I'd feel such disappointment over something like that."

Drew kept his attention trained on the road but Harriet could sense him mulling over everything she'd just said.

"It was a long shot anyway; I don't think it could be so simple as all that."

"Maybe," Drew said cryptically.

Sitting back against the seat, Harriet closed her eyes and tried to picture the shadowy figure that had stalked the children. How did you get close enough to them to know everything about them? It seemed impossible and yet their killer had done just that.

There was obviously something she was missing and it made her uncomfortable to know that someone out there was so many steps ahead of her. No matter how simple or obvious it seemed, no stone could be left untouched. The killer had obviously done his homework and Harriet had the feeling that it would be this that would help them finally catch up to him.

CHAPTER TWENTY-FOUR

IT WAS ALMOST impossible to make them understand that the world was a bad place that would never get better. They knew it was terrible, that the simple act of living was an act of extreme foolhardiness. And yet they kept trucking forward.

It baffled him.

Why fight to stay in a place that wanted nothing more than for you to disappear entirely?

Some people grouped themselves together. There was a kind of safety in numbers, he supposed, but it didn't change the fundamental facts at play. We were all alone and in the end that was how it would be.

For the lucky few he chose to help shirk the mortal coil they at least were not alone in the end. He was there with them, holding their hands as they fought.

But it was in the end when he stared into their eyes that he saw the truth. They wanted this; they were just too afraid to admit it out loud. That was the problem with people; we were too afraid to admit what we wanted. He wasn't afraid.

He wanted for nothing more than to leave this world behind and ascend to the greatness that awaited beyond. But there was nobody out there to help him cross over. No kindly soul that could take his misery from him and carry the burden along with their own.

He was the only one who saw the truth and with that knowledge came a weight that only he could bear. Of course, there would come a day when his body gave up and he longed for that day to come. He welcomed the thought of it. Just thinking about it was enough to bring a tear to his bloodshot eyes.

With hands that shook, he tied and retied the noose. He'd practiced it over and over and still, no matter how often he did it, he couldn't shake the fear that this time it wouldn't work.

This time it would be different. It needed to be different. But he was afraid. Not that fear was necessarily a bad thing. It kept him alert, kept him keen and aware and it was all of that that kept him going. He stayed one step ahead of those who would seek to destroy his work because of the fear.

Their stupidity and ignorance blinded them to the truth. They couldn't see the great work he was committing, couldn't see the truth of his mission and it was this that made them dangerous and gave his fear purpose.

This time would be different. There would be suffering but as with most things in life; from great suffering came the greatest joy. And while he wouldn't enjoy it, he knew it was necessary. A necessary evil. And afterwards, perhaps if he was lucky, he would sleep. He glanced down at the bear and smiled.

"Don't worry, we'll take you home soon enough."

CHAPTER TWENTY-FIVE

"WHAT DO you mean you think Sian's death is suspicious?" Nigel Thompson sat forward on the couch and pushed his wife's hand away. "How can you come in here and say something like that? I cut her down from the tree myself and she was—"

He covered his mouth with his hand as tears filled his eyes. "Do you know what that's like?"

"I can't begin to imagine how traumatic that must have been for you," Harriet managed to get the words in before he turned on her.

"And just who are you? What good is a psychologist now that Sian is dead? Where were you when she was stringing herself up?"

"That's just it," Drew tried again, and Harriet couldn't help but admire his tenacity. "We don't believe she took her life. We think someone made that choice for her."

Janet Thompson started to sob, and Harriet sat back in her chair and cast a quick look in Drew's direction. They were going around in circles. It seemed no matter how much they tried to steer the conversation back to Sian's death being a murder it triggered a round of accusations and questions demanding what good was it doing anyone now, Sian was still dead after all.

"How could they have killed her?" Janet said, raising her face to Harriet.

"I think they set it up to appear as a suicide. You said in your initial statement Sian showed no signs of being depressed, is that correct?"

Janet shook her head. "She was a pretty typical teen. She could be a bit moody but nothing out of the ordinary."

"Did you notice anything in her behaviour over these past recent months? Anything different at all?"

Janet shook her head. "She was a little bit more short-tempered than usual and I had a chat to her about her grades slipping. But she swore it was nothing, that she was just getting too grips with the curriculum."

"Do you think Sian was being secretive?" Harriet asked, studying Nigel and Janet's face as she asked the question.

"All teens are a bit secretive but I always told Sian she could come to me with anything." Janet dabbed at her eyes with the tissue in her hand.

"And what about you, Mr Thompson?" Harriet turned her attention to him. "Do you think Sian could be secretive?"

"They were very close," Janet interjected before Nigel could say anything. "She spent a lot of time talking to him, didn't she?"

Nigel shrugged. "We weren't that close but I did tell her if there was ever anything worrying her she could come to me."

"And did she ever come to you?"

"There was that thing with her boyfriend," Nigel cut in. "Nasty piece of work if you ask me. I tried to warn Sian off him. Said he was a no-good waster but she wouldn't hear of it."

"Aidan wasn't a bad boy," Janet said.

"He was a creep, trying to pressure Sian into sex —" Nigel buried his face in his hands and Harriet's suspicions rose.

"Well that sounds like you were close with her," she probed. "What about arguments between you, were there many of those?"

"Not particularly," Janet said. "We had our ups and downs like any parents have with their teens."

"I just can't believe she's gone," Nigel said, his voice cracking.

"Mr Thompson, perhaps you and I should get some air and maybe stick the kettle on," Harriet said, making a snap a decision to break the couple up. Handling them individually meant they might actually get some useful information from them and there was something about Nigel Thompson that set her teeth on edge.

"I can do it," Janet said, beginning to stand.

"Actually," Drew said, catching Harriet's eye. "I was wondering if you could help me create a list of Sian's friends."

"Oh well—"

Harriet pushed onto her feet. "Shall we?" She gestured to Nigel who stood and headed for the kitchen.

Once they were safely out of earshot of the living room, Harriet directed him to the table. "You sit, I can put the kettle on."

"Do you mind if I step out for a fag?"

Harriet shook her head. "I'll be there in a minute."

She busied herself with filling the kettle as Nigel stepped out onto the stone flags outside the back door. From the window, Harriet watched as he scrubbed at his eyes between drags on the cigarette he clutched between his fingers.

There was something about the entire situation that to her felt off somehow but what it was she couldn't quite put her finger on it.

With the kettle boiling, she stepped out onto the terrace next to him.

"It sounds like you and Sian shared a close bond."

He nodded. "As close as a step-father can be I suppose," he said guardedly.

"Did she confide in you a lot?"

He shook his head. "No, why should she have? Do you think she told me she was going to do this and I just—"

Harriet raised her hands as though to ward off his sudden defensiveness. "That's not what I meant, I'm sorry if it came across as insensitive. I was just referring to what you said earlier that Aidan was pressuring Sian for sex, that sounded like she was comfortable enough with you to discuss something so private?"

He shrugged. "She didn't really need to, you know? I asked her if he'd tried it on with her, I know what teenage boys are like around pretty girls."

"She was a very pretty girl," Harriet agreed. "Beautiful even."

Nigel nodded and took an unsteady drag of his cigarette. "If you'd seen pictures of Janet when she was Sian's age, the two of them were like twins of one another."

"Was Sian unhappy at all that you'd noticed?" Harriet asked, keeping her tone light and conversational.

"Not particularly. I think she was upset about the Aidan boy but she'd have gotten over that sooner or later. You know what teens are like, fickle as all get out."

"What about her friends?"

"What about them?"

"Did she have any arguments with them lately?"

"Her mother said there was a bit of furore but I took no notice of it. Girls can be bitches and they were just jealous of Sian anyway. She had every bloke in the county looking to hook up with her."

Harriet's discomfort intensified, a cold prickle of disgust that trailed down her spine.

"She told you that?"

"I've got eyes in my head, don't I? You'd need to be blind."

"And how did that make you feel?" Harriet asked, keeping her tone conversational.

"What do you mean?"

"Well that must have made you uncomfortable to think Sian was attracting so much attention?"

He took another drag of his cigarette and stared out over the garden. "Yeah. I didn't like it, I can tell you that. You know what I mean? Sian was under my roof."

"Of course, she was yours."

Nigel nodded. "Yeah. I didn't want other blokes thinking they could just come sniffing around her like that. She was so much better than that; Sian was special."

"And did you tell her that?"

"Course I did. Told her all the time that she was my special angel."

Harriet's blood ran cold in her veins but she kept her expression deliberately neutral.

"Did she like being your special angel?"

Nigel nodded and chucked his cigarette butt onto the ground before he ground it out with his boot. Before the sparks of his first cigarette were extinguished, he'd pulled another one from the packet and jammed it in his mouth.

"Sian liked knowing she was important. She liked the compliments, lapped them up, and I liked seeing her happy."

"When Aidan came on the scene, did she still like being your little angel then?"

Nigel's face screwed up into a sneer. "He was filling her head with all sorts of rubbish. Told her they were going to be together forever but it was just so he could get in her pants. But Sian knew it had to be special and she knew it wasn't special with him."

"What about you?"

"What do you mean, what about me?"

"Was it special with you?"

Nigel spluttered indignantly but there was a sly glint in his eyes that left Harriet cold.

"Well, you said it yourself that Sian shared a striking resemblance to her mother when she was the same age. It wouldn't be unusual for you being in a relationship with her mother to find Sian attractive too."

Nigel Thompson's eyes bulged in his head and

he started to choke and hack on the cigarette smoke he'd inhaled, part of Harriet hoped it choked him to death.

"What the fuck are you accusing me of?" He moved toward her, his face crimson with rage.

"You said it yourself she was beautiful. She was your special angel."

"She was but not like you're thinking. It wasn't like that."

"You made her feel special, isolated her from the others."

"I made her feel safe," he said.

"And then Aidan ruined it all. What did you threaten her with, Nigel? What did you do to keep her quiet?"

"You bitch," he said, and he lunged.

Harriet took a step backwards but her foot twisted over the edge of the stone flags and her ankle collapsed beneath her weight.

Nigel's hand caught her jacket, jerking her toward his thick bulk with enough force to cause her head to snap backwards painfully.

"You fucking bitch," he said his breath hot against her cheek.

"Did she beg you to leave her alone?"

"She was my daughter. I didn't lay a hand on her."

"When did it start?"

"Shut up!"

Nigel shook her violently and Harriet felt her teeth rattle in her head, reminding her of the night that had ended her career in clinical practice.

"She trusted you and you abused that trust."

His hand closed over her throat and Harriet's brain went into overdrive.

"Oi!" Drew's voice cut through the panic blaring in her head. Nigel released her abruptly and she stumbled backwards but her ankle refused to support her.

Harriet went down into the soft mud that made up the edges of the stone flag terrace.

"Nigel!" Janet Thompson's voice rose in hysteria and Harriet lifted her gaze in time to see Drew subdue the other larger man.

"I'm arresting you on suspicion of assault," Drew said, his voice quietly confident as he reeled off his speech.

"She needs to shut her fucking slag-mouth," Nigel said. "I would never touch a hair on Sian's head. I loved her. I wouldn't hurt her."

"That's a fine line," Harriet said as she pushed up onto her feet. "To you it was nothing more than love but for her it was a devastating betrayal."

Drew shot her a shocked glance but Harriet shook her head. There would be time to explain later, right now they needed to salvage a terrible situation but for once Harriet found herself unable to come up with a plan.

CHAPTER TWENTY-SIX

"WHAT DO you mean you've arrested the father of one of the dead teens?" Gregson kept his voice low but there was no denying the apoplectic rage that filled his eyes and caused the veins in his neck to stand out.

"I caught him in the garden trying to throttle Dr Quinn and—"

"Wait, why was she there?" Gregson asked, the unfriendly gleam in his eye made Drew uncomfortable.

"She's been assisting me with re-interviewing the families. It's with her guidance that we're finally starting to get somewhere on this."

"I had Dr Jackson on the phone to me this morning," Gregson said. "He's not happy about this either. Said you'd been over there digging into things you should keep your nose out of."

"I merely asked him to take another look at Sian's body, which he agreed to do."

"You're on thin ice here, Haskell," Gregson warned. "And I don't want that quack anywhere near the interview with the father. For all we know she hypnotised him into attacking her."

As Gregson turned away, Drew rolled his eyes. What was it about this case that was turning normally excellent officers into train-wrecks?

"Sir, I don't think that's what—"

"You heard me," Gregson said. "I don't want her in there."

"Well, I wasn't going to let her in there anyway, Sir. I was planning on taking Maz into the interview with me."

Gregson nodded. "That's good, let cooler heads prevail for once." Gregson paced in the small office space. "What have you got on him anyway?"

"Dr Quinn believes Nigel Thompson was abusing Sian."

Gregson's eyes widened and he pinched the bridge of his nose with his thumb and forefinger. "Fuck. Is there anyone around here not screwed up? What evidence has she got?"

"Well so far it's just her suspicion but, Sir, you should have seen how he was behaving. It wasn't right. During the first interview I did with the family I had Officer Crandell in with me, ask her how he was."

"So the man was upset, what has that got to do with anything?"

Drew shook his head. How was he supposed to explain a feeling to his boss when he couldn't even put it into words?

"There's the diary as well." Gregson shot him a dirty look. He was definitely grasping at straws with that one because unless Sian had explicitly written in her diary just why she hated her stepfather then it wasn't proof of anything other than a typical teen and a rocky parental relationship.

"We're going to take a run at the mother too," Drew said, drawing an incredulous look from his boss. "We need to know what she knows or if she was even aware of anything untoward."

Gregson nodded. "Fine. But this stays in here." He waved Drew out the door.

Before he could make it out of the office, Gregson called him back.

"Haskell, you better hope and pray that this doesn't all blow back on us like the shit-storm it's brewing up to be. It's all well and good for Dr Goody-Goody out there to poke her nose into other people's business and heads but we need more than just conjecture. I would hope you understood that."

"I do, sir."

"Then I expect you to bring her into line. In future if she has a suspicion, she should go to you first before she goes shooting off her mouth and bringing the wrath of God down on her head."

Drew nodded and pulled the door shut. He didn't entirely disagree with Gregson on this matter. If Harriet had just come to him before she'd gone wading into murky waters, then things might have been different. They could have treated the situation with kid-gloves instead of the ham-fisted way it had ended up.

Harriet caught his eye from the conference room. With a sigh, Drew crossed the office and tapped Maz as he passed his desk. "Can you come in here a minute? I need you to sit in with me on an interview."

"Sure." Maz began gathering up his stuff as Drew headed for the conference room.

He pushed open the door. "How's the foot?"

"It'll be fine," she said, waving his concern away. She had it propped on a chair opposite her, the ankle elevated with an ice pack draped over the bruised and rapidly swelling joint.

"Maybe you should get it looked at. For all you know it's fractured."

"It's not," she said dismissively.

"And you know this because you have X-ray eyes?"

"I know because I'm a doctor."

Drew sighed. "Not the same thing."

She shrugged and grinned at him. "What did the

DCI have to say?"

"Well he's not happy, that much is certain," Drew said, closing the door behind him before he tugged a chair out from under the large table and dropped down into it.

"I didn't think he would be," Harriet said. "Cases like these rarely make anyone happy."

"How sure are you that he was abusing Sian?"

"As sure as I can be," she said. "At least as sure as anyone can be without Sian to confirm it."

"What makes you so certain?"

"You don't believe me?"

Drew shook his head and planted his elbows on his knees as he leaned forward in the chair and let his hands dangle down between his legs. "That's not what I'm saying."

"Then Gregson doesn't believe me."

"He raises a good point, Harriet," Drew said. "What proof do we have? As it is right now it's a 'he said, she said,' case and those never work out."

"Look, I'm not saying I can definitively put my finger on it and say yes, here on these dates Nigel Thompson was interfering with his step-daughter. But I can say that after speaking to him today and the short pieces I read in Sian's diary, not to mention her grades slipping, her isolation from the family—" she ticked the items off on her fingers. "If he hadn't started to molest her then he was on the verge of it. He was grooming her, turning her into his perfect victim."

Drew closed his eyes. Things were definitely getting more complicated by the minute.

"Room for a little 'un?" Maz poked his head around the door with a wide smile on his face.

"Yeah, come on in," Drew said. "DS Mazer Arya, this is Dr Harriet Quinn."

Maz moved into the room and held his hand out toward Harriet. "Hey, Doc, you can call me, Maz, everyone around here does."

Harriet took his hand and returned his smile with a warm one of her own.

"Harriet," she said. "We don't need to stand on ceremony."

Maz's smile widened a little more and he sat in the chair next to her.

"What happened to your leg?"

"I had a run in with a garden terrace," she said wryly.

Seeing the two of them together, all jovial got under Drew's skin in a way he couldn't have imagined.

"If you two are finished getting all cosy, maybe we could get back to the situation at hand?"

Maz flushed up to his dark roots and Harriet cocked an eyebrow in Drew's direction.

"The DI here thinks I've messed up his case because I've uncovered a history of abuse in the Sian

Jones case."

"That's not what this is," Drew said. He cut himself off with a sigh and raked his hand back through his hair.

"I just think if you'd come to me before you started digging around with Nigel Thompson, we wouldn't be in this mess now."

"And if I hadn't started digging then we wouldn't be any the wiser about it. Not to mention the fact that if I'd tiptoed around it and just left it at that, he would have had a chance to talk his way out of it all."

"He didn't talk his way into it," Drew said in exasperation.

"But when you interview him, you'll have a better starting point. He's already off balance. The sooner you get in there and have a cosy little chat with him about his unnatural relationship and infatuation with his step-daughter the easier it will be for you to get the truth out of him."

"So wait, do we think Sian killed herself because her step-dad was abusing her?"

Drew shook his head. "No."

"It's possible," Harriet warned. "Until we hear back from the coroner on this, we need to approach it with an open mind."

"So you're changing your mind then?"

Harriet shook her head and Drew groaned into his hands.

"I haven't changed my mind. There's definitely

something going on here but you said it yourself we need proof and right now we've got pretty much nothing."

Drew hated to admit it, but she was right. However, he didn't appreciate her turning his words against him like that.

"Right, we're going in there with one goal in mind." He pushed onto his feet. "We've got to get Nigel to confess or we've got nothing at all."

"If you'd like me to talk to Janet," she started to say but Drew cut her off with a shake of his head.

"I'm afraid we've got to keep it strictly above board from now on."

"Another one of Gregson's arbitrary rules is it?"

He nodded. "Something like that. Maz and I'll take the interviews. You should get the leg looked at."

Harriet opened her mouth as though she was going to object and then seemed to change her mind. Was it disappointment he saw flash in her eyes as she grabbed her bag from the floor and dropped the ice-pack back onto the desk?

"I'll be off then," she said. "It looks like you've got it all under control here."

Drew caught up to her as she hobbled to the door. "Look, I'm not trying to cut you out here," he said, catching her elbow.

"Of course not," she said with false brightness. "You're just doing your job, like the rest of us."

"You've been a real asset in all of this. I couldn't have gotten this far without you."

Harriet smiled and patted his hand. "It's fine, Drew. I get it, I'm an outsider and that's all right. I'm not saying it to make you feel bad, it's just how it is."

If she wasn't saying it to make him feel bad, she was doing a bloody good job of it.

"I've got a lot of work at the university that I've been neglecting," she said. "When you need me, you know how to pick up a phone."

Drew nodded and took a step back, noting the way she shut him out with her professionalism. If they'd been getting closer to one another over the last two days, then obviously he'd been mistaken.

"I feel like you're taking this personally," he said.

Harriet shook her head as she pulled open the door. "There's nothing personal about it. You got from me what you needed. Now you need to hold up you side of the bargain and catch the person responsible."

"How should we approach the Thompsons?"

She hesitated and cocked her head to the side. "Try and gain his confidence. You know, man to man, that kind of thing. Deep down he doesn't see what he was doing with Sian was bad because he loved her. It's society in his eyes that's screwed up."

Drew sucked in a deep breath. "And if that doesn't work?"

Harriet gave him a grim smile. 'It'll work," she

said. "The man is so full of his own importance, he doesn't want to believe that he's sick. He wants people to empathise with him and if you can make him think that you understand why he did the things he did with Sian you'll have him eating out of the palm of your hand."

With that she pulled away from him and hobbled out into the main office.

"And Janet?"

Harriet didn't even look over her shoulder as she answered him. "Remind her that Sian was her baby—not that she'll have forgotten—but remind her all the same. And then ask her if Nigel ever commented on how Sian looked like her when she was younger."

"What'll that do?"

But Harriet was already gone out through the set of double doors that connected the office to the rest of the building.

"Shit," he swore under his breath before he turned back to face Maz. "Looks like it's just you and me."

Maz shrugged. "We don't need a head doctor to help us do our jobs," he said, flipping through the files laid out on the table. "She'd probably only just get in the way."

Drew said nothing as he moved back to the table and scooped up a file of his own. He wouldn't disagree with Maz aloud but he also wasn't going to agree with him either. Ever since he'd gotten Harriet involved, she'd caused him to view things in a new light. It was her insight into people that had helped him keep the case alive in the first place and it was with her help that they now had Sian's stepfather in holding.

None of those things would bring the dead teenager back. But at least that scumbag wouldn't get the chance to hurt anyone else and Drew had to believe that Sian would have wanted that.

"Right," he said, letting the file drop back onto the desk. "You ready?"

Maz rolled his shoulders, causing his neck to crack loudly. "Ready as I'll ever be."

CHAPTER TWENTY-SEVEN

HARRIET MADE it as far as her car before the pain in her ankle became too intense. As she slid in behind the wheel she groaned inwardly. Using her foot to change gears was going to be interesting to say the least.

But all of that paled in comparison to the pain she felt over being dismissed so thoroughly.

Placing her palms on the wheel, she pressed her forehead onto the backs of her hands. She should have seen it coming. At the end of the day, it made perfect sense for Drew to drop her once he had what he needed from her. In fact, it was something of a miracle that he had even allowed her to go out with him and do the interviews in the first place.

And maybe it was better this way. After all, this wasn't her real job and she'd been neglecting that in favour of doing this.

Starting up the engine, she gingerly pressed her foot down on the clutch and winced as the pain flared to life. It wasn't as bad as it had been walking out of the station but it wasn't great either. So long as she didn't need to do any emergency stops, she figured she'd get home just fine.

Without a backwards glance at the station, she pulled out into the flow of traffic.

BY THE TIME she made it into the house, Harriet's foot was on fire. Hobbling into the kitchen, she pulled a packet of garden peas from the freezer and wrapped them in a tea-towel before heading back into the living room. Propping her foot up on the couch next to her, she placed the peas over the unbecoming swelling that was made her ankle look more like a misshapen turnip than anything close to what it was supposed to be.

Reaching over to the coffee table she scooped her phone and dialled Bianca's number and listened as the ringing tone echoed in her ear. With no answer, Harriet let the phone drop back onto her lap and groaned.

Why had she been so stupid?

The answer was pretty simple. Working in the university wasn't enough for her. She enjoyed it, and for a time it had brought her some satisfaction knowing she was shaping the minds of the future.

But that had been short lived and now when she thought about work, it was a weight on her chest.

Grabbing the nearest case file, she flipped it open and studied the first page. But this had been so much more than that. It was new and exciting and for the first time since she'd started in the field of Forensic Psychology Harriet actually felt like she could make a difference to the world around her.

Perhaps by helping to understand the people who committed these kinds of crimes she could help prevent it happening in the future. It was of course pie in the sky. Crimes like these would always happen and there was nothing she could do to change that.

But it hadn't stopped her from feeling like she was making a difference, somehow, somewhere.

The phone next to her started to ring making her jump. Typical of Bianca to miss a call and then immediately return it.

"I was wondering when—"

"Harriet, it's Jonathan. I was calling to ask if you were running late or—"

Harriet pressed her hand over her eyes and swore silently under her breath. How could it have slipped her mind?

"Dr Connor, I'm so sorry," she said.

"You've stood me up," he said, not bothering to conceal the hurt and anger in his voice.

"No. Well, I did but it wasn't my intention."

"You could have had the courtesy to call," he said.

"I am very sorry," she said. "I'm only just in the door from work and there was an incident and—"

"Wait, you're not hurt, are you?"

"It's just a twisted ankle, I'll be fine. But—"

"Harriet, I'm so sorry. I shouldn't have jumped to conclusions. Is there something I can do to help?"

"No, no, I'm fine," she said wincing as she moved her foot into a more comfortable position on the couch "I'm the one who should be apologising anyway. Our meeting—"

"Never mind that," he said, cutting her off before she could finish speaking. "Our meeting is unimportant. Are you sure there's nothing I can do?"

"Honestly, I'll be fine. A little rest and I'll be right as rain in the morning."

"Well, if you're certain."

"I am." She was pleased to sound so decisive.

Dr Connor sighed. "Well, I best let you rest then."

"Thanks for calling," she said before ending the call.

Letting out a long breath, Harriet let her head flop back against the pillows. How had she forgotten the meeting? Of course, it didn't take a rocket scientist to work out why she'd let the meeting slip her mind. A combination of not wanting to go in the first place and the case engrossing her every waking moment.

Setting the phone down next to her, she reached over to the table and picked up another one of the files she'd brought home with her.

Drew had said he didn't need her help anymore but she had a feeling that it wasn't entirely true. There were things at play here that he couldn't hope to understand. Heck, she didn't even understand but she wanted to.

"Did you pick Sian because she was already isolated from her family? Did you know what her step-father was doing to her and if that's true then how did you know?"

It seemed unlikely that Sian would have confided in anyone. Although it was entirely likely she had confided the terrible truth in Aidan. But that would have been different for Sian. As far as she was concerned, he was her confidant, her boyfriend, her protector. It made perfect sense that she would have told him at least some of what was happening to her. And so, the question became: would he have told anyone?

Harriet flipped over the pictures of Sian and Aidan, laying them on her lap side by side. They were both so young, so terribly vulnerable to predators who looked for someone, anyone whose armour wasn't strong enough to withstand an assault.

And in Sian and Aidan he'd found two such victims.

Picking up the photograph of Aidan, she stared at it.

"What was your secret?"

"What made Sian trust you enough to tell you her darkest shame?" Harriet leaned her head back and stared up at the ceiling. "Did you share a secret with her? Is there something we don't know about you?"

Harriet paused and closed her eyes. "Well, I'd imagine it would have to have been equally as shameful as hers. She wouldn't have told you anything if your secret was something trivial. What is it, Aidan? What bonded you together?"

Grabbing a pen and pad of paper from her handbag, Harriet started to write down notes, small observations. It wasn't easy when all she had to go on amounted to little more than hearsay and gossip from those who had known the teenagers.

A loud knock on the door pulled her from her thought process. She paused, pen poised above the page and the knock came again.

"Harriet, it's me, Jonathan." The voice echoed in through the letterbox and into the hall and Harriet's heart sank in her chest.

What the hell was he doing here?

Scrambling to her feet, Harriet hobbled to the door before he could knock a third time. She tugged it open and came face to face with the handsome psychologist standing in her front porch.

The collar of his long wax jacket was pulled up around his ears and his salt and pepper hair was damp letting Harriet know it had started to rain since she'd gotten home.

His face broke out into a sympathetic smile and he raised a plastic bag in his left hand. "I thought if Mohammed can't come to the mountain, the mountain should come to Mohammed." He raised his right hand and presented a bottle of red wine to her.

"You really didn't have to," she said, doing her best to keep her smile friendly. The last thing she wanted to do was let him inside, the thought of entertaining him was beyond painful.

"Well, I figured you probably wouldn't be able to do much on that leg of yours," he said, as he cast a critical eye in the direction of her feet.

Harriet had the overwhelming feeling that he was testing her. Did he not believe her when she'd said she'd hurt herself? It felt a little petty and vindictive if it were true and there was a part of her that longed to disbelieve it.

"Can I come in?" He asked, waggling the bottle at her again.

Harriet hobbled aside and directed him to toward the back of the house. "Through the hall and into the kitchen," she said.

With the confidence Harriet had become accustomed to seeing in Jonathan, he strode through to the kitchen and began to set the food out on the granite countertop.

"Do you have cutlery? Plates? Glasses?" He raised a speculative eyebrow at her cupboards.

Harriet moved around the counter and took some dishes from the cupboard above her head, every time she moved her ankle protested painfully. Perhaps Drew had been right when he'd suggested a trip to the local A&E department but the thought of getting stuck there for hours on end was enough to make the pain bearable.

"I should be doing that," Jonathan said, but he made no move to take the plates from her or even really help.

He let her set the dishes down and Harriet grabbed two glasses from inside the dishwasher.

"Oh, did you have company?" Despite the nonchalant air to his question, Harriet could feel the undercurrent of curiosity in his voice.

"No," she said honestly. "I just haven't emptied the dishwasher in a few days."

"Here, let me," Jonathan finally made a move toward her and took the glasses from her hands before he filled them with wine.

Screw-top-lid, Harriet noted. Either he'd come prepared, thinking she might not have a corkscrew, or he hadn't wanted to waste too much money on a bottle of wine.

She settled onto the stool on the other side of the counter and watched him set the plastic containers out.

"I didn't know what you'd like," he said apologetically.

"So, you got a little of everything?" Harriet finished for him, staring at the amount of food he'd brought in surprise. Perhaps her earlier thought had been a little disingenuous. After all, why go to so much expense on the food and then skimp on the wine?

"Well, I know the woman who runs Daphne's," he said with a broad grin. "Surprisingly enough her name isn't Daphne."

Despite not seeing the humour in his little joke, Harriet felt compelled to join him in his laughter or run the risk of insulting him.

"So, what happened to your leg?" he asked, sliding a set of containers toward her. "I didn't think there was too much danger these days in academia, although maybe it's changed?"

Harriet smiled and shook her head. "No. The students didn't revolt if that's what you're thinking. I'm helping the police with a case and got a little overzealous when I was talking to one of the victim's families today."

Jonathan raised his face, his expression a mixture of concern and surprise. "Wait, you're helping the police now? When did that happen?"

"After I got back to the office yesterday, actually," she said, popping the lid on the box next to her. The smell of pasta spilled out and filled the air, caused Harriet's mouth to water.

The grapes and cheese from the night before hadn't exactly been a sustaining meal and the day had gone by in a flash leaving her no time to think of eating. She took a generous helping of the pasta before sliding it toward Jonathan.

"I don't understand, how did they find you?" There was a flicker of harshness in Jonathan's voice as he spoke, and Harriet glanced up at him through lowered lashes.

"I don't know," she said. "I guess they read some of my papers and liked what they saw."

"But I mean surely there are other more qualified psychologist's out there who could have helped them?"

Harriet smiled. "I'm sure there was but they came to me." She shrugged.

"What are you working on?"

She contemplated not telling him but decided against it. There was no point in alienating him and anyway it would probably prove useful to have another psychologist to bounce ideas off of from time to time.

"The three suicides up in Tollby," she said. "Three teens in just over three months."

"Was it bullying? Social media these days has

gotten really quite fierce and young minds find it difficult to separate out the present from the future."

Harriet shook her head. "We're not looking at bullying as the cause, although I think one of the cases could very nearly have gone that way."

"Then what?"

"Murder," Harriet said and watched as that one simple word sent a myriad of emotions flitting across Jonathan's face, the chief among them being jealousy.

"And the police have asked you to assist them? I'm sorry, I just don't understand it."

"What's not to understand?" Harriet kept her voice mild as she wound a forkful of spaghetti up and then proceeded to pop it into her mouth.

"I think you know exactly what I'm saying. You didn't spend very long working clinically and the amount of academic work behind you isn't exactly monumental."

She quirked an eyebrow at him. "I suppose you think you would have been a much better candidate?"

He nodded. "Well, yeah. Don't you?"

She set her fork down before picking up the glass of wine he'd poured for her. She twirled the stem around her fingers for a moment before taking a sip of the cheap merlot. It wasn't the worst she'd tasted, her student days had been filled with far dodgier bottles of plonk bought only with one intention in mind, to get as drunk as humanly possible. And given half an opportunity this would do exactly the same.

"I can't argue with you," she said. "You are much more experienced than I am."

Jonathan beamed proudly. "I'm not saying that you're not capable of giving them some guidance," he said.

"Just not as much as you think you could."

He nodded. "Of course. You said it yourself, I am much more experienced."

"Maybe they thought you were too busy," Harriet said, fighting to keep her voice neutral.

"Maybe," he said sounding more than a little unconvinced. "So why do they think these suicides are murder? It seems a little far-fetched to me."

"Nothing is set in stone," Harriet said, deciding to remain a little illusive. "They're exploring the possibilities is all."

"Ah," Jonathan said. "Maybe that's why they didn't contact me then."

Harriet inclined her head. "Why's that then?"

"They probably figured someone like me would have given them what for on wasting people's time. Whereas with you," he said as he smiled patronisingly. "Well, you're a little bit of a soft touch, aren't you?"

"That's not quite how I'd describe myself," she said, biting back the acerbic response that popped into her head.

"I hope you don't think I'm trying to insult you," he said, his face overcome with concern. "I would never do that."

Harriet nodded and turned her attention to the food in front of her. He wasn't trying to insult her, no, she could concede that point. He had however insulted her with his patronising mannerisms and his belief that just because she sought to heal through empathy that she was somehow a soft touch capable of being hoodwinked by even the most undiscerning of people.

"You wanted to discuss my mother's care," she said, changing the subject abruptly.

"I have insulted you, haven't I?" He reached across the counter and awkwardly patted the top of her hand the way an adult might try and console an errant child

"No," she said, curtly, sliding her hand away from him. "I just don't think it's appropriate to discuss the details of an ongoing investigation with someone who hasn't been cleared to hear said details." She smiled sweetly at him as she picked up her wine glass and took a deep mouthful of the bitter drink.

He shot her a wry smile as he nodded. "You're right, of course."

"So, what was it you wanted to discuss?"

He cleared his throat awkwardly. "As you know

your mother attacked another care-assistant," he said, setting his fork down on the side of his plate.

Harriet nodded. "She doesn't seem to see why it was a problem."

Jonathan's lips thinned. "She's not responding to the treatment the way she once was."

"Are you sure she's taking her medication?"

He smiled. "I thought you might ask that, and I went personally to oversee her medication being administered to her both last night and this morning."

"And she's definitely taking it?" Harriet couldn't keep the surprise from her voice. She'd been so certain yesterday in the hospital that there was something not quite right and the only thing in the whole scenario that made any sense was that her mother was somehow duping those administering her meds. Of course, it should have been impossible, but Harriet had long since learned that nothing in this life was truly impossible. Where there was a will there was a way and many people suffering similarly to her mother struggled to keep taking their medication.

It wasn't just defiance either. Many of them seemed to genuinely believe that the medication was somehow making them worse. Others believed incorrectly that they were now cured, as though their schizophrenia was somehow like an infection and that a course of medication could wipe it out much the way antibiotics could destroy bacteria.

"She's definitely taking it," he said. There was no questioning the certainty in his voice.

"I don't know then," she said, feeling a wave of hopelessness wash over her. "Do you think my visits are affecting her?"

He shook his head. "I honestly believe she looks forward to your visits, in her own way of course."

Harriet nodded. "Well what do you think we should do?"

Jonathan gave her a warm smile. "Well, I've been thinking about this and I was wondering what you might say to having her transferred to another facility?"

"Excuse me?"

"One with a little more security, for her safety along with everyone elses."

"I'm not sure how that's a good idea, she's been in there for twenty two years and—"

He shook his head. "But I think that's exactly the issue here. She has been here for twenty-two years, that's a long time by anyones measure and I'm starting to believe that your mother is beginning to go somewhat stir-crazy."

"But that's—"

"Harriet, I need you to put aside your personal feelings in this matter for a moment and imagine what is best for your mother."

She nodded. "Don't you think that's what I'm doing?"

Jonathan gave her a withering smile. "I think you're allowing your feelings to get wrapped up in what's practical."

"How is moving her practical? You and I both know it could set her back. Routine and familiarity is vital to someone like her."

"Familiarity also breeds contempt," he said. "And it's my professional opinion that your mother's familiarity with her surroundings is causing her to act out. Perhaps in an environment where she didn't feel so in-control, it might cause her to reset, mentally."

"You're talking absolute rubbish," Harriet said pushing up onto her feet. Forgetting her foot, she placed her weight on the injured leg and a jab of shooting pain ripped up through her calf causing her to gasp aloud.

She crumpled forward and grabbed the counter for support, tears momentarily blinding her.

Jonathan was there in an instant.

"Here, let me help," he said as she tried to swat him away.

"I'm fine," she said, through gritted teeth.

He didn't let her go, his hands, holding her tight as she straightened up with the support of the counter to balance her weight.

"Let me take you inside," he said, his hand sliding down to grasp her waist.

Harriet shrugged him off and took a hobbling step toward the living room. "I said, I'm fine," she said pleased to discover the hitch in her voice had disappeared.

He followed her into the living room and Harriet scooped up the papers and files she'd left strewn over the couch before he had the chance to examine them.

"Are those the case files?"

She nodded but bit down on her tongue to keep from snapping at him.

He set her wine glass down on the coffee table before he joined her on the couch. He folded his lean legs up beneath his body, angling his torso so that he faced her. He wore a sympathetic expression and Harriet remembered it only too well from the early years when she'd been a teen visiting her mother. She'd hated it then and she hated it now.

"Harriet, I think you're allowing your emotions to cloud your judgement."

"Don't patronise me."

He looked at her, shock filling his eyes. "I never would."

Harriet leaned over and picked up the glass. Her hands shook and she fought to control her temper. Was it the pain that was affecting her judgement or because Jonathan seemed to be needling her? It was probably a combination and Harriet was too tired to try and analyse it too closely.

"If you can't see how this might benefit her then

you're not the psychologist I thought you were." His words were a slap in the face and Harriet sucked a sharp breath in through her teeth. "I'm your mother's doctor first and foremost, everything I say is for her benefit."

"And how does this benefit her if it triggers another break?"

He leaned forward earnestly. "I don't think it will."

"But you can't say with any certainty that it won't."

"Well, no but—"

"So why take that risk?"

"Because if I don't, I think she's going to kill someone."

"Someone else you mean," Harriet said softly as she turned her head away and took another mouthful of the wine. It seemed the more of it she drank, the less it tasted of bitter vinegar. When she'd been a student, she'd found the same to be true then too.

"I'm sorry, I didn't mean to upset you like this," he said with a deep sigh. He leaned back on the sofa and gave her a rueful smile. "I screwed all this up, didn't I?"

"What do you mean?"

"Oh, you know," he said, the meaning in his words unmistakable.

"I never led you to believe that this would amount to anything," Harriet said.

He shot her a disappointed smile. "I know you didn't, but you can't blame a guy for trying."

"I'm not interested, Jonathan, not like that."

He nodded. "I understand."

Harriet shook her head and dropped her gaze to the glass in her hands. "This won't affect your ability to care for my mother, will it?"

"How could you think that of me?" He forced as much hurt into those few words that Harriet felt instantly guilty. How was he so good at always turning the tables on her? It wasn't the first time he'd done it and it always seemed to catch her off guard when it happened.

"No. My care for my patients always come before any personal attachments I might have," he said softly.

"Good."

"Harriet," he said, leaning forward.

She glanced up at him and was surprised to find him so close. Before she could move, his lips found hers. It was nothing like she'd imagined it might be. His lips were cold and wet and they slid against her mouth as his hand pressed into her hair.

With her free hand, she planted it against his chest and pushed, hard. Instead of releasing her, Jonathan tightened his grip on her hair and Harriet cried out in pain.

It was all he needed and he thrust his tongue into her mouth with enough force to make her gag.

He moved closer, his weight pressing into her and Harriet reacted. Clutching the wine glass, she tipped it over his crotch.

"Christ," he said jerking away from her to stare down in disgust at the bright red stain spreading across the front of his beige chinos.

Harriet scrubbed her hand over her mouth in an attempt to rid herself of the taste of him.

"What the hell do you think you're doing?" Harriet spat the words out as she shifted backwards on the couch to put as much distance between them as was humanly possible.

"What am I doing? Shouldn't I be the one asking you that question? Look at what you've done to me?"

Harriet glanced down at the spreading red stain on his trousers and felt a flicker of satisfaction light insider her chest.

"I told you I wasn't interested and you said you understood. I thought I was pretty clear on this?"

He shook his head and stared at her with incredulity. "You're unbelievable, you know that?" Jonathan snorted in derision as he climbed to his feet. "You women are all the bloody same. You smile and flick your hair while batting your lashes at us poor bastards and we're supposed to just ignore it all like you're not flirting your bloody arses off."

"I wasn't flirting with you," Harriet said, fighting to keep her temper in check. "In fact, if you think what I was doing with you could be even slightly construed as flirting then I pity any woman you've ever had any contact with."

"You're just a frigid bitch," he spat, temper getting the better of him as he dabbed at his trousers with a white handkerchief.

"Sticks and stones, Jonathan," Harriet said before she sighed. "And you call yourself a psychologist, yet you can't read when a woman isn't interested in you. How does that work?"

"I was going to talk to the board about getting you into the hospital when your mother was moved out but I won't bother now. In fact, you'll be lucky if you ever work clinically again when I'm done with you."

"So that's what all this was about?" Harriet stared up at him in shock. How could she have been so naive and stupid? He'd spent years trying to talk her into working at the hospital but there had always been the barrier of her mother being an in-patient.

But if he succeeded in shipping her mother off somewhere else then there wouldn't be anything stopping her from taking up a position in the hospital; he was obviously more calculating than she'd given him credit for.

Had he been counting on her feeling beholden to him for his help as a way to get her into bed?

It seemed too far-fetched, yet as she stared up at him, she couldn't shake the feeling that it was the truth.

"You'd risk the welfare of your own patient, for what?"

"Don't you come the high and mighty with me, you arrogant bitch," he said, leaning down toward her. "I wasn't the one who let a patient get the jump on me and causing the death of another member of staff."

"That's unfair and you know it," Harriet said. His words cut her to the quick and she hated the wobble it caused in her voice. "Mr Joyce wasn't my patient."

"No," Jonathan said. "He wasn't and you shouldn't have been in that room with him. But it doesn't alter the fact that you screwed up. There's blood on your hands, Harriet, so don't sit there and pretend you're better than me when you're really not."

He strode from the room and she listened as he gathered his things from the kitchen. It wasn't until the front door slammed that she released the breath she'd been holding onto.

He was an arrogant asshole but he was right about one thing. She did have blood on her hands. If she hadn't been so arrogant and let her desire to be the best get in the way, then Joyce's nurse would still be alive. It was her fault, and nothing would change that.

Reaching over to the table, Harriet grabbed the bottle of wine and emptied the rest of it into her glass before she took a mouthful. How was she supposed to help the police when she hadn't even been able to help those who relied on her?

She stared into the glass and not for the first time wondered if perhaps the answer could be found at the bottom of it after all.

CHAPTER TWENTY-EIGHT

WITH TILLY TUCKED up in bed, Bianca made her way downstairs to the quiet living room. Pulling her laptop from the table and onto her lap, she settled back against the cushions and stared at the Skype request.

Ryder1980 wants to add you.

At least this way if she did add him and they spoke over video chat there could be no confusion come Saturday. He was either who he said he was or...

She clicked accept request and waited. It took only a moment for the screen to light up and the sound of a ringing phone filled the room.

Tugging a pair of headphones from her handbag she connected the call and stared at the blank black screen.

"Hello?" She felt stupid talking to a blank screen but it was either that or just hang up.

The screen lightened and she found herself staring at the same man from the dating site. The image was grainy but he at least looked as she'd imagined.

"Hey, babe!" He grinned and the image froze with his hand halfway to his face.

"Ryder, the picture is really bad. Is it your end or mine?"

"Sorry," he said, the picture failing entirely. "I've got hotel wi-fi and I don't think it's very good." His voice at least came through crystal clear and Bianca felt the knot of tension she'd carried with her all day slowly unravel.

"I got to see you for a minute," she said with a smile.

"I can still see you," he said. "And my god but you are a cool drink on a hot day."

Bianca cringed at the cheesy compliment and covered the screen with her hand.

"Hey!" Ryder said.

"You can't say stuff like that," she said.

"Why not?"

"It's cringey, that's why." Bianca pulled her hand away and grinned.

"Your hair is shorter than the picture you put up," he said. "

"Yeah, I got it cut since then." Bianca pulled the

end of her hair and stared down at the red locks. "I needed a change."

"Yeah, I get that." There was a sound on the other end of the line as though Ryder had changed position.

"Are you in bed?"

His masculine chuckle slid down the line into Bianca's ear. She curled her toes against the carpet and felt the butterflies in her stomach erupt.

"Why would you like it if I was?"

"Seems a little early is all," she said aiming for nonchalant and managed only to sound ridiculous instead.

He laughed again. "I've got an early one in the morning," he said.

"Another shareholder meeting?"

"Yeah. God save me from those bloody shareholders." He sighed. "Anyway, enough about that. What were you saying earlier about being nervous?"

Bianca sighed and slid down on the couch, it was weird talking to a blank screen but Ryder's familiar voice in her ear was soothing.

"I don't know," she said. "It's probably just my own weird neuroses."

"No go on, you can tell me."

"I feel like I'm being unfaithful," she said. "You know to Tom."

Silence greeted her on the other end of the line and Bianca's heart sank. Clearly, this was a step too far for Ryder. Not that she could blame him, it wasn't his place to take on someone as screwed up as she was.

"Do you think he'd want you to think like that?"

"What?"

"Tom, do you think he'd want you to look at it like that?"

"Well no," she said. "But it's how I feel."

Ryder sighed. "You know, if it's too much for you, we don't have to meet on Saturday. If you're not ready, I understand."

"That's not what I'm saying," she said and closed her eyes. "Or am I? I don't know anymore."

"Well, let's start with what you do know," he said softly. "I don't want you think there's any pressure on my end."

"You see, when you say stuff like that you make me feel bad," she said as she started to laugh.

"Why?"

"Because it proves you're one of the good guys."

He chuckled and Bianca fought the urge to squirm.

"You don't need to worry about that," he said. "I'm definitely not a good guy."

Bianca rolled her eyes dramatically. *Well, you could have fooled me.*

"Mommy!" Tilly's voice cut the air and Bianca jumped.

"I've got to go," she said, ending the call without waiting for Ryder to say anything.

Her heart thudded violently in her chest as she took the stairs two at a time, reaching the landing in record time.

Tilly stood in the doorway, her Dora the Explorer pyjamas askew and her dark hair standing on end.

"What's it, baby?" Bianca said, crossing the floor to her daughter.

"I can't find, Gruff," Tilly said, scrubbing her hands over her eyes.

"What do you mean, I thought he was on the bed with you?"

"That's what I thought too," Tilly said, her voice hitched as the first of her tears began to fall. "But I can't find him."

"Well, was he in the bed with you when I read you your story?"

Tilly shook her head and stared up helplessly at her mother. "I don't know. I don't remember."

Bianca sighed as her phone downstairs began to ring. "Well he's got to be in here somewhere," she said, taking her daughter by the shoulders and turning her around to march her back into the room.

"You didn't move him, did you mommy?"

Bianca ran back over the events of the morning. She'd made Tilly's bed and Gruff had been where her daughter had left him that morning, hadn't he?

She could have sworn that he was definitely on the end of the bed but that was the problem with doing the same things every day; each task had the uncanny ability of bleeding into one another and this was no exception.

"No, I'm sure he was on the bed when I made it," she said, flicking on the overhead light.

"You didn't put him into wash?" There was no denying the hopeful note in her daughter's voice.

"No," Bianca said. "But you hop into bed and I'll have a look for him."

It took only a couple of minutes for Bianca to realise her daughter's most prized possession wasn't anywhere to be found in the room.

"Can you check the washing machine?" Tilly asked. "Just in case..." Tilly was on the verge of tears and Bianca found it impossible to deny her daughter that request.

"You stay here, I'll be back in a minute."

Hurrying down the stairs, Bianca passed the couch and caught sight of Ryder's messages of concern that lit up the screen. He could wait.

Heading into the kitchen, she tugged open the washing machine and stared into the empty drum. Not that she actually expected to find anything inside anyway. That was definitely something she'd remember. Grabbing Tilly's school bag from the table, she unzipped the pink bag and peered at its contents. Nothing.

With a frustrated sigh, Bianca set the bag back on the table This was the last thing she needed.

Moving back to the stairs, Bianca grabbed her phone and took it upstairs with her.

"Did you find him?"

Bianca shook her head. "Sorry, kiddo, there's no sign of him."

Tilly's face crumpled. "Where is he?"

"You didn't take him to school, today did you?" Tilly knew the drill, Gruff wasn't supposed to leave the house. After the incident involving a train journey the summer before an appeal online had seen the little brown bear returned in one piece, luckily. From that moment on, the rule had become Gruff didn't leave the bedroom except for special occasions but that rule hadn't stopped Tilly from trying to take him to school on more than one occasion.

"No," Tilly said, crossing her heart. "I wouldn't."

Bianca dropped down on the pink coverlet next to her daughter. "I don't know," she said. "He's bound to turn up. He's just waiting somewhere for us to find him and we will."

"Promise?"

"I promise," Bianca said, snuggling in next to her daughter. "Now, come on, you need to get some sleep or come the morning you won't want to get up."

Tilly nodded and slid down in the bed. Her eyes were still watery and as Bianca stared down at her small serious daughter a tear slipped from the corner of her eye and slid down onto the pillow.

"I just hope he's all right," Tilly said. "I don't want him to be scared."

"He's a big bear," Bianca said. "And big bears don't get scared. Remember, you tell him to look after me every day before school, so he's not scared of anything."

Tilly nodded. "That's true. He's a protector bear."

Bianca smoothed down her daughter's hair and nodded. "Yes, he is. Now get some sleep."

"Will you stay here?" Tilly's voice was already thick with oncoming sleep.

"Of course I will."

Tilly snuggled down into her mother's arms and within a few minutes had drifted off. Bianca lay there next to her and ran back over the day's events. As far as she was concerned, Gruff had been on the bed when she'd made it, the only trouble was she couldn't swear to it. But if she was right and he'd been on the bed before she left the house, then where was he now?

CHAPTER TWENTY-NINE

DREW SCRUBBED his hands over his eyes and listened to Maz repeat the question for what felt like the millionth time.

"Let me get this straight, Nigel. You expect us to believe that you never had a thing for your stepdaughter?"

Nigel shook his head, the picture of innocence. "I wouldn't do that. And it's just messed up that you would even think that I would."

"Nigel," Drew said, sliding a photograph of Sian across the desk toward the other man. "I know you loved her, it's perfectly understandable."

Nigel shook his head. "Not like that, I didn't. I never crossed the line with her, never."

"But you wanted to?" Maz interjected.

"That's not what I—"

"I mean, come on, how could you not. She's

gorgeous," Maz continued on as though the other man hadn't spoken at all.

"I bet she was a bit of a flirt too?"

"Mate, you've crossed the line there," Drew said, addressing the DS.

"Yeah, that's not on. That's my step-daughter you're talking about." Nigel's voice went up several octaves.

"Have I?" Maz picked up the picture. "I mean, come on. Look at her. Anyone who looks at her and doesn't think she's a stunner needs a reality check."

Drew shook his head. "DS Arya, do you think maybe you could step out and grab us a cup of coffee?" He turned to Nigel. "Do you want anything, Mr Thompson?"

Nigel looked between the two detectives as though he couldn't quite decide if he should trust either of them. "A coffee would be great," he said uncertainly.

"And a coffee for, Mr Thompson. Sugar? Milk?"

"Two sugars, please," Nigel said, straightening up a little in his chair.

Drew waited until Maz had left the room before he turned to Nigel again. "I'm sorry about my colleague there. He can be a little overzealous sometimes."

Nigel nodded. "Yeah, he was coming off a little creepy. Sian was a good girl."

Drew dropped his gaze to the file in front of him.

"You met Sian's mother four years ago, is that correct?"

Nigel settled himself a little more comfortably in the chair. "Yeah, that's right."

"How did you two meet?"

"Through a grief group," Nigel said. "My mother passed away and I was attending the meetings when I met Janet. I was on the verge of giving up and then one day in she walks." He smiled fondly. "I mean, you've seen her. I'm a very lucky man."

Drew smiled. "Were you ever married before?"

A cloud passed over Nigel's face and he shook his head. "Never married, no."

"But you were in a long-term relationship before you met Janet?"

Nigel shrugged. "So? What of it?"

"I'm just trying to get some background information here, Mr Thompson, that's all."

"I don't see what my background has to do with Sian's death."

Drew leaned back in his chair. "To be honest, Nigel, can I call you Nigel by the way?"

The other man nodded. "Why not?"

"To be perfectly frank with you, Nigel, your background has nothing to do with Sian's murder. But when such a serious allegation has been made, we've got to follow up. You understand, right?"

Drew studied the other man as he spoke, watching as his emotions flooded across his face. No wonder Harriet had found it so easy to read him, he was practically an open book.

"That crazy bitch made that shit up about me. I never touched Sian and if she were here she'd tell you I never did nothing to her."

"But that's the unfortunate part in all of this," Drew said. "Sian isn't here to tell us. We only have your side of the story."

"You've got to believe me. I wouldn't hurt her." Spittle formed at the corner of Nigel's mouth as he spoke.

"And I do believe you," Drew said with as much sincerity as he could muster. "You cared deeply for Sian, that much has been plain to me from the beginning."

"Yeah, I did. I loved her like she was my own."

"All you ever wanted to do was protect Sian, isn't that right?"

Nigel nodded vehemently. "That's right. When she met that Aidan boy and he was trying to get in her knickers I told her that. I said, don't you go throwing yourself at him. You're worth more than that."

"That makes perfect sense," Drew said. "It can be so hard with kids these days. They grow up so fast, girls especially, with all that make-up and doing their hair, and the clothes they wear. I've seen some sights let me tell you."

"You're telling me?" Nigel snorted. "The

amount of times I had to tell Sian to get back upstairs and put something more decent on. I didn't want her to give the blokes in the area the wrong idea. She was my princess and I wanted to keep her that way."

"And what did Sian think of all this? I don't suppose she took it too well?"

Nigel started to laugh and took the empty polystyrene cup he'd been drinking from and began to tear the sides of it. "She didn't like being told what to do. She could be a bossy mare when she wanted."

"But you were the man of the house," Drew said softly.

"And she knew it." Nigel's lips curled up at the corner into an unpleasant smirk. "I think sometimes she'd do it deliberately, you know?"

Drew shook his head.

"You know what I mean; dress a bit provocative to get a rise from me. She liked being the centre of attention, craved it and I didn't mind giving it to her. It was like she wanted me to be firm with her, testing boundaries and whatnot."

"And that changed when she met Aidan, did it?" Drew asked, keeping his tone nonchalant despite the discomfort churning in his stomach. Harriet was right to be uncomfortable around him.

"Yeah, it was like she didn't need me no more."

"In what way?"

"We used to spend Saturday mornings together,"

Nigel said. "Janet used to take Paul and Clare swimming and I'd stay home with Sian."

"And when she met Aidan, she didn't want to spend her time with you anymore?"

"She threw a tantrum one morning when I said she couldn't go out to meet her friends. She locked herself in her room and didn't come out until Janet came home."

"What happened after that?"

"I took the lock off her door. We didn't know what she might do in there on her own."

"When you said, Sian needed a firm hand, what did you mean?"

Nigel's gaze became hooded and he glanced toward the door. "When is he coming back with that coffee, I'm parched here."

As though on cue, Maz poked his head back in the door. "Guv, can I have a word?"

Drew pushed up onto his feet and followed Maz out into the corridor.

"Well?"

"We've done a little digging on him. He's originally from Southampton that's why it's taken so long to track him down."

"What did you get?"

"There was a complaint made by a Melody Curtis," Maz said, handing Drew a file. "She dated Nigel briefly in 2012. She didn't go ahead with charges but there was a whiff of inappropriate behaviour toward her ten-year-old daughter."

"Why didn't she press charges?" Drew asked, scanning the file quickly.

"It says there in the file that she couldn't be sure. She says her daughter was prone to imagination and she didn't want to ruin a man's life on something that might not be true."

Drew swore under his breath. "Do we know what kind of inappropriate behaviour?"

Maz shook his head. "I've been trying to get her on the phone but so far I've had no luck."

Snapping the file shut, Drew nodded. "Fine. You keep on that and I'll ask him about Melody."

"Do you want me to get the coffee for you?"

Drew shook his head. "No. Let him wait a little longer for it, see if we can't shake something loose."

"Do you really think she was right then?"

"Don't you?"

Maz shrugged. "Well that makes it more likely, but I don't know."

Drew turned back to the door. "Well, it's still our job to get to the bottom of it."

Pushing open the door, he smiled at Nigel. It was going to be a long night.

CHAPTER THIRTY

"JANET, I know this isn't easy," Drew said, passing a box of tissues across the table to the quietly crying woman who sat opposite him.

"My daughter is dead," she said between sobs. "And now you've arrested Nigel. What else are you going to take from me?"

Drew gave her what he hoped was a sympathetic smile. But sympathy had never been his strong suit and he glanced down at the table before he could terrify the woman any more than she already was.

"I have to ask you some questions now which you're going to find uncomfortable."

"Why?"

"Because certain things have come to light and I'm hoping we can get to the bottom of it." He glanced up at her, but Janet stared at the wall, her expression blank. "If I'd just gone into her that night and talked to her."

"Did you ever notice any tension between Nigel and your daughter Sian?"

Janet shook her head. "If I'd just gone and spoke to her then maybe—"

"Mrs Thompson, I'm asking for your help here."

"She's dead, isn't she? This won't bring her back, none of it will."

"But it might help us understand who did this, and why."

Janet turned her attention back to Drew. "Do you think Nigel had anything to do with it?"

"I don't know. That's why I need you to answer these questions as honestly as you can."

"He loved her," Janet said. "He wouldn't hurt her."

Drew sighed and pushed his hand back through his short hair. This was getting them nowhere and it wasn't as though it would give them a suspect for Sian's death even if they did manage to get the truth out of Janet Thompson. Harriet had pushed them down a rabbit hole and made his job a million times more difficult than it already was.

"Was Sian particularly unhappy in the run up to her death?"

Janet's eyes brimmed with tears, that slowly tipped over the edges of her lashes and tracked down her hollow cheeks. "I didn't see it," she said. "I should have done; what kind of mother doesn't see their child is so unhappy that they would..." She trailed off and knitted her fingers into the sleeves of her jumper before she raised her face to Drew. "But she didn't though, did she?" There was a kind of hope in her voice that Drew recognised from his own guilty conscience. "Take her own life I mean. You said she was murdered."

"We're exploring that possibility, yes," Drew said gently. "Which is why I need your help."

She nodded. "Ask your questions."

"Was she unhappy in the run up to her death?"

Janet swallowed hard and shook her head. "Not that I particularly noticed. She'd gotten a little moodier lately. Especially after Aidan's death; that hit her hard."

"And what about yours and Nigel's relationship with her, how did that seem to you?"

Janet shrugged. "Normal, I guess. We fought like all parents do with their teenage children."

"Did you notice Nigel's relationship with Sian changing?"

"They fought more," she said. "Stupid stuff. He'd tell her to do something and she'd refuse. She was so pig-headed sometimes. Nigel said we were like mother like daughter."

"What else did Nigel say about the two of you?"

Janet glanced up at him. "What do you mean?"

"Did he think you and Sian were alike in other ways, perhaps?"

"I don't know. I guess..." She trailed off and started to chew her fingernails.

"Did he ever remark on how alike you looked?"

"What are you getting at here?" Janet blurted out suddenly. "Nigel's a good man. He wouldn't have hurt Sian."

"We're just trying to understand some things that Mr Thompson mentioned," Drew said carefully.

"Some things like what?"

"He seemed to think that the men in the area were all after Sian. That she was becoming sexualised." Janet stared at him in shock and not for the first time Drew wondered if perhaps he had crossed the line. After all, Janet wasn't the suspect in all of this, it was her husband.

"He wouldn't have said that," she said softly.

"He told us that you both looked alike, that Sian was almost a carbon copy of you when you were younger." Drew noted the way she swallowed and ducked her gaze and instinctively knew he'd hit a nerve. "Is that true, has he said that to you in the past?"

Janet shrugged. "So what? We do look alike... Did look alike." She corrected herself.

"But that's different for you to say it, isn't it?" Drew said. "You're Sian's mother after all, it makes sense that you would be proud of the resemblance you shared with your daughter." Drew sighed. "It just strikes me as odd that a man who isn't related to Sian can make the comparison between the woman he's married to--the woman he admittedly finds sexually attractive both now and when he's seen pictures of you younger--and her daughter who bears a striking resemblance to her."

"I never saw anything inappropriate between them," Janet said. "Do you think I'd be with a man who would do that?"

Drew shook his head. "No, I think you're the type of woman who if she knew would do anything in her power to protect her babies."

She nodded. "I would."

"Was Sian uncomfortable around Nigel?"

The blood seemed to drain from Janet's face and Drew felt his stomach drop into his shoes.

"He used to take them all swimming," she said quietly. "And then Sian said she was giving it up, that she felt weird in a bathing suit and didn't want people to see her." She swallowed hard, her attention laser-focused on her hands in her jumper. "I thought it was just her being a typical teen." She raised her face then. "I thought she was just going through an awkward phase."

"What happened, Janet?"

"She was happy enough the first week, Nigel took Clare and Paul with him and then..." She choked up, her eyes tearing at her memory. The moment passed and she coughed, clearing her throat as she scrubbed her hand over her face. When she spoke again, her voice was clearer, stronger.

"The following week, Nigel said he wasn't feeling well and asked if I'd mind taking Clare and Paul swimming. I thought nothing of it, and I did it. After that it just seemed to become routine. And then Sian asked me when Nigel was going to go back to doing it."

"And what happened?"

She shrugged. "Nigel said he was getting a lot of work done on a Saturday morning and I didn't think much of it. Then a few weeks ago I came home with the kids and found Sian crying, she said, Nigel had broke her door and took the lock off it."

Drew kept his expression deliberately blank, the least little thing he said could throw her off and that was something he didn't want to happen.

"When I asked him, he said they'd had a fight and she'd threatened to kill herself before she locked the door and wouldn't let him in. Nigel took the door off its hinges to get in there to her." She sucked in a deep breath. "He was just looking out for her."

"Are you sure?"

Janet opened her mouth before she closed it again with a snap. She shook her head, violently. "She'd have told me if there was something wrong. She'd have come to me..."

Drew pushed onto his feet as Janet started to

rock back and forth in her seat. He made it to the door before she spoke again.

"If he hurt her, I'll kill him," she said, her voice low. Drew glanced back at her and what he saw in her face left him in no doubt as to the veracity of her claim.

"I hope for both our sakes it won't come to that," Drew said, before he left the room.

"Did you get anything from her?" Maz asked as he met him in the hall.

"Well, nothing concrete but there's something here that's just not right."

"So how do we break him?"

Drew shook his head. "I don't honestly know," he said. "But if we can't pull this off then we're going to have to let him go."

CHAPTER THIRTY-ONE

SITTING on the edge of her couch, Harriet buried her face in her hands. How could she have been so stupid? All she'd done was give Jonathan ammunition with which to destroy her. Many would see her treatment of him as an overreaction, hysterical even. While others still would look at her with suspicion and wonder just what she had done to lead him on.

That was the problem with society. Without meaning to, people tended toward victim blaming. Harriet had seen her fair share of cases of sexual violence where the victim was asked what they were wearing at the time of the assault, or how much had they to drink? As though their clothes and or levels of intoxication somehow made them more deserving of the crime perpetrated against them.

Societies simplistic views on certain matters made things more difficult to navigate and made those who were victims of a serious crime less likely to come forward.

She, by extension, was lucky. Dr Connor had been deterred by a simple glass of wine to the crotch but his entitled behaviour was indicative of the world surrounding them. Despite hearing her say she wasn't interested, in his mind that refusal was a green light for action.

There was a knock on the door and Harriet sighed as she pushed onto her feet. Her ankle throbbed painfully and for a moment she wobbled back and forth, a nasty combination of too much wine and an inability to balance on one leg.

Hobbling to the door, she paused as the shadow outside the frosted glass moved and her heart sank. If he had come back for round two, he was in for a rude awakening.

She tugged the door open and opened her mouth to speak but instead of Jonathan on the doorstep, she came face to face with DI Haskell.

"What do you want?" Her voice was curt and he blinked at her in surprise, reminding her of a deer caught in the headlights.

"Is this a bad time?"

She shook her head and rubbed her eyes. "No, not really," she said, feeling somewhat childish for her initial outburst. "Sorry, it's been one hell of a night so far."

"You and me both," he said with a huff. "I had to

let Nigel Thompson go," he said. "I wasn't getting anywhere with him."

"So you just let him go like that?"

Drew shrugged his shoulders helplessly. "I'm not disagreeing with you. There's definitely something there and even if he's innocent this time I wouldn't put it past him for the future."

"But you couldn't get anything on him?"

He shook his head. "We took his computers, phone, tablets, the works but it's going to take some time to go through them."

Harriet nodded. She knew only too well just how slowly the wheels of justice moved. She'd seen enough people get caught in the flow to recognise that he might never even be charged for the abuse, let alone convicted of anything.

"Anyway," he said, holding a blue folder aloft. "I just came over here to give you this."

"What is it?"

"Sian's diary." Harriet took the folder and flipped it open. The pages within were photocopies of the ones she'd seen in Sian's diary.

"Thanks for this," she said, her eyes already scanning the top page. "Did your people find anything?"

Drew shook his head. "Nothing conclusive. There are too many sets of fingerprints, mostly Sian's. If Nigel got his hands on her diary, I'm sure we'll match his fingerprints to the ones they've managed to lift from the pages."

"Do you want to come in?" Harriet asked, stepping to the side.

Drew started to shake his head.

"I've got the remnants of a bottle of wine," Harriet said. "And my head would really appreciate it in the morning if you'd help me finish it?"

He smiled and stepped inside the door. "I'm not much of a wine drinker," he said. "More of a beer drinker if I'm honest."

Harriet wrinkled her nose in disgust and let the door slam shut. "That's one beverage I've never been fit to tolerate."

He grinned at her. "Well, I'll have to bear that in mind in case you drop by my place." Drew paused in the living room doorway, and Harriet studied his profile as his gaze swept the room.

"Well, at least you're consistent," he said finally.

"What does that mean?"

"This place is just as messy as your office." He grinned at her as Harriet hobbled past him and swept some of the papers aside to make a space for him on the couch.

"I've been a little preoccupied." She stacked a couple of books she'd used for research on the coffee table. "It's not normally like this."

Drew shot her a knowing smile before he sat tentatively on the edge of the couch.

"Just leave your coat on the back of the chair,"

she said, gesturing to an armchair in the corner. "I'll get you a glass."

"I can get one," Drew said as she started to hobble toward the kitchen. "You need to stay off that foot."

She pulled a face at him and stepped into the kitchen. He followed her and paused in the doorway, from the corner of her eye as she washed up a second wine glass, she could see him taking in the take-away boxes.

"Did you have company?"

"Unfortunately," she said, turning back to him with the glass in her hand.

"That bad, huh?"

Harriet smiled. "You have no idea. There's food there that hasn't even been opened if you're hungry."

Drew shook his head. "I'm fine thanks, I grabbed a sandwich at the office."

Harriet knew a polite refusal when she saw one, but she wasn't going to push him. "So, what did Nigel have to say when you questioned him?"

Drew's expression changed instantaneously, his shoulders tightening almost imperceptibly.

"The usual crap to be honest. I loved her; I wouldn't hurt her. That kind of thing."

Harriet nodded. "I thought he would. Like I said, in his mind what he did wasn't wrong. It's just that society has misunderstood him."

Drew's face screwed up in a grimace. "How do you deal with that?"

"What do you mean?"

"Well, you're so calm about it all. Put me in a room with one of those blokes and it's difficult not to knock their heads off."

He spoke with such passion that Harriet was forced to hide a smile behind her hand she reached over to the half empty bottle of wine on the table to pour him a glass.

"It's my job," she said.

"Yeah, and it's my job too. Doesn't change the fact that I find it hard to hide my disgust."

She sighed. "If I let them know I was disgusted by them I wouldn't be doing my job."

Drew gave her a sceptical glance. "How does that work?"

"If they come to me as a psychologist, I have a duty of care to help them in any way I can."

"But they're sick, perverse."

"But they don't see it that way. To them, their proclivities are just at the opposite end of the spectrum to you or me. If I let them know I was disgusted by everything they told me they would be less likely to want to confide in me. And that's not a healthy working relationship to have. They need to trust me to open up to me and if I abuse that trust then I shouldn't be doing this kind of work."

"But it must make you sick?"

Harriet shrugged. It was very difficult to explain to someone like Drew who saw the world only in such stark black and white colours.

"Of course I don't like it," she said. "But I can't allow myself to think like that. When I do, I lose all ability to gain the trust of my client."

Drew stared at her like she'd grown a second head and Harriet sighed. "You don't need to understand, DI Haskell, suffice to say I try to do good with my job."

He shook his head and stared down at his hands. "I mean, I thought that what I do is hard. Obviously, I had it all wrong."

Harriet gave him the ghost of a smile before she turned her attention to the glass in front of her. "So what really brought you around here?"

He looked up, startled. "I brought you Sian's diary."

"You did but that could have waited until the morning. There must have been something else on your mind to bring you around here so late."

"I'm that easy to read?"

Harriet shrugged and scooped up the glass. "You've got an honest face," she said tactfully.

Drew started to laugh, and the sound warmed her from her toes all the way up to the tips of her ears. It was good to hear him laugh. He had struck her as the type of man who needed to laugh more, maybe even for his own sanity.

"Is that shrink code for: I can read you like a book?"

Harriet didn't bother to conceal her grin. "Maybe."

Drew's laughter died away as he grabbed his own glass and downed the contents of the wine in two large mouthfuls. She sat and waited for him to finish, her impatience growing with every second that slipped by. There was obviously something bothering him but unless he told her what it was, she wasn't going to guess for herself.

"I'm starting to think we've been barking up the wrong tree after all," he said ruefully.

"What makes you say that?"

"Where's the evidence?" He set the glass down heavily on the coffee table and Harriet winced. "I mean all we've really got to go on is my gut instinct and so far it's gotten us diddly squat."

"I wouldn't say that," Harriet said softly. "You're making new lines of enquiry all the time. A case like this, such a complicated beast requires patience."

He shook his head and buried his face in his hands. "I asked the mother like you suggested about whether there was anything missing belonging to Sian."

Harriet held her breath.

"There was a locket on the necklace she usually wore," he said. "You know the one we found wedged in her hand."

Harriet pursed her lips. "In the crime scene photos, I don't remember seeing a locket anywhere."

Drew shook his head. "That's because there wasn't one. At least not one that got logged in by forensics from the scene."

"What about in her bedroom?"

Drew shook his head. "I've asked them to go over the place again but I'm not sure we're going to find it."

"So why are you suddenly doubting your own gut instinct?" She stared at the man who didn't seem able to bring himself to meet her gaze. It was the break he was after, so why wasn't he happier about it?

"Because whoever is doing this is like a fucking ghost." He cringed. "Sorry, I didn't mean—"

Harriet cut him off with a dismissive wave. "I've heard worse, Detective."

"Seriously, call me Drew already."

She grinned at him. "Fine, Drew. I've heard worse."

He smiled at her then before he ducked his head and returned his attention to his hands. "They're a ghost. We've got nothing to go on. Hell, until you came on board there was no case. And even now it's just all hearsay and gut instinct. I can't bring a case with just that. I need more, we need proof."

"And we'll get it," Harriet said. "We need time."

"He'll kill again," Drew said softly. "He's gearing

up to murder some other poor sod and we're sat here chasing our tails."

Harriet couldn't argue with him there. Every bit of knowledge she had told her their killer was only going to escalate. And the sad part about her job was that the more people he murdered the more chance she had of figuring out just who he was and why he was doing the things he did. More bodies on the ground, meant opportunities to catch him and a greater risk that he would make a mistake. That was the sad part about the job she did. It wasn't preventative, at least not entirely. It was prescriptive.

"As his kills escalate, he'll make more mistakes," Harriet said, sounding more sure of herself than she truly was.

"And if he doesn't?"

"We're going to catch him."

Drew nodded and glared down at his hands. "I hope you're right, Doc, I hope for everyone's sake you're bloody right."

CHAPTER THIRTY-TWO

SUNLIGHT PEEKED in through the curtains and fell over Drew's face. His head felt like someone had taken a hammer to it and his tongue—he was almost positive—had grown fur overnight.

He stretched and his leg bumped something solid. This definitely wasn't his bed, he thought as he opened his eyes and stared up at the ceiling overhead. The plaster moulding was unfamiliar, as was the height of the ceiling. His apartment definitely wasn't kitted out with original Victorian features.

He straightened, pushing upright and wasn't particularly surprised to find himself still wearing yesterday's clothes. Ever since he'd caught the case, he'd been so dead on his feet that he hadn't been making it to bed before dropping off on the couch. However, this was a new low even for him.

Reaching up to his head, he ran his fingers through his hair and scanned the room.

He'd called around to the good doctor's house the night before.

"Bugger," he said, sliding the blanket she'd draped over him at some point during the night off himself. He folded it neatly and was in the process of sliding his feet back into his shoes when the tantalising aroma of freshly ground coffee hit his nostrils.

This definitely wasn't the same black slop they drank down the station, that was for sure and certain.

Cautiously, he moved toward the kitchen and toward the sound of someone moving about out there. Tugging open the door, he came face to face with Harriet. She glanced over at him and then did a double take before shooting him a wide grin and gesturing to his head.

"Slept well, did you?"

He rolled his shoulders, half expecting them to protest over the position he'd contorted himself into the night, but he was pleasantly surprised to find them pain free.

"Actually, I did," he said, unable to keep the surprise from his voice. He had slept well, better than he had in a long time and he found himself wondering if maybe the doctor had slipped him something in his wine.

He stepped out into the kitchen and caught sight of his reflection in the metal cooker hood.

"Christ," he said gruffly, doing his damnedest to smooth his hair down that seemed to be determined to stand up in all directions.

"There's a shower through there," Harriet said directing him to a small corridor off the kitchen. "Feel free to use it."

He shook his head. "I should go home and get changed there."

She shrugged. "It's up to you. I've just brewed some coffee if you'd like some?"

Coffee was something Drew could always get on board with and he nodded enthusiastically. Before he sat down, he nodded toward the bathroom. "I think I'll use your loo though, if it's all right with you?"

Harriet shrugged. "*Mi casa es su casa.*"

Retreating to the bathroom, Drew locked the door behind him and paused in front of the sink and stared at his reflection in the mirror. He hadn't drunk a whole lot of wine the night before but he looked like a man who'd been out on a pub crawl.

Starting up the tap, he splashed cold water up onto his face, the icy chill sending a shockwave through his body that saw his breath catch in the back of his throat. He needed to get a grip. This case wasn't really any worse than the others he'd worked on in the past. It was a comforting lie but a lie none the less. It wasn't really about one case being any worse than another.

It was the method of the crimes and the victims themselves that made it so hard to stomach. Who in their right mind went around the place staging the suicides of teenagers?

He could wrap his mind around a crime of passion. Even opportunistic murders made more sense than this, whatever it was.

Sighing, he wet his hands and smoothed it over his rumpled hair. A quick coffee and then he would go home, shower, change, and finally get shaved before returning to the office. Maybe doing all of that would help him get his head straight, approach the case with a fresh mindset.

Leaving the bathroom, he returned to the warm kitchen and plonked himself down on one of the stainless-steel barstools that lined the breakfast counter.

"You only just moved in?" He asked casting a look around the bare walls and almost empty counters.

"Actually, I've been here three years." Harriet kept her gaze trained on the coffee pot she was pouring from.

"Oh, right," he said, accepting the mug she pushed over the counter to him.

"Work keeps me pretty busy," she said, and Drew couldn't help but wonder why she felt the need to explain herself to him. It wasn't as though he could judge. He'd lived in his place for going on a year and a half and still treated it more like a crash pad than a home. If it wasn't for Rita, the woman who came in to clean for him once a week he dreaded to think what the place would actually look like.

"It's a nice place," he said, and inwardly cringed.

"Do you want milk, or sugar?"

He nodded and watched as she moved over to the fridge and took a pint out. The fridge itself was practically empty, although he did spot the take-away boxes from the night before stacked neatly on the shelves.

He loaded his cup up with sugar and topped the black coffee off with a generous helping of milk before lifting the cup up to his mouth. The coffee was rich and hot and Drew felt his tiredness slowly slip away as the caffeine hit his veins.

"This definitely beats the crap we get at the office," he said, with a grin.

Harriet had taken up a position at the other side of the kitchen and she sipped her coffee delicately. She smiled and shrugged.

"Coffee is the one thing I take very seriously."

"You and me both," he said. "I don't think I'd get through even half a day without one."

"What are—" Before she could get the words out, Drew's phone began to ring shrilly in the other room. Scrambling out of his seat, he hurried into the living room and snatched up his coat. The call ended before he could fish the phone out of his pocket and he swore beneath his breath.

"I've got to return this."

"Sure," she said. "I'll head upstairs and finish getting ready anyway."

He nodded and waited as she climbed the stairs quickly before he turned his attention back to the phone. The number on the screen was all too familiar to him and he hit the redial button before the noise of Harriet's footsteps had completely receded.

"Dr Jackson, sorry I missed your call. I was—"

"I don't care about what you get up to in your spare time, Detective," the long-suffering tone of the coroner echoed in Drew's ear. "I've got some news."

"What is it?" Drew snapped, unable to keep the impatience from his voice. He'd waited so long for this and he was damned if he was going to wait a moment longer.

"Can you come by my office?"

Drew sighed. "Can't you just give me something?"

The man on the other end of the line huffed. "I'm going to tentatively agree with your thoughts," he said. "Don't get too excited mind, I still need the other results to come back."

"But something changed your mind?"

"We had some more in-depth results return today from the initial sets of bloods I sent off and while strictly there's nothing particularly abnormal I took a second look and what I've found is concerning."

Drew bit his tongue to keep from babbling. He sucked in a deep breath and closed his eyes before he answered. "I can be there in twenty."

"Make it fifteen," the coroner said. "I've got to be in court in an hour." He hung up before Drew could answer.

He stood in the middle of Harriet's sitting room and his stomach clenched. He was right. This was foul play and if the coroner was correct then this was the evidence he'd been waiting for.

Grabbing up his coat, he slipped it on before he headed for the front door.

"I've got to go," he called up the stairs and without waiting for a response he pulled the door open and stepped out into the crisp morning air.

He could tell Harriet later, once he had something more substantial to tell her.

CHAPTER THIRTY-THREE

"CHRIS, if you were to sit a patient down and confront them the way you've suggested in your report, all you'd end up with for your trouble is a blank wall. People don't want to feel like you're against them. They want to know that no matter what they say to you, you cannot be shocked. You're their confidante, their sounding board. You listen and offer insights that they might otherwise overlook themselves. It's not your job to judge their behaviour."

"But how can I not? If I've got someone who comes to me and tells me they've killed a bunch of people, then surely you don't expect me to just sit there and nod at them."

Harriet smiled and dropped her gaze back down to the sheaf of papers in front of her. This wasn't exactly how she'd planned on spending her morning but it wasn't as though she had a choice in it.

"No," she said, struggling to keep her tone patient. If this was the best they had to offer when it came to the future of psychology, then Harriet wasn't entirely sure the world was on the right track. "I don't expect you to just sit there and nod at them. But the moment you let them know that you're no longer on their side is the moment they view you as a threat."

Chris rolled his eyes. "I'm sure I could take them."

"With that kind of arrogant attitude, I'm sure you wouldn't last very long," she snapped.

He stared at her in shock. "You can't say that to me."

"Why not? It's the truth. If you're arrogant enough to believe that if you came face to face with someone truly dangerous that you could as you so aptly put it, 'take them,' then I'd be remiss in my duty not to point out the error of your way."

"Yeah, but you didn't need to be mean about it." There was a petulance to his voice that brought Harriet's exasperation to the surface. How was she supposed to get through to people like this?

The phone on her desk began to shrill and she jumped. Raising her hand in Chris' direction as he climbed from his chair, she picked the phone up.

"Dr Quinn," she said, keeping her voice light.

"Harriet, it's DI Haskell, I tried calling your mobile but it kept sending me to voicemail."

"Yeah, sorry about that. I've been in meetings all morning. What's up?"

"Is it all right if I call in and have a chat?"

"Sure. I was going to break up for lunch anyway."

"Great." The line went dead and she stared at the phone in surprise for a moment.

"Chris, I want you to work on your attitude. If you're serious about this."

He shrugged as he pulled open the door to her office and stepped out into the main reception. Harriet hurried after him and was surprised to see Drew waiting for her on the chairs outside.

"I didn't know you were actually here," she said.

He shrugged. "We've had a bit of a break-through..." he trailed off and glanced over at Martha's desk. "Can we speak in your office?"

"Do you mind if we walk and talk?" Harriet said, pulling her coat off the rack inside her door. "I've only got thirty minutes to eat before my lecture this afternoon."

Drew nodded and Harriet retrieved her bag and the pile of notes she'd locked in her desk drawer. When she returned a moment later, she smiled at him and gestured to the door.

"After you."

Drew shot her a lopsided smile as he moved out

into the hall. The place was heaving with students and it took a few minutes before they were free of the main throng.

"So, what was it you wanted to discuss with me?"

"The phone call this morning. It was the coroner."

Harriet felt her heartbeat stutter in her chest. It wouldn't take much to kill their fledgling investigation before it had even really gone anywhere.

"He's taken a second look at Sian and he's willing to back us and say that her death was the result of foul play. He found traces of a benzodiazepine in her body during the initial toxicology report."

"And this didn't raise a red flag why?" Harriet asked.

"Because Sian had been taking benzos according to her own doctor to treat some anxiety she'd begun experiencing."

Harriet's fingers tightened around the strap of her handbag but she kept silent.

"Because I asked him to, he ran a follow up on the samples and found traces of flunitrazepam in her body."

"Rohypnol…" Harriet felt her stomach clench. "This is excellent news," Harriet said and then caught the look of discomfort that flashed on Drew's face. "It is great news, right? I mean it's the proof you were looking for."

"It's good insofar as it confirms what I've been

saying all along. However, once the press get hold of this, they're going to have a field day with it."

Harriet grimaced. She'd had her fair share of run ins with the press herself and she definitely wasn't a fan. Their desire for larger readerships left them blind to common decency.

"Are you going to exhume the first two victims?"

Drew shook his head. "Dr Jackson thinks any traces of the drug in the body will be long gone by now. And he says he has enough tissue and hair samples to test for traces of the drug anyway."

Harriet felt the tension in her shoulders relax. The thought of having to approach the families for something like an exhumation order left her cold.

"So, what are you going to do?"

He shrugged. "Gregson wants to keep everything as quiet as he can but that's not going to last long. Especially now that we've had to release Sian's step-father pending further investigation. He's already threatened legal action against us for slandering his good name.

"I wanted to talk to you about that," she said. "After you fell asleep last night—"

"Listen, about that. I'm really sorry. I shouldn't have imposed on you like that."

Harriet shook her head. "It's fine, honestly I didn't mind. You saved me a raging headache by finishing off the wine." She smiled up at him and had the sudden urge to reach out and touch his arm.

Harriet pulled herself up short before she could, everything was far too complicated between them without further muddying the waters. Once he figured out the truth, he wouldn't want anything more to do with her, of that she was certain.

"Well, if you're sure?"

"I'm positive. But while you were asleep last night, I had a chance to review Sian's diary. Well a little of her diary anyway."

"Anything we can nail that bastard down with?"

"Not so far. Sian hints at things but part of me wonders if maybe her reticence to put her true feelings down in print is that she's worried he'll find the diary?"

Drew nodded. "It's possible. She definitely had it hidden well enough in her room, but I don't see why he couldn't have gone in there and dug it out."

"That's what I was thinking too. It might even explain why there was some pages torn out too. After a section in the diary that has been removed, Sian grows increasingly cryptic in her entries."

"We're never going to catch a break, are we?"

"Well, that's the thing. Sian does mention a group that both she and Aidan were members of online."

"What kind of a group?"

"From her diary, I have the impression that it's a message board of sorts for teens to share their thoughts. Probably akin to Reddit or one of those places. If we could get access to it, I reckon we would have all the proof we needed to find out what was truly going on in Sian's life."

Drew scrubbed his hand over his jaw and Harriet couldn't help but notice that he hadn't yet shaved. His morning had obviously been as active as her own.

"You don't think their killer could have used this board to track them down, do you?"

Harriet nodded. "It's possible. Some of the diary entries make mention of a Jumpsuit67 and a Lifeis-HELL333 and some private chats she was having with them."

"It's worth chasing down," Drew said as she paused outside one of the smaller campus coffee shops. "And now that Jackson is on board, I think it'll be easier to get Gregson to release some more manpower to throw at it."

"Do you want a coffee?" Harriet asked as she slipped her purse from her handbag.

"Nah, I owe you for this morning. Let me get this. What do you want?"

"Large black coffee," she said with a smile.

She watched him head inside before she grabbed a small table beneath the shelter of the coffee shops striped awning. Despite the sun beaming down on the pavement, there was a nip in the air that spoke of winter's claws insidiously sinking into autumn's hide.

Harriet pulled the notes from her bag and began

to read some more of the diary entries. Mostly it was typical teenage stuff, how unfair her parents were, how much she loved Aidan and more recently how concerned she was about upcoming exams.

The diary entries ended abruptly after the date of Aidan's death which Harriet found both intriguing and worrying. Surely after the death of her boyfriend, Sian would have more to say, not less.

Drew returned a couple of moments later and set a large coffee cup down in front of her.

"I don't know how you can drink that black," he said, eyeing her suspiciously. "You know, I read somewhere that people who prefer to drink black coffee are secretly psychopaths."

Harriet didn't bother to hide her smile as she popped the lid on her cup in an attempt to let it cool down faster.

"Whoever told you that clearly doesn't know how to appreciate a good coffee."

"So, you really think Sian might have been in contact with her killer beforehand?"

Harriet dropped back against the aluminium chair and folded her legs, giving herself time to think before answering.

"Her killer knew her somehow."

"Yeah, but couldn't he have just stalked her?"

She shrugged. "He could but it's not like Sian was someone famous. I know teens these days have a propensity for posting every little aspect of their lives online but there's still a limit to the amount of knowledge you could gather that way."

"What are you saying?"

"I'm saying that Sian's killer knew her and the others well enough to make their death's look like a suicide. Now either he lured them outside at nighttime, which seems far too risky for our guy—he's careful, methodical almost—or he was in their houses with them and subdued his victims until everyone was asleep." She sighed. "In both scenarios, our killer is going to need a working knowledge of the houses, and the victims in order to carry out his plan undetected."

"So he scouted them out ahead of time."

Harriet nodded. "Now, I would have expected him to take trophies from their houses. Little souvenirs to tide him over until it was time."

"Sian's mother said she used to wear a locket around her neck with a picture of Aidan inside all of the time."

Harriet nodded. "And we know it's gone. But I think our guy would take things before the murders even, maybe even move things about. But our teens aren't going to tell their parents about it because they already feel somewhat isolated from them. They maybe even assumed that the missing or moved items were done by their parents."

"Maybe that's why Sian ripped the pages out of her journal and taped it up under her locker."

"Unfortunately, the only three people who could have told us that are dead."

"I'll get the tech guys onto the computer stuff immediately. If our killer was in contact with them then we'll find him."

Harriet stared down into her coffee cup and watched the black liquid swirl around. She wanted to believe that DI Haskell was correct that it would be as easy as he suggested but she couldn't shake the nagging feeling that no matter how much she wanted it to be true, their guy wouldn't be so easily caught.

CHAPTER THIRTY-FOUR

ADELAIDE DAVIS WATCHED as her grand-daughter hugged her mother one last time and smiled. She looked so much like Tom that it was uncanny. But seeing her granddaughter was always one of those bitter-sweet moments and as much as Adelaide cherished them, they never ceased to cause her pain too.

"I love you," Bianca said, squeezing Tilly close.

"Mommy, you'll squeeze the air out of me," Tilly said, breathlessly her words tumbled over one another in her haste to get them out.

"I'd never do that," Bianca released her daughter with a grin.

Tilly turned to Adelaide, her expression utterly serious. "I can't bring Gruff with me today."

"Oh, why not?" Adelaide asked. After Tom's

death she'd had a momentary lapse in judgement and hadn't wanted anything to do with Tilly. It was stupid and selfish but a part of her had almost blamed the little girl for her loss. She had come along and her son had left, as though he'd made way for his daughter.

It was a stupid thought and Adelaide had regretted them ever since. Now though she would make it up to Tilly.

Even if she had to spend the rest of her life making it up to the granddaughter who painfully reminded her of everything she had lost she would do it.

"Because Gruff has gone missing," Tilly said, and her lower lip wobbled.

"Of dear, perhaps he had teddy bear business to attend to," Adelaide said making her voice as equally serious as her granddaughters.

"Like what?"

"Well, I don't know," she said honestly. "I've never been a teddy bear. But I'd imagine it's very important."

Tilly regarded her for a moment, her large brown eyes the mirror image of Tom's.

"I suppose so," she said, thoughtfully. She turned to her mother. "Do you think Gruff is doing teddy bear business?"

Bianca nodded. "I think Nana is right."

The confirmation seemed to be just what Tilly

needed and she smiled up at them both. "I hope he comes home soon though and tells me all about it."

"I'm sure he will, love," Bianca said. "Now you be good for Nana Adelaide and Grandpa."

Tilly grinned. "Can I see Freddie?"

Adelaide returned her granddaughter's smile with a warm one of her own. "Of course you can, Freddie is waiting for you to take him on his walk this evening. Now you go and hop in the back seat and I'll be there in a minute to strap you in."

"Why?"

"Because I just need a quick word with your mommy."

Tilly shrugged and skipped across the path to the station wagon parked on the drive.

Adelaide turned to her daughter in law and noted the dark circles beneath her eyes.

"Is there anything I should know?"

Bianca shook her head. "She doesn't have swimming or piano tomorrow so you can bring her straight back here after school."

Adelaide nodded abruptly. "I suppose you're still going on that date on Saturday?"

Bianca actually had the good grace to look uncomfortable and Adelaide couldn't stop a small thrill of satisfaction from spreading through her. It was perverse. Tom was barely cold in the ground and his wife was already looking to replace him. Simply thinking about it was enough to cause a lump to form in the back of her throat.

"I am." She looked awkwardly at the ground. "I know you don't approve," she said. "But I need to do this for both of us."

"Well, I don't know how you could," Adelaide felt her temper rising and tried to suppress it. Trevor had told her that starting an argument with Bianca was pointless and he was right. But that didn't take the sting out of it all.

"Look, I didn't tell you so you could berate me over it," Bianca said suddenly.

"Then why did you tell me?"

"Because I care about you and Trevor," she lowered her voice as she cast a glance toward the car where Tilly was sitting. "I love Tom and if you were honest about it you know it's true."

"Well, you have a funny way of showing it. How could you go out and dishonour him like that? He was always so faithful to you and then you—"

"He's not coming back," Bianca said, her voice hoarse. "I have to think of Tilly and my future; our future."

"Don't you dare!"

"It's the truth. He wouldn't want us to live like this. He'd want me to be happy and you know it. He loved me, loved Tilly and he'd want us to move forward—"

"Not like this he wouldn't." Adelaide harrumphed and tossed a glance back over her shoulder at Tilly. "I'll concede he'd want you to be happy but—"

"Would he want me to be alone?" There was such pain in Bianca's voice that it took Adelaide by surprise and she snapped her attention back to her daughter-in-law's face. What she saw there cut her to the core, but Adelaide's pain was such that she'd long since left behind the ability to fully empathise with anyone else. Part of her longed to reach out and comfort Bianca, to tell her that it was all right, that what she was doing was okay. But as she stood there on the front step, she just couldn't bring herself to do it.

"Loneliness is the price you pay for loving someone," Adelaide said, inwardly cringing at the harsh severity in her tone. "It's the risk you take, the risk we all take."

"That's not what Tom would—"

"How do you think I feel?" Adelaide cut in, leaning in toward Bianca so as not to raise her voice. "He was my only son. I can't run out and replace him."

"It's different," she said. "I can't imagine how painful it is for you but, he was my partner and now I have no-one. You still have Trevor."

Adelaide shook her head. "That's not how it works. When you love someone that doesn't just go

318

away and you can't just run out and get yourself another model."

Anger flared in Bianca's eyes, dampening the pain and sadness she'd seen there a moment before.

"I don't need your approval or your blessing," she said. "I loved Tom. I still love him now. And even if I go on a million dates, I won't stop loving him."

"And when you meet someone and fall in love with them? Will you get married again, have more children? What happens to Tom then, does he just become an inconvenient and painful memory you put away in the back of your closet?"

"Don't you dare," Bianca said. Her eyes widened a little and she shifted her gaze from Adelaide's face. Adelaide turned and caught sight of Tilly standing on the drive observing the two of them with her too serious expression and a bottom lip that jutted out.

"Are you fighting?"

Before Adelaide could form the words, Bianca was out the door and moving toward her daughter.

"Of course not, Tills. We were just having a conversation."

"It looked like you were mad at each other," she said. "I don't want you to be mad at each other."

Adelaide moved to her granddaughter's side and brushed her dark hair back from her wide tear-filled eyes.

"You don't need to worry, pumpkin. Sometimes grown-ups have very serious conversations and it can look like they're arguing but they're not. Not really anyway," Adelaide plastered a smile onto her face for the benefit of her granddaughter.

Whether the little girl actually believed her was debatable and it cut at Adelaide. How could another human being be so much like Tom? It seemed impossible and yet the proof was currently staring back at her with scepticism on her small face.

"Were you arguing about me?" Tilly asked. "Because if you were then—"

"We weren't arguing about you," Bianca said. "We all love you so much. You don't need to worry about any of that. Nana Adelaide is right, sometimes grown-up conversations can look like an argument but they're really not."

"Will you hug and say sorry to each other then?" Tilly asked, her voice heavy with sincerity. On any other child, Adelaide might have wondered whether that kind of emotion was legitimate or not but with Tilly she knew the truth.

Bianca looked up at Adelaide but whatever she saw reflected there caused Bianca to sigh and then shake her head.

"I don't think so, Tills. It's not always as simple as that."

"But why not?"

"Because we weren't arguing," Adelaide said quickly. "We better hurry up and head home or

Freddie is going to miss his walk and he was so looking forward to it."

Tilly glanced uncertainly back at her mother and panic wormed its way into Adelaide's heart. It would be all too easy for Bianca to cut her out of her granddaughter's life if she so chose to. And if Tilly kicked up too much of a fuss now, there was nothing stopping Bianca from balking.

"We can stop at McDonald's on the way home if you'd like, Tilly?" It was a low blow and Bianca stared back at her with disgust as Tilly's face lit up, the last of her uncertainty evaporating as though it had never been there at all.

"Yes!" Tilly said as she squirmed out of her mother's arms and raced toward the car. "Will I get a toy with my happy meal?"

"You betcha," Adelaide said. She smiled thinly at Bianca as she followed her granddaughter to the car. The sooner they left, the less chance there was for anything to go wrong.

Bianca hovered at her shoulder as she strapped Tilly into the back seat. Closing the back door, she turned to face Bianca.

"Don't you ever manipulate her like that again," Bianca said, through a grudging smile.

"It's not a manipulation if it's the truth," Adelaide said. "I'll take her to McDonalds and we'll walk Freddie this evening. And in the end, we'll have a lovely visit and when she comes home to you tomorrow, she won't remember any of this unpleasantness."

"But I will," Bianca said. "And she's not as gullible as you think. Tilly is sensitive. You think you've pulled the wool over her eyes this time, but it won't last. Sooner or later, she'll see you for what you really are."

Tilly chose that moment to tap on the window and Adelaide swung toward her granddaughter with a wide smile.

"I'm coming," she said, ignoring the tears that filled Bianca's eyes as she waved to her daughter.

"You have fun," Bianca said, her voice cracking over the words.

Adelaide slid in behind the wheel.

"Are we ready?" She cast a look back at Tilly who nodded enthusiastically.

Adelaide started the car and backed slowly off the drive, ignoring Bianca as she followed them. From the corner of her eye, she spotted a blue Rav-4 parked down the road. There was no on in the car, at least not that she could see and the biter part of her that resented Bianca's ability to just move on wondered if Bianca had invited her fancy piece over now that Tilly was out of the house. It would be just like her too. Always so selfish, thinking only of herself and her wants and needs. What about Tilly in all of this? How would she cope when Bianca brought her new boyfriend? Would she make her call him daddy?

Shaking her head, she turned and gave a sharp smile to Bianca.

"Say goodbye to mommy, Tilly!"

"I love you!" Tilly said, her childish voice high and singsongy as she waved to her mother.

Without looking back Adelaide accelerated. The sooner she got Tilly away from here the better. But as she drove down the street, Adelaide couldn't stop a small kernel of guilt from forming in the pit of her stomach.

Perhaps she was too harsh with Bianca? After all, if there was one thing her deeply held faith had taught her it was that forgiveness was all important. But nowhere in the bible did it mention how you should forgive your daughter-in-law when she moved on when your own grief still held you firmly in its grip.

CHAPTER THIRTY-FIVE

HE SAW HER PAIN, witnessed it from the shadows. It made his heart ache and he longed to go to her, to wrap his hands around her and tell her that soon it would be done.

Instead, he kept to the shadows and watched as she waved her daughter goodbye. Did she know of the path that had already been laid for her? Had someone whispered in her ear and told her what was expected of her? It seemed impossible and yet, there was no denying that it was all working out as though something greater, something divine had intervened to make it happen.

He had no aversion to ending the suffering of children but unlike the adults who cared for them they didn't yet understand the hardships that awaited them in the world.

But he'd been prepared to do whatever was

necessary if it had been expected of him. The fact that it wasn't allowed a little relief to creep in, just the smallest flicker.

She turned away, raising her hand at the car moving off the drive and he spotted his opportunity. It wouldn't come again.

Keeping to the shadows, he crept up the side of the house and let himself into through the back door.

CHAPTER THIRTY-SIX

BIANCA HEADED BACK into the empty house and stood with her back against the closed front door. This was the bit she hated the most. The utter and complete silence that always followed Tilly's absence. It would get worse too as the evening wore on. The hours stretched out before her, empty and unfulfilled.

Most evenings it was a cram to get everything done on time. The little rituals and routines that they'd discovered together after Tom's passing.

Homework, then dinner, a little television before it was bath-time and straight into bed for a story. Bianca tried to push away the emptiness that clawed at her and failed.

She slid down the door and buried her face in her arms as her tears started to flow a little more freely.

Who did Adelaide think she was, swanning in

with her judgements and her anger? She didn't know what it was like to be alone, to crave the company of another human being who didn't rely solely on you for their survival. At the end of the day she had Trevor to go home to every evening. Their grief over the loss of their son was something they could share together. And no matter how hard, Bianca had tried to get closer to them they had locked her out at every turn.

When Tom had died and they'd ignored Tilly for months, it had taken all of Bianca's strength not to shut the door on them. But when they'd come crawling back, begging to be allowed to spend time with their precious granddaughter she'd let them back into their lives again.

Scrubbing her hands over her face, Bianca climbed back onto her feet and headed for the kitchen. The last thing she needed to do was waste the little free time she had now on upset and tears over the guilt trip Adelaide had tried to lay on her. She had work to finish up and it wasn't going to get done with her in an emotional ball.

Flicking on the kettle, she made herself a coffee before she headed upstairs to the make-shift office she'd turned the box-room into. She sat down in front of the lap top and stared at the blank screen before her fingers began to move over the keyboard.

The sooner she got the article done, the sooner she could relax for the rest of the evening.

But no matter how much she tried to concentrate on the words on the screen, her mind kept replaying the argument with Adelaide.

Finally frustrated, she pushed away from the desk and headed for Tilly's room.

She pushed open the door and stared at the bed. The little brown bear stared back at her, seemingly as bemused as she was by his sudden reappearance.

"Where have you been?" she said, crossing the carpet to scoop the bear up off the bed. Tilly was going to be thrilled when she realised Gruff was back.

Fear slithered down Bianca's spine. Just how had he gotten here? She'd made the bed and searched the room from top to bottom while Tilly was at school but there had been no sign of the worn brown bear she now held in her hands. He hadn't been on the bed, he hadn't been underneath it and there was no way that Tilly had found him and left him here on the bed...

Or was there?

Was this her daughter's way of leaving behind her protector?

As she stood at the bottom of the bed, the teddy bear clutched in her hands, Bianca's phone dinged an incoming message. Her hand automatically moved to her pocket and she slipped the phone out as a hand clamped over her mouth.

Shock momentarily rooted her to the spot, fear causing her skin to break out in a clammy sweat.

Opening her mouth, she inhaled a noxious substance that burned her lips and throat. She tried to scream but the gloved hand holding the cloth over her nose and mouth pressed harder. Desperate for air, she pushed backwards but her attacker was a solid mass behind her that refused to move, and the knowledge sent her heartbeat skyrocketing with panic.

The phone slipped from her fingers and bounced beneath the edge of the bed as her legs started to buckle.

What was wrong with her? She needed to fight.

She willed her body to obey but whatever she was breathing spread through her panicked body—carried on a wave of adrenaline and her wildly beating heart—like a wildfire that left nothing in its wake untouched.

Bianca moaned and slithered toward the floor, her eyes rolled in her head as she fought to stay conscious. Her attacker moved with her, cradling her against his broad chest as her head lolled back onto his shoulder and took his hand away from her face.

"Why?" The word was almost incoherent and in the foggy recess of her mind Bianca wondered if she'd even asked the question aloud. The man holding her nodded as though he could still understand her. Or maybe it was just that for him the question wasn't unexpected.

"Because you're in pain, sweetheart, and I can make it go away."

Darkness gathered at the edges of her vision as she stared up at the man cradling her on the floor of her daughter's bedroom. There was a serenity to his expression as he brushed her hair back from her face and instinct told Bianca that whatever he had planned for her wasn't going to be pleasant.

The darkness she'd fought so hard against at last swallowed her and Bianca's last thought was for her daughter.

Who would look after her? Who would protect her now?

CHAPTER THIRTY-SEVEN

EVEN WITH HER EYES CLOSED, he could feel her acceptance, her acquiescence, and it humbled him. The others had been terrified and it caused him to wonder if what he was doing was the right thing after all. But as he sat on the beige carpet and smoothed her dark hair from her face, the serenity of her expression told him everything he needed to know.

He really was helping.

Carefully, he folded the cloth with his home-made chloroform back up and slipped it into the plastic sandwich bag he'd brought it here in. Re-sealing the top of the bag, he pushed it into the bottom of his rucksack and took his tools out. She wouldn't stay unconscious for very long and a thrill raced through him as he considered the ramifications of what he was about to do.

Moving out into the hall, he tossed the rope and noose over the staircase and watched as it pooled on the hall floor below. The others had the chance to see the world before they stepped off the wheel. Bianca would not get that luxury and for that he was sorry.

Hurrying back into the bedroom, he picked her up carefully and carried her down the stairs. Like Sian she was slight and for that he was grateful. Despite still being alive, her body was nothing more than a dead weight and there was nothing easy about carrying her.

The sedative he'd used on the others had made things easier, making them more malleable. If he'd been forced to carry either Aidan or Jack outside his plan would have fallen apart at the first hurdle.

As he reached the bottom step, Bianca stirred in his arms. A low murmured moan that told him his time was running out. He laid her out on the cold floor and secured the noose around her throat. The movement seemed to draw her further from her unconscious state and panic caused a cold sweat to break out on his skin.

"Tilly..."

As he secured the rope around his waist and arms he moved backwards, testing the strength of the banister above. Would it be that way for him too? Would his final thoughts be for his child when his time came? He hoped it would. Satisfied the staircase would hold he waited, holding his breath in his lungs until he was sure they would both burst.

He watched as Bianca's eyes fluttered open, her confusion a kindness for what was about to happen next. She caught sight of him and started, her mouth opening into an 'o' of horror. He moved swiftly and the rope tightened cutting off her air supply before she could make even a squeak of sound.

"Don't fight it," he said but even as the words left his mouth, he knew they were futile.

CHAPTER THIRTY-EIGHT

SWEAT CAUSED the gloves he wore to stick to his fingers. This was the part he hated the most. Being forced to wear gloves created a distance between him and the ones he freed. If he could just reach out and touch them...

He curled his fingers into a fist and tucked himself up on the bottom step of the stairs. She'd long since ceased to struggle and the life had drained from her in the blink of an eye. The others had been almost peaceful, but she had not.

She had fought against the inevitable. Tears clouded his vision and he buried his face in the crook of his arm and let his sobs overtake him. Had it been a mistake? Was he wrong?

Was this not how it was supposed to be?

The evening light faded and the shadows extended their reach across the floor. He sat and watched over her. It was easier here. With the others, he'd been forced to abandon them once the deed was done. The risk of getting caught was too high. But here, in the safety of her house, it was easier.

The air chilled and the scent of death permeated the space. The kind of scent that once you had it in your nose you never could shake free of it.

Closing his eyes, he let his exhaustion wash over him and sweep him under.

The shrill of the telephone dragged him from the pleasant dream he'd been having. His heartbeat exploded in his chest as he realised where he was. Glancing down at his watch, he sucked a sharp breath in through his teeth.

Stupid. So stupid.

Light pooled on the floor and Bianca's body cast an odd shadow across the hall as he pushed upright. His body was cramped, the muscles of his legs protested as he crossed the floor and paused to stare up at her.

She was an angel now, just like the others. Free of her pain and suffering. It was done.

He turned as the answer machine kicked in and Bianca's voice flooded the house. It was eerie and the hairs on the back of his neck stood to attention as he listened to her speak.

Bianca's voice ended and the abrupt beep that followed tugged him from his silent contemplation.

"Bianca, it's me. That's twice now I've tried you.

Is everything ok?" Her voice was sorrow personified and his heart constricted in his chest. Gasping for breath, his knees buckled and he dropped to the floor.

He knew that voice. He'd heard her on the answering machine the few times he'd visited Bianca's house before yesterday. They were friends but who she was, he had no clue. All he knew for certain was that he wanted to know who she was. It was important. He could feel it in his bones.

There was no denying the pain in her voice. A deep-seated sorrow that spoke to his own.

The desire to pick the phone up, to speak to her rooted him to the spot. With her it would be all too easy to forget what was at stake here.

He closed his eyes and waited for the telltale click of the call ending. When it came, he climbed back onto his unsteady feet and glanced back at Bianca.

"Who is she?"

Bianca was silent, her bulging bloodshot eyes stared straight ahead.

Moving through the house, he worked quickly, searching through Bianca's handbag until he found what he was looking for. He tugged her address book free and scanned the contents. She didn't have many friends and for that at least he was grateful, it would make his job much easier.

He jotted down the telephone number that

blinked on the answering machine and slipped the pink book into his jacket before he checked on Bianca one last time.

"Sleep well," he said, and his voice echoed in the silence of the hall.

CHAPTER THIRTY-NINE

HARRIET CARRIED her mug downstairs and set it on the kitchen counter. Grabbing her phone, she dialled Bianca's number and listened to the familiar sound of the call as it tried to connect. The answer phone kicked in and Harriet sighed.

"Bianca, it's me. That's twice now I've tried you. Is everything ok?" She ended the call and immediately regretted leaving the message at all. It wasn't unusual for Bianca to take her time to get back to her but there was also usually a pretty good reason for her tardiness. Had she upset her more than she'd let on the other night? Insulted her because of her choice of boyfriend perhaps?

It wouldn't have been the first time. Bianca was a little on the sensitive side of things, particularly since Tom had died. It had affected her more than she was willing to admit to and the only reason Harriet knew was because she'd known her for so many years.

She could always go up a day early. Surprise both her and Tilly...

It was a nice thought but Harriet squashed it as soon as it had occurred to her. She'd already taken more time than she should have off from the college. Any more time away from her real job and Baig would have a legitimate reason to be pissed at her. As it was, she was already skating on thin ice.

Sighing, Harriet grabbed her bag and coat before she gathered the notes she'd made on the case so far. After Drew had fallen asleep, she'd taken the opportunity to review a little of Sian's diary and while there wasn't the smoking gun they'd been after regarding her stepfather, Sian had certainly alluded to some kind of inappropriate behaviour. Of course, she'd also mentioned an online group they'd all been a part of where they'd shared their traumas and upsets. If she could just get a look at the laptop then perhaps it would give her the information she needed.

Harriet fished her car keys from her purse and headed for the door. They would just have to make do with her being present in the office, albeit a little more distracted than usual.

CHAPTER FORTY

BLEARY EYED, Adelaide turned her car onto Tilly's street.

"Mommy said we're going to make chocolate chip cookies and watch movies tonight," Tilly said excitedly from the backseat.

"That'll be nice, pumpkin," she said as she indicated and drove up onto Tilly's driveway. She parked her car next to Bianca's and killed the engine before she turned to look back at Tilly who bounced in her car seat.

"Can I go in?" She had already unbuckled her seatbelt and Adelaide tutted her disapproval.

"What have I said about taking your belt off before I say it's safe?"

Tilly had the good grace too look chastened and Adelaide found it almost impossible to stay angry at her young granddaughter.

"Fine, you go and knock while I get your bags."

Tilly grinned from ear to ear and waited patiently for Adelaide to get out and open her door before she bounded up toward the front door.

Adelaide pulled open the boot, her body on autopilot as she tugged the bags out.

Tilly hadn't slept a wink the night before from worrying and fretting about Gruff and Adelaide had spent her time trying to reassure her that Gruff would come home. She was beyond exhausted as she pulled the small school bag and overnight bag from the car and slammed the boot shut.

Turning toward the door, she frowned. Tilly was stood on the front step, her small face bunched up in consternation.

"Aren't you going to knock?" Adelaide asked as she started up the path. It took her a moment to realise that Tilly was peering in through the letterbox.

"I see you!" Tilly said, the excitement in her voice unmistakable. "I see you, Mommy!"

AS ADELAIDE KNOCKED BRISKLY on the front door, Tilly let the letterbox snap shut with a decisive thud.

"She's there, Nana, I saw her," Tilly said, the confusion on the little girl's face apparent. "Why won't she answer?"

"You've probably just seen a reflection," Adelaide dismissed Tilly's questions with a wave of her hand. "She's probably nipped out for something and lost track of time." She didn't add what she really thought Bianca was up to, there was no point in upsetting the child further, not when Bianca could do that all on her own. No, as far as Adelaide was concerned it was better that Tilly see her as the solid reliable nana she was.

Sliding her phone out of her handbag, Adelaide stood back from the door and dialled Bianca's number. It rang and rang but there was no answer.

Tilly has returned to her previous position at the door, her little face jammed against the letter box.

"Nana, I see her. She's flying!"

"About time," Adelaide muttered beneath her breath as she ended the call.

"Mommy, I'm home!"

Frowning, Adelaide turned her attention to her granddaughter. "What do you mean you can see her?"

"She's right there." As she spoke, Tilly pushed one small finger in through the letterbox. "I don't think she can hear me because she's flying."

Frustrated, Adelaide, set the bags down on the doorstep and crouched next to Tilly; ignoring the ominous creak her knees gave as she bent down. Arthritis the doctor had said; just another sign that the clock was ticking ever forward and not backward as she'd wished.

"Where is she?" Adelaide pressed her face next to Tilly's the scent of the little girl's strawberry scented shampoo wafting up to tickle her nose as she squinted through the letterbox.

From her vantage point, there was a shoe lying discarded on the floor directly inside the door, a battered tennis shoe that had seen better days. Typical Bianca, she never was particularly neat and tidy when Tom had been alive either. Clearly old habits died hard.

"I don't see—" Adelaide cut off abruptly as two legs came into view. The shoe remaining on Bianca's left foot was a match for the one on the floor but there was something so terribly odd about the situation, almost as though her feet weren't actually on the ground at all. Adelaide's brain refused to put the pieces of the scene before her into focus.

It wasn't— It couldn't be. What she was seeing wasn't real.

Her gaze travelled up over Bianca's body, the small view through the letterbox cut her off at the waist but not before Adelaide caught a glimpse of her unnaturally coloured fist by her side.

"Oh good, God!" Adelaide fell backwards from the door as her mind finally put all the pieces together.

"Mommy!" Tilly called.

Bile, acidic and bitter poured up Adelaide's throat as she grabbed Tilly by the shoulder and tugged her away from the door.

"No," she said, her voice hoarse with emotion. Tears blurred her vision as she wrapped her arms around her bewildered granddaughter and began to weep.

CHAPTER FORTY-ONE

WITH HER LAST lecture for the day finished, Harriet killed her engine and stared at the pile of paperwork that filled the passenger seat of her car. She was falling behind, and as much as she wanted to feel bad about it, she couldn't quite bring herself to feel the emotion. The case was too strong a lure and over and over, she found her mind straying back to it.

Drew had suggested she call by the office once she was done for the day with the promise of reviewing some of Sian's correspondence the IT department had managed to retrieve.

She grabbed her bag and headed inside.

"DI Haskell is expecting me," she said, to the desk sergeant.

He nodded and buzzed her through. Harriet met Drew in the corridor beyond.

"I came as soon as I could," she said.

Drew grinned at her and directed her into the conference room they'd sat in the evening before. "And not a moment too soon," he said. "We've got so much documentation to go through here we're practically drowning in paperwork."

She set her handbag down at the table and slipped her jacket off. "Where do you want me to start?"

Maz pushed a stack of folders across the wide table toward her. "I can't make head nor tails of this here," he said. "Let's see if your luck is better."

"What is it?" She eyed the stack curiously and dropped into the chair Drew had pointed to.

"All of Sian's emails, text messages, and online correspondence with any kind of group she was a member of."

Harriet felt her stomach drop. "All of this?"

Maz shook his head and relief flooded through her.

"That's only the first pile," he said. "They're still pulling things off her hard-drive."

"How are we supposed to wade through all of this?" She pulled the first folder down and stared at the conversation thread.

"Well, that's where we were hoping you would help us narrow it down," Drew said.

"Short of knowing who her real-life friends are in all this narrowing it down isn't going to be easy."

Drew nodded. "I was afraid you would say something like that."

"I've arranged a meeting with the school principal tomorrow and I'm hoping they'll be able to assist us in narrowing the pool of information further."

"That's smart thinking," she said. "Have they found any chat scripts between a Jumpsuit67 and Sian, or a LifeisHELL333 yet?"

Drew inclined his head toward a much smaller pile of folders. "Already pulled them out for you."

"Any luck on working out who is behind the monikers?"

Drew shook his head. "They're working on tracing the IP addresses back to their sources but unless we find something in all of this—" He gestured to the piles of paperwork surrounding them— "Then I think we're barking up the wrong tree."

Harriet grinned at him. "Well, if you don't mind, I think I'll make a start with them."

"Well, who's going to go through all of this then?" Maz asked indicating the stacks of paper.

"I wouldn't trust anyone else with the job," Drew said, as he pushed the stack back toward the centre of the table. It was the most jovial and animated Harriet had seen him since he'd called to her office and she was almost certain she could see a glimpse of the man he had been before his life had fallen to pieces.

She settled back into her chair and opened the

folder. It was then that it hit her, there really was nowhere else she would have preferred to be at that moment. At least if she could never bring herself to work clinically again, doing this kind of work meant she could still help, albeit in a different capacity.

CHAPTER FORTY-TWO

DREW PUSHED up from the desk and headed out into the main office. He made it as far as the coffee station when the phone in his pocket buzzed.

With an empty coffee cup in one hand, he tugged the phone free and answered without bothering to check the number.

"My office, now," Gregson said, his voice cool.

Drew knew that tone of voice too well but he couldn't think of a good reason why his boss would be pissed off at him. Setting the cup down, he headed to the Monk's office and rapped on the door.

"Come in!"

Drew didn't need to be told twice and pushed open the door and stepped inside. The Monk sat behind his desk and the look on his face said it all. Drew's heart sank.

"There's another one isn't there?"

Gregson sighed and slipped his glasses off before he scrubbed a meaty knuckle into his left eye.

"We got the call about five minutes ago," he said. "Another suicide."

Drew's hands tightened into fists. "Sir, with all due respect I think we need to stop referring to these as suicides."

Gregson nodded. "They're saying this one doesn't much look like a suicide anyway. There's signs of a struggle upstairs in the kid's bedroom and the setup is different."

"Wait, the victim, how old are they?"

"It's a woman, early thirties. Her mother in law called it in. Said she was bringing her granddaughter home after she spent the night with them and found her hanging in the hall."

"Shit," Drew said. "Did the kid see anything?"

Gregson shrugged. "I don't know. Uniforms are there now and forensics are already on the scene. I need you to get down there and contain the situation."

"Sir, permission to bring DS Arya with me. And Dr Quinn."

Gregson opened his mouth but Drew cut him off before he could get the words out.

"Sir, I think she could be a real asset in all of this. Especially when it comes to interviewing the victim's family."

Gregson sighed. 'Fine. Just don't let her

anywhere near the press. I don't want to wake up tomorrow morning to an even bigger shit-show than we've already got."

"I'll keep her clear of it," he said before he headed for the door.

Drew made it back to the conference room in record time and grabbed his coat.

"We've got to go," he said.

"Has there been another murder?" Harriet was already on her feet before he'd even finished speaking.

"Yeah. This time it's an adult."

"That's an unusual escalation," she said. "I would have expected his victims to get younger but not older."

Drew pulled his car keys from his pocket. "I'm beginning to think that nothing about our guy is straight forward. Maz, let's move."

CHAPTER FORTY-THREE

HARRIET SAT in the back of Drew's BMW and stared out of the window. She'd offered to follow him but he'd seemed strangely insistent that she ride with them. Not that she particularly minded. Sitting back here and staring out as the countryside flashed by gave her the chance to formulate her thoughts a little more clearly.

The killer's escalation both in time and his choice of victim suggested he was beginning to devolve. Had this newest victim been chosen because the opportunity had presented itself and it was just too good to pass up? Or had he taken his time and stalked her like the others?

As the surroundings grew more familiar, Harriet sat up a little straighter.

"Where did you say this new victim was from?"

Maz pulled a notebook from inside his jacket.

"The town of Kirkbridge," he said. "It's a few miles north of Tollby."

Harriet dug her fingers into the car seat in front of her as her heartbeat began to pick up speed. "Do you have the name of the victim?"

"Why?" Drew asked, breaking his silence in the front of the car.

"Because a friend of mine lives in Kirkbridge," she said.

Drew cast a glance back over his shoulder. "And?"

"And she's a single mother, Drew."

"The victim's name is a Bianca Sommerland," Maz said.

Harriet's heart flip-flopped in her chest. It couldn't be true. They'd made some sort of mistake.

"Harriet?" Drew said. She caught his eye in the rear-view mirror and the concern she saw etched on his face sent an icy wave of emotion barrelling though her chest.

"You're wrong," she said. "I spoke to her the other day. I'm supposed to go and see her tomorrow..."

"Shit!" Drew swore violently and swung the car off the road and into a lay-by.

She was numb, her body cold as she fought to try and wrap her brain around what she was being told.

Drew tugged open her car door and she stared up

at him in surprise before she glanced back at the driver's seat.

"Harriet, are you all right?"

She shook her head but her voice failed her. The words—like her tears—refused to form.

"Guv, what am I supposed to do?" Maz asked.

"Call ahead and tell them we're running late."

Their voices were very far away and Harriet blinked up at Drew. The feeling of numbness and disassociation was the same feeling she'd experienced when she was ten. The doctors had explained to her that it was shock, her bodies way of trying to process the loss of her brother and her mother's attempt on her life.

The rational part of her brain recognised it for what it was. Not that it could do anything to change the situation.

"Harriet, can you hear me?"

It took her a moment to figure out that Drew was still talking to her. Her feet were on the gravel of the lay-by the cold evening air swirled around her legs but she barely felt it. She was leaning forward, her head pressed to her knees and she glanced up at the man crouched next to her.

"Are you all right?"

"This can't be happening," she said, finally managing to get the words out past her frozen lips.

"I'm so sorry," Drew said, brushing his hand against her arm.

Harriet jerked, her stomach turning violently.

"I'm going to be sick," she said decisively. She leapt to her feet and raced toward the bushes that lined the side of the road.

The gravel was rough beneath her knees as she hit the ground and vomited it into the grass verge.

This was wrong. It was all wrong. It wasn't supposed to happen like this, not like this. Bianca was at home right now, helping Tilly with her homework.

As the thought of the six-year-old popped into her head, Harriet felt the first prickle of tears behind her eyes. She had already lost so much and now this...

It wasn't fair.

"I've called for a car to come and pick you up," Drew said from directly behind her.

"No," she said, her voice little more than a pathetic squeak.

"I'm so sorry, Harriet. If I'd known she was your friend I would never have—"

"No," she said again, this time a little more forcefully. The taste of bile was still potent in her mouth and her stomach threatened to rebel again, but she ignored it as she scrubbed her hand over her lips. She pushed up onto her feet, the pain in her foot no longer even registered. It was amazing what a little bit of shock could do for an injury.

"I want to come with you," she said.

Drew shook his head and stared at her sadly. "I'm afraid that's not possible. This is a murder investigation, Harriet, your close personal relationship with the victim demands I send you home."

"I'm not going," she said. "If you don't take me with you then I'll find my own way there."

Drew groaned in frustration and shoved his hand back through his hair, causing it to stand on end.

"You know I can't let you," he said through gritted teeth. "I know this is hard for you but you need to let me do my job."

Harriet shook her head. "I know I should, but I can't. Just let me come with you. I won't get in the way, I promise. But there's Tilly to think of and—"

"Who's Tilly?"

"Bianca's daughter," Harriet said, her voice rough. "She's going to need someone on her side and I'd at least like to know that she's all right."

Drew stared off into the distance for what felt like an age before he nodded abruptly. "Fine. But when we get there you stay out of the way, do you understand?"

Harriet nodded and allowed herself to be directed back to the car.

"Guv, I'm not sure this is a good idea," Maz said, his voice heavy with scepticism. Not that Harriet blamed him; he had to think of the investigation and as much as she hated to admit it, she had now become a liability to the entire operation. The simple fact that Drew was allowing her to go with them at all was a huge no-no as far as protocol dictated.

"Neither am I," Drew said. "But what am I supposed to do? Leave her here on the side of the road?"

As she climbed into the back of the car, she felt Maz's gaze boring into her back. Harriet could already imagine what he was thinking. What kind of hold did she have over his boss that allowed her to sway his decision-making process this way? But it wasn't like that at all. Drew was a good man; the more time she spent with him, the more she had come to realise it. He deserved better and more than that, he deserved the truth from her.

But now was not the time for it. She needed him to have his head in the game. Bianca was dead and the man responsible for it was still out there, probably looking for his next victim.

Maz grumbled beneath his breath as he slid reluctantly back into the passenger seat. Drew got back in behind the wheel and started the engine. As he pulled back out onto the road and into the steady flow of traffic, he glanced surreptitiously at her in the rear-view mirror. Harriet studiously avoided his gaze, keeping her eyes on the scenery as it passed outside the glass.

She wanted to cry, scream, yell, anything but the terrible aching empty void that had opened up inside her chest. Bianca had been the closest thing to family she'd had in a very long time and now she was gone.

Clenching her hands into fists, Harriet closed her eyes as the red and blue lights from the other police cars lit up the sky.

CHAPTER FORTY-FOUR

DREW PARKED NEXT to two other police cars. Before he got out, he turned to Harriet, who sat with her eyes closed in the back of the vehicle. She wasn't asleep, that much he knew, but her skin was pale, almost translucent, in the strange red and blue glow that lit the evening sky.

"You remember what I said?" He dug his fingers into the leather steering wheel. "About keeping out of the way?"

Her gaze was even more piercing than usual, the unshed tears making the blue of her eyes stand out.

"I remember," she said coldly. "You don't need to worry about me, Detective Inspector. I won't embarrass you."

"That's not what I meant," he growled, frustration gnawing at his insides. "But if anyone finds out about this, it'll be more than my job's worth."

Harriet ducked her head and stared down at her hands folded neatly on her lap. "I'll stay out of your way."

Drew turned to Maz. "You see that she does," he said. He forced the car door open and stepped out as Maz's protests followed him.

"Guv, come on, you can't put me on babysitting duty and—"

Drew turned on him, frustration and rage colliding inside him to create an emotion he hadn't felt since Freya had driven them into the lake.

"Just do as I ask, Maz. Please."

The other man huffed his displeasure but nodded. "Fine."

Sometimes it was like working with a petulant teenager and not another adult officer of the law.

Drew approached the house cautiously, the red brick building squatted against the backdrop of other houses just like it. Uniform rows that all looked identical. What had made his killer look at this house in particular and decide the people within needed to be touched by his own personal brand of insanity? Because as Drew saw it, only a total nutter would do the things this guy was doing.

He caught sight of Officer Crandell up by the front door, the same uniform officer he'd worked with on Sian's case. He slipped beneath the cordon tape.

"Keep these people back," he said to the nearest officer who was stood next to the crime scene tape.

The young man jumped as though Drew had appeared out of thin air and he knew the officer's attention was divided.

"What's your name?" Drew said, his voice crisp.

"Officer Williams, Sir," the officer snapped to attention as though returning from a trance and met Drew's gaze head on.

"How about keeping your eyes on the people you're supposed to be keeping out of the crime scene?"

"Shit, sorry, sir," he said as he turned away from the house and back out toward the sizeable crowd of onlookers who had gathered.

"We need names, addresses and contact details for everyone here," he said. As though summoned, Officer Crandell appeared at his elbow.

"Sir, is there something I can do?"

Drew moved toward the house, inextricably drawn forward. He paused in the doorway and swallowed around the lump in his throat as he peered in at the pitiful sight spread out in the hall.

At least the bushes and shrubs would keep the gossip mongers at bay and prevent them from getting a bird's eye view of the horror that had unfolded in this small unassuming house at the end of the cul-de-sac.

"Sir?"

Drew nodded. "Start door to door enquiries, I want to know if anyone saw anything around here. I find it hard to believe that in a built-up area like this that our guy wasn't spotted lurking around. If anyone saw a fly so much as take a shit near here, I want to know about it."

If she was surprised by the tone of his voice or the language he used, she didn't show it. Instead she inclined her head. "I'll get some of the uniforms together."

"He won't have been seen," Harriet's voice was hoarse, and Drew turned to face her.

She stood just a few feet away, her sight pinned on the scene that lay directly behind him. Her eyes, while still a little too wide from shock, held a steely resolve. She tore her gaze away and met his. "You said it yourself, Drew. He's a ghost. They won't have seen or heard anything. Bianca's a fighter—" She swallowed hard. "Was a fighter. She was a fighter but that won't have deterred him. He'll have come with a plan to subdue her quickly, make her compliant just as he did with the others."

"What did I say to you," he said, cutting her off. "DS Arya, make sure—" He cut off. "Where's Maz?"

"You need me on this," she said, ignoring his question. "You can't just shut me out. I can help you find him."

Drew shook his head. "You don't know what you're asking," he said. "He crossed the line and made sure you couldn't help on this. You have to understand that."

"She was family. You can't just expect me to sit idly by while he runs rings around you all."

Her words stung but Drew had to admit she was at least partially right. Without her help there wouldn't be a case to speak of. This crime would have been easily dismissed as too different in comparison to a cluster of teenage suicides.

"Harriet, if you don't leave now. I'm going to have you removed."

She glared up at him. "You're going to let him get away with this, for what?"

"Because I have to follow the law. Without that, we've got nothing at all."

Maz reappeared. "Sir, that was the IT guys. They got a hit on the IP addresses from the chat logs."

"And?"

"And it's a dead end. Jumpsuit67 belonged to a boy from Tollby who died a year ago."

"And the other one?"

"Aidan Wilson, sir."

"Shit..."

"You see, you need my help," Harriet interjected. "Please, let me be useful."

"Maz, have one of the uniformed officers take Dr. Quinn home."

Drew ignored the flash of annoyance that crossed over the DS' face before he turned to Harriet.

"Come on," Maz said, his tone patronising as he laid a hand on her arm.

Harriet shook him off, but she had eyes only for Drew.

"You're making a mistake," she said. "I can be useful."

"And under normal circumstances, I would agree," he said. "But come on, Harriet. If you were in my position, what would you say about someone who had just suffered the kind of shock you have?"

Her gaze shifted away. "But this is different."

"Is it?"

She covered her face with her hands. "Yes, this is different because I'm—"

"You're what? Because you're a psychologist? I would have thought that would have made you understand the difficulty I'm presented with even more."

"No," she said. "Because I can get inside this guy's head."

Drew shook his head. "Nobody can do that," he said. "And even if they could, after what you've seen here, why would you want to?"

"It's because of what's happened here that I want to."

Her voice was becoming increasingly desperate as Drew refused to budge over her demands.

"Harriet, go home. I'll call you tomorrow, I promise."

"I just—"

"GO HOME," he said. Then he sighed, regretting the firmness of his tone, and said, "I'll call you if I have anything."

She nodded and Drew felt a weight lift off his shoulders. "You promise you'll call?"

"I'll call."

Only then did she allow Maz to take her arm and direct her away from the house. Drew watched them leave and as she was helped into the waiting squad car, he felt the tension he'd felt in the centre of his chest slowly loosen.

Christ, what a mess.

DREW SCRUBBED his hand back through his hair as he watched Harriet leave. He let go a sigh of relief. Just having her here was a conflict of interest and the Monk would have his ass thrown off the case faster than he could blink if he found out.

"Guv, what do you want me—"

"DI Haskell?" One of the forensics team appeared in the doorway. The woman pulled her mask down, revealing a sharp aquiline nose and full lips. "We found a phone underneath the bed." She held a plastic bag out toward him. "We've dusted it for prints and other residues but it's been ringing."

Drew slipped on a pair of gloves and took the bag from her hands before lifting it carefully free of the protective plastic. He pressed the home key and the phone lit up revealing a long list of missed calls.

"Maz, I want you to get a trace on this number. Find out who this Ryder is," he said. Drew clicked into the message box and was surprised to find the phone wasn't locked. "Looks like Bianca was having quite a bit of back and forth conversation with the guy. I want to know who is and whether he's in any way connected to all of this."

Maz nodded and jotted the number down before he started away leaving Drew behind on the doorstep.

He glanced back into the hall and shuddered. Whoever had done this was beyond cruel and if it killed him, he would hunt them down and bring them to justice before they laid a finger on another person.

CHAPTER FORTY-FIVE

HE SET the notebook down on the desk next to the computer and typed the name *Dr Harriet Quinn* into the laptop. The search engine took only a moment to return thousands of entries.

He clicked on the top one and found himself staring at a serious-faced young woman. It was there in her eyes; the sorrow he'd seen in the others. He'd heard it in her voice on the answering machine. He clicked through the pages and found a newspaper article dated several years ago.

He'd been right to think she was in pain. It was there in black and white. He read on and as he did, his heart rate picked up speed. She was next. And the end would come only too soon.

CHAPTER FORTY-SIX

HARRIET CURLED UP DEEPER beneath the covers, tugging the heavy duvet over her head in an attempt to escape the daylight streaming in through the open curtains. The night had passed like all things eventually do, but sleep had been as elusive to her as peace of mind often was to the people she treated.

The phone rang downstairs but she ignored it. There was a part of her that demanded she get out of the bed, that by staying here she was allowing the monster who'd stolen Bianca's life from her to win. But she couldn't bring herself to do it.

What would be the point anyway? Drew was right; she was tainted now by her association with one of the victims and no amount of knowledge of predators, or the crimes they committed, would allow her to help the investigation.

She was utterly and completely useless.

She recognised the self-defeating spiral for what it was; self-pity.

The answer machine kicked in and Harriet tugged the pillow over her head to block out the noise.

The hours dragged by and as the morning turned into the afternoon Harriet finally pulled herself from the bed. Drew might not want her help but that didn't mean she couldn't continue to work. It was all she had left; the only thing she was any good at.

Dragging herself downstairs, she settled onto the couch with a black coffee and pulled open the files she'd brought from the office.

Jumpsuit67: I'm goin 2 fail my exams. I know it already and my dad is goin 2 kill me.

Pixiedust05: You don't know for sure. I thought I was failing last year and it was fine. At least ur dad cares. Mine only wants 1 thing.

LifeisHELL333: Pixie's right. U'll be fine.

Jumpsuit67: You don't know what it's like. The pressure I'm under. My dad thinks I'll be just like him. That I'm smart like he is.

Pixiedust05: You'll get through this.

Harriet scanned the pages of transcripts. The chat logs all seemed to follow a similar pattern, day to day the teens seemed to share their woes. Skipping ahead, one particular line jumped out at her.

Pixiedust05: He raped me last night.

Harriet's heart stalled in her chest and she read the line over and over.

LifeisHELL333: I'll kill him. I'm goin 2 fukin' kill him!!!

Pixiedust05: I don't know what to do.

LifeisHELL333: Go 2 police. I'll come wit u. I love u.

Pixiedust05: I can't go police. My mom luvs him and it wuld kill her if she knew the truth.

Harriet stared at the date on the transcript and her mouth went dry. The 19th of September. Two weeks before Aidan was murdered.

Her gaze moved down the page and another entry caught her attention.

Jumpsuit67: LifeisHELL333 knows there's nothin goin on between us. I wuldn't lie to him like that. I no u 2 are 2gether.

As she sat there on the edge of the couch, something niggled in the back of her mind. But the events of the evening before were clouded by an unpleasant fog that refused to lift.

It was her brain's way of trying to protect her from the trauma of seeing her friend like that.

"Think, Harriet, think!" She buried her face in her hands and pushed up from her place on the couch to pace around the room. They'd been right outside Bianca's house when Maz had dropped the bombshell of the transcripts being nothing more than a dead end.

Jumpsuit67, whoever he was, couldn't have been sending those messages to Sian, not when he'd been dead for a year already. Harriet flipped back through the pages gripped in her hand. His name was all over the transcripts, entire conversations that had occurred long after he was allegedly deceased. It seemed unlikely that Maz, and by extension the IT department had made such a grievous error but if it wasn't Jumpsuit, then who the hell were they talking to all this time?

Harriet scrabbled over the books scattered across the floor and grabbed her phone from the coffee table. Dialling Drew's number, she closed her eyes and tried to imagine the kind of mind it would take to pull something like this off.

The phone rang out without an answer and she groaned. There was only one choice left to her. As much as Drew wanted her to stay as far away from the case as possible, he needed to know what she'd discovered.

She set the papers down and raced back up the stairs to shower and change.

CHAPTER FORTY-SEVEN

GREGSON STOOD at the window of his office and beckoned Drew over.

Drew crossed the floor and pushed open the door. "Sir?"

The DCI was behind the desk now, his gaze trained on a pile of papers in front of him.

"I've got the preliminary report here from the coroner," he said. "Looks like he decided to change things up a bit."

"What do you mean?"

"He found fibres in the victim's airways conducive to a cloth being placed over her nose and mouth. Dr. Jackson says here the burns around her nose and mouth are in keeping with the use of chloroform. Did you find any evidence of that at the other scenes?

Drew shook his head and took the report

Gregson offered him. "There's bruising around the nose and mouth," Drew mused as he studied the file. "It looks like he's escalating."

Gregson groaned. "Great, just what we need. A nut job who's getting more violent. As though killing kids wasn't enough."

Drew closed the file as the DCI dropped into his swivel chair.

"Any new leads on the enquiry into Mr Thompson?"

Drew nodded, his expression grim. "IT have passed the laptop over to the child pornography team. They found some files on it that corroborate Dr. Quinn's theory of abuse."

"Christ, what a mess."

Drew nodded. "I couldn't agree more."

"Any new leads on this case?"

"DS Arya is bringing a suspect in now. We got his details from the victim's phone. They were supposed to meet this weekend but phone signals actually put him quite near the crime scene on the day of Bianca's murder—" Drew shrugged. It was definitely a lead but until he had more information, he wasn't willing to put his arse on the line by saying they definitely had their guy. There were too many loose ends to try and match up and this Ryder—or as he'd learned his real name was Jim Tate—just didn't answer all the questions raised in the case.

Of course, if Harriet had been here he could have

spoken to her about it all. But as it was, she wasn't picking up her phone. Not that he could blame her. She'd been through a shock. If she didn't get back to him by the evening then he was going to swing by her place and see how she was coping. Or at least he would if he ever got out of the bloody office.

Maz strode into the office and gave Drew a thumbs up.

"Sir—"

"Yes, yes, go." Gregson waved him away as he turned his attention back to the pile of paperwork on his desk. "And Drew."

"Yes?" Drew paused in the doorway.

"Make sure you nail this bastard. I don't want any cock-ups."

Drew nodded. "That makes two of us, sir."

DREW FOLLOWED Maz back to the interview suites.

"When we told him she was dead, he cried like a little baby—" Maz babbled excitedly.

Drew paused outside the door to the interview room and peered into the room.

"His girlfriend wasn't too pleased, neither."

"He has a girlfriend?"

Maz nodded. "He says she'll give him an alibi for the times and dates but I'm not so sure. When I told her what we were taking him in for, she seemed pretty certain he wouldn't get a damn thing from her."

"But that doesn't mean he's not telling the truth."

Maz shrugged. "Only one way to tell."

Drew opened the door and stepped into the interview suite.

Jim Tate sat at the table, his face swollen and blotchy. Snot dangled from the tip of his nose and he swiped it away with the back of his hand. He looked up as Drew entered and his eyes teared up again.

"I didn't do this, I swear!"

Drew held his hands up in a placating gesture. "Relax, Jim. We want to get to the bottom of this as much as you do."

"Is she really dead then?"

Drew nodded. "Afraid so."

The other man nodded and buried his face in the crook of his arm. "I just can't believe it."

"Can you tell me about your relationship with the victim?"

"We didn't really have one," he said. "A bit of sexting here and there. We were going to meet on Saturday night and—" He trailed off and stared down at the table. "You must think I'm a right scumbag?"

Drew shrugged. "I don't really care much what you get up to in your spare time, Jim. I only care about the victims of the crime and getting justice for them."

"Like I told the other detective, you can ask

Justine. She'll tell you I was with her on the dates you're talking about."

"My colleague is verifying that now, Jim. But Justine doesn't seem to remember you being with her on those dates."

Jim's face crumpled and his tears overflowed again. "That's only 'cause she's pissed at me for cheating. But I swear I didn't kill anyone."

"But your phone puts you near Bianca's house yesterday. What were you doing there?"

Jim stared down at his hands. "You hear about people being catfished all the time. I wanted to make sure she was who she said she was, you know?"

Drew shook his head. "But you aren't who you said you were, Jim. I mean you told her your name was Ryder Tate for one thing and you said you were single."

"I know," he said. "I'm an asshole. But I swear I didn't kill anyone. I just wanted to know if she was fit."

Drew glanced down at the file in front of him. He was inclined to agree with the man sitting across from him. Jim Tate just didn't strike him as the type to murder a fly never mind three teenagers and an adult.

"You have to believe me," he whined. "I haven't killed anyone."

Drew pushed up from the desk and shoved the file under his arm.

"Where are you going?" Jim's voice rose hysterically. "You believe me, right?"

Drew stepped out into the hall and closed the door behind him. He'd seen suspects before who were capable of turning the water works on when it suited them. But this was a whole new level. If Jim Tate turned out to be their guy, then he would eat his hat; or least he would if he wore one.

CHAPTER FORTY-EIGHT

AN HOUR LATER, Harriet sat outside the police station, the papers next to her on the passenger seat of her Mini. It would be all too easy to turn around and leave but what would it accomplish?

Pushing open the car door, she hurried across the car park and into the station. The place was teaming with people, various different people from the media and newspaper journalists all crowded into one corner of the waiting area. Clearly something big was going down to have them all down here, circling like sharks who had just scented blood.

Harriet pushed her way to the front and smiled at the greying officer on the desk. The white shirt he wore strained over his ample stomach and he peered at her through a pair of wire-rimmed glasses.

"I'm here to see DI Haskell," she said.

"You and the rest of them," he said, gesturing to the reporters gathered behind her.

"I'm not with them," she said. "If you could just ask him, you'll see that I'm—"

"That you're not here wasting my time like those other vultures?" The officer behind the counter glared at her. "I'll tell you what I've been telling that lot. When the DI and his team want to make a statement about their arrest, then they'll call a press conference. But not until then."

Harriet stared at him, shock causing her mouth to drop open and it took her a couple of seconds to recover her senses sufficiently to actually form a coherent thought. They'd made an arrest. They'd made an arrest and Drew hadn't called like he'd promised.

"Who?" she said, leaning over the counter toward the Perspex glass that separated her from the officer.

"Who, what?"

"Who have they arrested?"

"What do you take me for?" he asked, looking at her like she'd just sprouted a second head from her neck. "I told you, when—"

"Yeah, I got that part. Can you please just ask DI Drew Haskell to come down here? Tell him it's Dr. Harriet Quinn and—"

"Look, I don't care if you're Father bloody

Christmas, I have my orders. DI Haskell will make a statement when—"

"Dr. Quinn?" Maz's voice cut over the desk sergeant's tirade and Harriet's heart leaped for joy.

"Oh, thank God, a friendly face," she said, despite noticing the distinct lack of a friendly expression on the Detective Sergeant's face.

"I need to speak to Drew but the desk sergeant here said you were all too busy and—"

Maz gestured her over to the door and buzzed her through. As she stepped through the entry way, she spotted some of the reporters eyeing her up. It wouldn't take long for them to figure out who she was.

"Why are you here?"

"I told you, I want to speak to Drew."

Maz shook his head. "I told him not to call you."

"He didn't," she said, unable to keep the bite out of her words. "He said he would, but he didn't. I hear you've made an arrest."

Maz nodded and Harriet couldn't help but detect a subtle amount of pride as he straightened his shoulders, pushing his chest out. It reminded her of the wildlife programmes she watched about King Penguins and their mating rituals.

"We did. And we managed it all without your input," he said.

Harriet kept her expression deliberately blank.

There was no point in allowing him to score points off her, not like this anyway.

"Can I ask you who it is?"

He shrugged. "Free country. But remember, just because you ask, doesn't mean I'll tell you."

Harriet tilted her head to the side. "Why do I intimidate you so much?"

Maz took a step backwards, shock and unease making his expression that much easier to read; not that he'd been particularly difficult to read to begin with.

"You don't intimidate me," he said. "I just happen to think that messing around in people's heads is never going to beat a bit of good ol' fashioned police work. Boots on the ground kind of work that you wouldn't understand."

Harriet smiled at him and shrugged. "I'm not going to disagree with you there," she said. "But this isn't a competition for me. I don't need to be better than you are at your job because I'd be a fool to think I could ever be. However, all I've ever wanted to do is help people. And all I've ever wanted to do since Drew approached me about this case is help you catch the person responsible."

"You psychologists are all the same; glory-hounds looking to make a name for yourselves."

Harriet couldn't stop the bubble of laughter that escaped her then. "DS Arya, if I wanted to make a name for myself, do you really think I'd try to do it off the back of a police investigation?"

He shrugged and looked sheepishly at the floor. "You might. There's plenty of supposed profilers always vying for attention on the telly every night of the week."

Harriet couldn't argue with him there. The world had gone mad on murder, their desire for every salacious detail made for brutal viewing.

"Look, I'm not here to change your mind."

"You couldn't."

She inclined her head toward him. "Maybe not. But it doesn't matter anymore though now does it? You've made an arrest and that's the important thing. I'm just trying to put some of the pieces of the puzzle together."

"Like what?"

"Like in the transcripts between Sian, Jumpsuit67, and Aidan she admits that her step-father raped her."

Maz's colour fled, leaving his normally coffee coloured complexion ashen. "She says that in the chat logs?"

Harriet nodded. "That's not the only discrepancy," she said. "Would it be possible for you to tell me the name of the young man behind Jumpsuit67?"

Maz screwed his face up into a grimace. "You're not working this case anymore. It's as good as done."

Harriet nodded. "I know that. But I've still got

some questions I'd like to look into. Namely, who was using the Jumpsuit67 login details to talk to Sian and Aidan up to just a couple of days before Aidan died?"

"That's got to be a mistake," Maz said. "IT tracked it back to an IP address." He pulled a notepad from his suit pocket and flipped through the pages quickly.

"Here, see," he said, pointing to a scrawled piece of writing on the page. The name Trevor Burton jumped out at her and Harriet managed to catch a glimpse of the word Tollby before Maz flipped the notepad shut preventing her from reading the other information he had. "He's dead. It's just some kind of analog issue."

Harriet smiled at him. "I suppose you're right," she said as she turned back toward the door. "You'll tell Drew about Sian's logs though. It's proof at least that we're on the right path with her step-father."

Maz nodded. "I'll tell him."

"And congratulations on the collar."

Maz beamed proudly, a dimple appearing in his left cheek which made him appear more boyish than he actually was.

"Maybe you're not the worst," he said as he buzzed her out into the main reception.

Harriet shrugged at him as she walked away. "Maybe not."

She made it to the door of the police station

without attracting the attention of the reporters who were waiting none too patiently. Maz was definitely wrong if he thought she was out to make a name for herself. The very last thing she wanted to do was draw the attention of the press. The thought of them digging into her past and plastering it all over the tabloids for the world to gawp at left her cold.

She slid back in behind the wheel of the car and dragged her phone from her pocket. Pulling up the internet she quickly typed in the name Trevor Burton and the word obituary. Within seconds she had all the listings for all the Trevor's who had died. She narrowed the results by area and finally by age, eliminating everyone until she had just one name.

Trevor Burton, formally of Tollby. Aged 16. Survived by his parents, Robert and Lucy Burton.

She scanned the entry and her palms grew sweaty as she realised the date of his death.

August 4th, 2018. A year to the day before Jack Whitly's death. The coincidence was too great to ignore, especially when she took into consideration that his login details had been used to contact Sian and Aidan before their deaths. Had his friends taken over the account after his untimely death and if that were true, were they also at risk?

Drew might have made an arrest in the case, but Harriet still wasn't entirely satisfied. There were too many inconsistencies and until she could get to the bottom of them, she wasn't going to give up.

Jotting down the address for Trevor's parents, Harriet started the engine and entered the address into her sat-nav. Drew might have left her out of the arrest, but she was damned if he was going to completely cut her out of the investigation.

CHAPTER FORTY-NINE

THE RAIN PATTERED SOFTLY against the windscreen as Harriet parked the car across the road from Trevor Burton's house. She switched off the engine and the rain instantly blurred her view of the dark red brick house set back from the road. The wall facing the street was almost entirely covered in ivy. The creeping plant encroached on the windows and Harriet couldn't imagine what it must be like to live inside it all.

Grabbing her bag, she slung it over her shoulder before she jumped out of the car and hurried over to the door. There were no guarantees that Trevor's parents even still lived here but what little searching she'd done on the Internet hadn't turned up any new addresses for the broken family.

The doorbell was lit up and Harriet pressed it, huddling under the small porch in an attempt to stay out of the rain that slanted across the driveway in sheets.

The sound of the bell echoed ominously inside the house. There was a light on in there somewhere, she surmised as she peered in through the stained glass that made up the part of the door.

"Hello, Mr Burton, Mrs Burton?" She called out as she rang the bell again.

It was difficult to hear over the sound of the rain as it fell on the gravel drive but as she raised her hand to try the bell again, she was almost certain there was some kind of movement from inside. Something shifted behind the door and Harriet stepped backwards as the door swung inwards and revealed a stooped man with sandy brown hair.

He was tall and lanky, his body hunched in on itself as though he were afraid to take up too much space or he spent too much time at a desk and his body had grown accustomed to that position and now refused to straighten.

"Can I help you?" When he spoke, his voice was soft and unassuming, and Harriet found herself having to strain forward to catch his words.

"Are you Mr. Burton?" She tilted her head to the side and took note of the beige chinos he wore and the green sweater vest that had definitely seen better days.

"Yes, and you are?"

Harriet held her hand out toward him. "My

name is Dr Harriet Quinn," she said. "I'm a psychologist at St George's University in York."

Mr Burton took her hand in his much larger one. His grip was firm but not uncomfortable as he pumped her hand gently.

"How can I help you, Doctor?"

"Please, call me, Harriet," she said. "I was hoping maybe I could come in and have a small chat with you about your son, Trevor."

His expression which up until then had been a mixture between bemused curiosity and polite indifference shifted. He narrowed his gaze, his shoulder's rounding over almost imperceptibly as though she'd dealt him a blow and not asked if she could step in out of the rain.

"My son is dead," he said, his voice flat and devoid of emotion.

"I'm aware of that and I am so very sorry for your loss," she said.

"If you know then why are you here?"

"I was hoping to have a small conversation with you regarding your son," she said, inwardly cringing at her lack of sensitivity.

He opened his mouth as though to protest and Harriet saw her opportunity to get to the bottom of it all slipping away from her.

"Please, Mr. Burton. I realise this is painful for you but I'm worried your son's death might have a connection to the murders of three teenagers and more recently the death of a young widowed mother." Harriet dug her nails into the palm of her hand in an attempt to keep her voice steady. Just thinking about Bianca was enough to cause a lump to form in the back of her throat. But if she fell apart now, it wouldn't help anyone, least of all her dead friend.

His eyes widened and he stepped back. "Murder?"

Harriet nodded. "I'm afraid so. Would it be all right if I came in out of the rain?"

As though he'd noticed the weather for the first time he started and stepped back before he gestured for her to step inside.

"I'm so sorry. You took me by surprise and I suppose my manners fled. Please, do come in." He scrutinised her carefully and a prickle of unease raced over Harriet's scalp.

"Can I get you a towel?"

She smiled her thanks and let him lead her into the house. He directed her into a small living room. "I'll get you that towel. Get comfortable, I'll be back in a moment."

Harriet nodded and moved into the room. Her gaze swept over the framed pictures that decorated the walls. Typical family photographs of holidays spent in the sun. Trevor as a happy smiling child who grinned up at the camera.

It took her only a moment to realise there were no pictures of Trevor as a teenager. Instead, he was frozen in this between place of childhood and prepubescent boyhood; as though his life had ended when he was ten or twelve and not when he was sixteen.

"That's Trevor," Mr Burton said, his silent return made Harriet jump and she turned to face him, but he had eyes only for the pictures on the wall.

"He was a very handsome young man," she said.

Mr Burton nodded and held the towel gripped in his hands out toward her. "He was. Lucy always said he'd grow up to be a real heartbreaker. We didn't know then how right she was."

Harriet nodded. "Where is your wife now, Mr. Burton?"

"Please call me, Robert," he said. "Everyone else does."

Harriet returned his smile with one of her own. "Ok, Robert."

The smile on his lips hovered only for a moment before he moved over toward the chair opposite the couch and dropped into it. Harriet copied him, choosing a seat on the couch that angled her body toward his without being so close that he might feel overwhelmed.

"Lucy is dead," he said. "She died four months ago. I always said it was a broken heart after Trevor but the doctors said it was an aneurysm. They don't think she suffered but..." He shrugged and splayed his hands out in front of him. "That's not much of a consolation when I know she suffered after Trevor died."

"I am very sorry," Harriet said, setting the towel aside. "I can't imagine how difficult that must have been for you; to lose both you son and your wife."

He nodded and raised his tear stained face. "I still wake up expecting them both to be here, you know? As though I'll go to bed one night and find out it was all just a terrible nightmare."

Harriet nodded sympathetically. "It must be terribly lonely for you," she said.

Robert rubbed his hands back over his face. "I feel close to them here. That probably doesn't make any sense, I know. But it's the truth."

Harriet had heard others in the thick of the grieving process say the same thing.

"Just being here brings me comfort." He smiled thinly at her. "Listen to me, bending your ear about something you don't want to hear."

Harriet shook her head. "I don't mind listening," she said. "Sometimes I think it's the only thing I'm truly good at."

Robert smiled at her and rubbed his hands vigorously on his thighs. "What was it you wanted to talk to me about?"

Harriet slipped the papers of the transcripts from her bag. "During the course of the investigation we discovered your son appeared to be in contact with a number of teens in the months directly proceeding his death."

Robert shook his head and stood. Harriet drew her legs up in an attempt to prevent him from brushing against her as he moved around the couch to the pictures on the wall behind her.

"Was he?" Robert seemed genuinely surprised and Harriet found herself wondering just how much time he'd actually spent with his son.

"Did he have many friends?"

"Some," he said. "Trevor could be a little bit of a loner."

"Would it be possible for me to take a look around, Trevor's room?"

Harriet kept her smile warm and inviting despite the sense of foreboding that was slowly beginning to creep over her.

Robert glanced down at the floor and she half expected him to shake his head and decline her request. Instead, he swallowed hard, his Adam's apple bobbing violently in his throat before he nodded his head.

"Of course. I'll take you up there."

Part of her wanted to ask if she could go upstairs herself but she knew it would be asking too much.

He directed her to the stairs and Harriet moved ahead of him. The stairs creaked and groaned as Harriet's shoes tapped against the dark hard wood.

"It's down here," Robert said, touching her arm gently.

Harriet's fingers tightened over the handle of her handbag as she swung around the top of the landing and moved down the wooden hall.

Robert paused at the door. He sucked in a deep breath, his eyes closed, as he seemed to compose himself as his hand hovered just over the door knob.

"I can do this alone," she said gently. "If you'd prefer?"

He shook his head. "No. I don't mean any offence, but I don't like having strangers in Trevor's room. It feels wrong."

"We don't have to do this if it makes you too uncomfortable?"

Robert smiled and shook his head. "Trev would want me to do this. He'd want to help. I've got to honour that, do you know what I mean?"

Harriet nodded. "I can understand that."

"Have you lost someone close to you too?"

"My brother," she said.

"I'm sorry. How did he die?"

"Car accident," Harriet said simply. It was easier to boil everything that had happened with her mother down to something simple. It was too complicated a story for most and the last thing she needed to do here was confuse the situation with her own trauma.

"That must have been very difficult for you," he

said. "I didn't have any siblings myself so I've never had that kind of bond. It must have been terribly traumatic for someone so young."

Harriet nodded, her eyes intent on the door but his words brought her up short.

"Excuse me?" She kept her smile in place.

"Forgive me," he said. "I only meant that you're still so young to lose a brother."

"Of course."

Robert shook his head. "Shall we get this over with?" Before she had the chance to answer, he pushed the door open.

Dust motes swirled in the grey light that filtered in through the windows. Robert stood back and gestured to the room.

"Go ahead. I'll wait here."

Harriet nodded and stepped into the room.

A large set of mirrored wardrobe doors sat against the back wall of the room giving it a sense of space it wouldn't ordinarily have enjoyed.

A large wooden desk dominated the wall beneath the window; an iMac sat pride of place, with books and other notepads scattered around.

Harriet turned slowly and drank it in. Her gaze came to rest on the bed and she paused. It was immaculately made. The corners of the sheets were tucked in beneath the mattress in a macabre mirroring of Sian's bedroom.

"He loved his computer." Robert's voice cut

through Harriet's thoughts and she jerked her gaze back to the man silhouetted in the doorway.

"He was always doing something on it and if he wasn't tapping away on the keys then he was taking them apart to see how they ticked. I always said he was a chip off the old block in that sense."

"You work with computers?"

He nodded. "Technical support," he said. "If you need a new hard drive installed, then I'm your man."

Harriet glanced down at the papers in her hands as bile crept up the back of her throat. It meant he would have had both the means and the opportunity to gain access to his son's accounts online.

"Would your son have told any of his friends the login details for his online forums?"

"No. He knew how important internet security was. He would never be so stupid."

"And is it possible his friends were as equally interested in computers as he was?"

Robert shrugged. "I don't actually know. Like I said downstairs Trev was a bit of a loner in school. He was athletic, and intelligent. He was handsome too and it should have made him the most popular boy in his year but—" Robert shrugged. "I don't know what to say. I think he was just more interested in his virtual life than the one he was actually living."

Harriet nodded and schooled her features into a smile. "Would it be possible for me to use your bathroom, Robert?"

"Of course," he said. "Third door down. I'll meet you downstairs."

"Thank you."

She let him escort her from the room, skirting carefully around him in the doorway. There was no doubt in her mind that whoever Drew had arrested was the wrong man. The one they were looking for was right here and she was standing in his house alone. No one knew she was here.

The precariousness of her situation flashed through her mind as she walked down the hall.

She needed to get word to Drew before Mr Burton realised what she was doing. And then what? She had no proof. Pointing to a bed and the way it was made was proof of nothing more than a man who liked to keep his house neat and tidy.

No, she needed proof too; Drew and Maz wouldn't give up their suspect so easily.

"It's just there," he said politely.

Harriet pushed open the bathroom door and stepped inside before she locked the door behind her.

She leaned her head back on the door as she closed her eyes and swallowed back the fear that threatened to overwhelm her. She couldn't give up now, not when she was so close to the truth.

She dropped her bag into the sink and proceeded to scrabble around in the contents in search of her phone. Her fingers closed around it and she jerked it free. With hands that trembled she dialled Drew's number, the phone ringing in her ear she waited with bated breath.

"Please pick up," she murmured.

The voicemail kicked in and Harriet's heart sank. Why couldn't he just have picked up his phone this once?

The shake in her hands intensified as she dialled the number of the station. The call was answered after the first ring.

"My name is Dr. Harriet Quinn," she said. "I need to speak to either DI Drew Haskell, or DS Maz Arya, please it's urgent." She spoke quickly in hushed tones, her mouth cupped over the mouthpiece in an attempt to keep her voice from carrying.

"Miss, I—" The woman on the other end of the line hesitated.

"Are you all right?" Robert Burton's voice seemed to carry ominously through the house and a cold sweat broke out on Harriet's skin.

"I'll be just a minute," she said.

"Are you in trouble?" The female operator said.

"I think so," Harriet said. "Please, I just need to speak to DI Haskell, this is pertaining to his case."

There was a click on the line and Maz's voice cut over the operator.

"Dr. Quinn?"

"Oh, thank God," she said quickly. "I know you don't want to hear this, but I think you've got the wrong man." Harriet's gaze snagged on her reflection in the cabinet above the sink.

She barely recognised herself; eyes ringed with dark circles, skin pale and milky in the poor light that poured in through the small frosted glass window behind the toilet. Her heartbeat thrummed in her chest and the panic she'd fought so hard to control since the incident in the hospital insidiously crept through her veins.

Maz sighed. "You just don't give up do you?"

"I'm in his house," she said. "His name is Robert Burton. He lives at 62 Ashfield Drive in Tollby."

"Dr. Quinn, I think—"

"Listen to me, damn it," she said. "I'm in his bloody house. I know you don't believe me but I need you to tell Drew. He'll understand that what I'm saying is true. His son committed suicide a year ago. His wife died four months before the murders began and I think that was his trigger."

"I don't understand," Maz interrupted. "Why are you in his house?"

"Because he's Jumpsuit67," she said. "Well, his son was the original Jumpsuit but he took it over."

"How do you know all of this?"

As he spoke Harriet pulled open the door of the cabinet and peered in at the contents. There was a razor and shaving gel, cotton buds and aftershave lotion. And interspersed among the normal items that take up space in a bathroom were bottles of prescription medication. Harriet's hands shook as she lifted down the nearest bottle and studied the label.

Flunitrazepam. The same kind of benzodiazepine drug the coroner had found in Sian's system.

"Dr. Quinn?" Robert's voice came from directly outside the bathroom door and it took every ounce of strength Harriet had not to let the bottle of pills fall from her hands.

"The same medication they found in Sian's body. It's here in his bathroom," she said. "It's got his son's name on it."

"Dr. Quinn, I—"

"Harriet..." Robert's voice was low.

Harriet set the bottle of pills back in the cabinet as he rattled the doorknob.

"Just a second."

"Tell Drew," she said into the phone. She ended the call and slipped the phone back into her bag. Smoothing her hair back from her face, she tried to calm her heart rate as she moved toward the door. She flushed the toilet hurriedly and tugged the door open and found herself face to face with Robert Burton.

He was framed in the doorway and he peered past her into the room as though he expected to see someone else in there with her.

"I thought I heard you talking to someone," he said.

Harriet shook her head. "I'm sorry. It's a hazard

of the job. Sometimes I like to talk my thoughts aloud. Articulating them helps me to see a situation more clearly."

He smiled but it never reached his dark eyes. "And what has this visit helped you to see more clearly?"

"This was more of a fact-finding mission," she said. "I'm trying to understand all the elements at play a little more clearly."

"And?"

He didn't budge from his spot. Harriet's palms had begun to sweat but her voice at least remained steady.

"I think the person we're looking for has his reasons for his actions."

"They said on the news that they've made an arrest," Robert said, his voice completely flat. "The reporters don't believe the man responsible could have a reason. They called the deaths, senseless. A pointless waste of human life. They're calling him a murderer. Do you think that's true, Dr. Quinn?"

"You should call me, Harriet," she said gently as she took a small step backwards. "And no, I don't agree with them. This man is not murdering these people, he's helping them."

Robert closed his eyes and nodded, his face breaking out into a broad smile. "I knew you'd understand..."

She didn't wait for him to finish. With her hand

still on the door she slammed it shut in his startled face.

"Dr. Quinn, what are you doing? I thought you understood."

He rattled the door as Harriet flipped the lock into place.

"Open up, Dr. Quinn. I don't want to hurt you."

"Robert, I need you to listen to me," she said, quickly. "I do understand what you're doing."

"Then open the door so we can finish this." There was a thread of something harder in his voice as he spoke.

"Why do you think Trevor took his own life?"

Robert ceased his assault on the door and Harriet sucked in a deep breath as she waited for him to answer.

"He said in the note that he was unhappy. That he didn't want to be a disappointment anymore."

"And how did that make you feel?"

"How do you think it made me feel?" He snapped back. "I was never disappointed in my son. I don't know where he even got the idea from."

"But you read all those messages he sent to his friends," she said. "You got the chance to get a glimpse into your son's mind. That's not something most people get, Robert."

"It gave me a glimpse into the unhappiness of those other children too," he said.

"Tell me about them, Robert," she said. If she

could just keep him talking, then it would give the police a chance to get here...

That was of course if they were actually coming at all. She definitely hadn't managed to convince Maz of her suspicions but he was a good police officer and she needed to believe that he wouldn't let his dislike for her outweigh his desire to do his job.

"The boy, Aidan Wilson; his father is a drunk. Beats his wife and Aidan too. I don't know how any man could do that to his child. Our children are precious, a gift from God. We're supposed to protect them."

"And that's what you were doing, is it?"

Something hit the door with a bone-shaking crash and Harriet jumped. She backed up and collided with the edge of the sink. Turning toward the cabinet again, she tugged it open and searched among the shelves for something, anything, that she could use as a weapon. She snatched up the razor but being a safety razor meant it was as good as useless. Finding nothing else, she turned her attention to the rest of the room as another earth-shattering bang sounded from the door and the wood around the lock began to crumble.

"Robert," she said. "Just talk to me."

She hit redial on the phone in her bag and prayed for the call to connect.

"I know what you're doing," he said as he hit the door again. The lock finally gave way and the door opened, slamming into the plaster wall with a dull thud.

Harriet spotted a cloth in Robert's hand as he stepped into the room toward her.

"I know what you're doing," he repeated. "But everything will become clear soon enough."

Harriet shook her head. "You don't need to do this," she said softly as the sweet scent of the chloroform caught her nose.

Panic flared inside her chest. She knew what would happen if he rendered her unconscious. She couldn't let that happen.

"Don't fight me," he said. "It'll go so much easier if you don't; for both of us."

He lunged toward her and Harriet darted beneath his arm. She made it to the open doorway before he crashed into her, knocking her sideways into the wall. Her head bounced off the splintered doorframe and pain flared bright and blinding behind her eyes.

The impact of hitting the ground jolted her back to the present and she tried to scramble away as Robert crawled over her and pressed her into the hardwood floor. He straddled her, his knees pinning her in place as he planted his hand with the cloth over her nose and mouth.

At this point, going unconscious was an inevitability but there was one thing she could do and that was attempt to control the length of time she was actually unconscious for. However, it meant fighting against every adrenaline-soaked nerve ending in her body.

She tried holding her breath as she let her body go limp. She slumped against the floor hoping and praying he took the bait. The sooner he thought she was unconscious meant the less time he would keep the rag pressed to her face.

She held her breath for as long as possible but her body screamed for oxygen and she had no choice but to breathe in the sweet scent of the chloroform. Her eyes rolled back in her head as the chemical rendered her useless.

"Shh," Robert said, smoothing her hair out of her face. "It'll all be over soon. Don't you worry."

Darkness rolled over her and tossed her beneath a wave of black. And Harriet had no choice but to hope that the call she'd made had connected and that Drew would get the message. If not, then everything she had done had been for nothing. She would die here, alone and afraid in the arms of a man who thought he was releasing her from a world that had so far treated her with nothing but contempt.

CHAPTER FIFTY

THE TASTE of metal in her mouth was the first sense that returned to Harriet as she crawled back toward consciousness. Her head felt as though someone had lifted her brain out of her head with a rusty ice-cream scoop before replacing it with cotton wool. Groggily, she struggled to open her eyes as the sound of something shuffling nearby reached her ears.

"I was wondering when you would wake up."

Harriet finally managed to pry one eye open, the other one felt heavy and refused to budge. She tried to lift her hands from the floor but they were like lead weights at the end of each arm.

Her vision was blurred. Her surroundings swam in and out of focus but after a minute of trying, she finally managed to pinpoint Robert in the space.

The room was small, the ceiling low overhead,

and he was even more stooped than usual.

Harriet shifted and discovered she was propped up against a wooden beam which pressed painfully in against her spine. She tilted her head back and the rope around her throat scratched at her skin.

It took every ounce of concentration she had—which, considering how much her head pounded, wasn't a whole lot to begin with—to keep from letting her panic overtake her. If she did that, then she was as good as dead.

"It's the basement," Robert said by way of an explanation. He gestured to the room and sighed. "Trev and I spent a lot of time down here taking computers apart. I thought he was happy in those days."

"Why are you doing this?"

Robert shot her a quizzical look. "What do you mean, why am I doing this? You said you understood."

Harriet shook her head and the world ran in colourful streamers. Her head had started to pound and just keeping one eye open was painful.

"I lied. I don't understand any of this. Do you really think this is what your son would have wanted?"

Robert glanced down at his hands. "He doesn't get to choose," he said. "He took that decision into his own hands the day he decided to come down here and hang himself from that beam."

Nausea washed up the back of Harriet's throat.

"And your wife, is this what she would want you to do?"

"Why do you think I'm doing this at all?" He exploded, his face turning an unbecoming shade of red as he stalked across the room. It wasn't until he started to move that Harriet realised he was holding the other end of the rope in his hands. As he got closer, the noose tightened on her throat.

He caught himself and paused and Harriet felt his gaze on her as she gagged and spluttered, her brain screaming for oxygen.

Robert stepped back and the tension disappeared. Harriet sucked down clean air into her lungs and the pain in her head increased until she was sure it would explode.

"Your wife," she said, coughing to clear her raw airway. "She didn't die of an aneurysm, did she?"

Robert shook his head. "No." He turned away and the rope went slack as he moved over to sit on the bottom of the stairs.

"She was so unhappy after, Trev," he said. "And then she was diagnosed with breast cancer." He shrugged. "She got sicker and sicker. And then she was palliative; it all happened so fast and she didn't even try and put up a fight."

"And that's when she asked you to help her die," Harriet finished for him.

He raised his tear-soaked face to her and smiled.

"I was afraid. Afraid to be alone. Afraid to help. I didn't want to hurt anyone but she helped talk me through it all. She'd been a nurse, so she knew what she needed to take."

He rubbed his face on the sleeve of his white shirt. "I stayed with her until it was over. And then when they came and got her body; I thought this is it, Robert. They're going to know what you did but—"

"But they didn't."

He shook his head and smiled. "I knew then it was a sign. A sign that I could help others who were hurting. I knew then that this was what I was supposed to do."

"But your wife made a choice," Harriet said. "The position she put you in it wasn't right, but I can understand why you helped her but the others. They didn't want to die. They were still fighting."

He snorted his derision and shook his head. "They wanted it. Whether they knew it or not, I gave them what they were too afraid to do for themselves."

"Bianca, has a daughter—"

Robert nodded. "I know. Her name is Tilly and she's six years old. Bright as a button."

"And you've taken her mother from her. The only parent she had left."

Robert shook his head. "Bianca didn't know how to get through her own grief, never mind help her daughter deal with hers. I've done that child a favour."

"You're wrong." Harriet shuffled against the beam. "You're wrong and you can't see it yet. But you will. One day you'll understand the level of devastation you've brought these people."

She struggled to get her legs beneath her. If she could just stand up...

Her legs refused to cooperate, her muscles were jelly and the more she tried to force them to work, the more exhausted she became.

Robert shook his head. "No. I freed them. I helped them. They couldn't do it themselves. They wanted to but they couldn't do it and I helped them."

"They had their whole lives ahead of them."

"They were broken!" His voice was hoarse with unshed tears. "You don't understand at all. You're just a liar. You're lying to me and you're lying to yourself."

Harriet opened her mouth to answer but he cut over her.

"Don't try to deny it. I know all about your past. I know all about what your mother did to you and your brother. You would have been better off if you'd stayed in the car that day. She was only trying to spare you the grief, the hardship of growing up knowing you were unloved and unwanted."

It took Harriet a moment to find her composure. He knew who she was, knew about her past and Kyle. Had he known all along or had he discovered the truth while she'd been out for the count?

"You think I don't understand what pain is. That I can't fathom it, well you're wrong. I know what your pain is, and I know how to make it stop. Just like I knew how to help the others."

He grabbed the rope and began to wind it around his arm.

"Wait," Harriet said. "What if I don't want it to stop?"

Her question seemed to catch him off guard and he sneered at her. "Don't be ridiculous."

She shook her head. "I'm being serious. What if I like it; the pain, I mean?"

"Nobody wants to be in pain."

Harriet shook her head and stared at her feet. "Now who's being ridiculous? There are plenty of people in this world that thrive on pain. Who actively seek it out just so they can get off on it."

"That's not who you are."

Harriet shrugged. "No, it's not. But my pain is my own and I don't want it to just go away."

"Why not?"

"Because it has helped create me. Without that crucible I wouldn't be the psychologist I am. I wouldn't help people; or even want to help people who are suffering because I wouldn't understand what it's like to walk in their shoes."

Robert shook his head. "You're stalling for time and I don't believe you." He punctuated his words by tightening his hold on the rope.

Harriet managed to get her legs beneath her and pushed onto her feet. He cut her off with a sharp jerk, he pulled the rope taut and the knot tight around her throat.

Harriet thrashed, fighting against the ever-tightening noose on her neck. She dug her fingers into the rope in an attempt to get her fingers inside the noose but all she succeeded in doing was gouging at the flesh of her throat. Stars burst behind her eyes as her oxygen was depleted. Her pulse pounded in her ears and still she fought against the noose.

There was a crash above her head and the veins in Robert's neck stood out as he heaved and pulled the rope tighter. Harriet felt her feet leave the floor as the edges of her vision turned black. Her heart rate slowed, the noise thundering in her ears as she gasped for air.

"Police!"

The shout seemed to come from far away; too far away to be of any use to her as darkness ate at her vision.

The rope went slack and Harriet hit the ground hard; the jolt and sudden rush of air enough to make her dizzy. She opened her eyes to see Robert on the floor, pinned beneath two uniformed officers.

"Harriet!" Drew's face swam into focus and she opened her mouth to speak but there was no sound.

She blacked out.

When she came around, Drew was sliding the

noose from her neck and the pain was enough to shoot through her nerve endings and set them alight.

"Harriet, can you hear me?" He crouched over her, cradling her gently against his chest.

She tried to speak but the effort was too much. The adrenaline flooding her body sent her heart rate into overdrive and the world lost its colour. She gasped and clutched at her throat again, the sudden rush of air she'd drank down only moments ago no longer enough to sustain her.

Shock. She was going into shock. She'd heard it could happen to those who'd suicide attempts had been thwarted by loved ones, but she'd never thought she would find herself on the receiving end of it.

Her back arched as she struggled to find the oxygen necessary for survival and she clutched at Drew's jacket.

"Where's the ambulance?" Drew shouted.

"Is she dead?"

Harriet wasn't sure but she could have sworn she heard an edge of triumph in Robert's voice as he was picked up from the ground and dragged up the stairs.

"Is she dead? Did I free her? Tell me!"

"Harriet, help is on the way. Just stay with me..."

She couldn't speak. Couldn't breathe. The adrenaline in her body spiked as panic robbed her of her senses and she succumbed to the darkness that swallowed her whole.

CHAPTER FIFTY-ONE

WHEN SHE AWOKE, the room was almost completely dark; only the faint light from the monitor above her bed cast a glow over the space. A monitor beeped and it took her a moment to realise the beeping was the sound of her heartbeat.

Her head throbbed as she stared up at the white ceiling tiles above her head.

"We thought you were a goner." Drew's voice drifted over to her from the darkened corner of the room. The beeping monitor beside the bed gradually picked up its pace.

"Hey," Drew said, sitting forward on his chair. "It's all right, no need to panic." He grinned at her and Harriet could just make out his haggard expression tinged blue from the screen.

"How long have I—" She trailed off. Her throat felt like she'd swallowed a whole packet of razor blades. She swallowed past the pain and tried again. "How long have I been in here?"

"Twenty-four hours," Drew said as he scrubbed his hand over his face. "They thought they would have to intubate you but they managed to stabilise you on the ride over in the ambulance with oxygen support." He sighed. "You frightened the crap out of me, you know?"

Harriet smiled at him but her face was sore and it felt more like a grimace than an expression of happiness.

"What about Robert?"

"Full confession," Drew said. "The bloke wouldn't tell us anything at first. He just kept on asking if you were dead."

"And you told him I was?"

Drew looked up at her in surprise. "Actually, that was Maz. He came up with the bright idea to give the guy what he wanted so he told him you were dead and that we were charging him with your murder. He soon changed his tune after that. Said we were too stupid to understand what he was trying to do. So Maz asked him to explain and the guy spilled the lot."

Harriet's smile faded. "And your other suspect? The one you arrested without telling me about..."

"We let him go. What do you mean I didn't tell you?"

"You said you'd call me. That night outside Bianca's house, you said you'd call and you never did."

"Yeah, I did. I called your house and there was no answer so I left a message on your machine."

Harriet shook her head. "It doesn't matter now."

"Yes, it does," Drew said indignantly. "I kept my promise, Harriet."

"Ok." She nodded and her mind drifted as her eyes slid shut.

"I should go and let you rest," Drew said.

"What?"

"I'll go and let you rest…"

The thought of being left alone filled her with dread and she reached out to him in the dark. "Please. Stay."

He studied her face for a moment before he nodded. "I'll stay."

Satisfied, Harriet dropped back against the pillows. Her eyelids were heavy and she let them drift shut as the sound of the machines next to her beeped.

CHAPTER FIFTY-TWO

HARRIET SAT on the side of the bed, with her bag of meagre belongings packed up next to her.

"When did they say they'd discharge you?" Drew asked from the chair in the corner of the room. He glanced down at his watch.

"If you have to be somewhere else, I can make my own way home." She grinned at him. "I'm not an invalid, you know."

"I never said you were. But it's okay. I can wait another while longer."

"Has there been any news on Robert's case?"

Drew shook his head. "The defence is looking to enter a plea for insanity."

Harriet lifted her gaze. "But he's not insane."

Drew shrugged. "He's not all there either."

"An insanity defence only works if you can prove that your client doesn't understand their actions. Robert Burton knew exactly what he was doing."

Drew gave her a helpless look. "It's not up to me now. We sent our information off to the CPS. It's for them to proceed."

Harriet pursed her lips and glanced up at the door and her heart dropped as she spotted the salt and pepper haired man heading in their direction.

The moment he'd found out about the incident with Robert Burton, Jonathan had rushed to her side. She'd politely told him she didn't need his help but as he'd proven before, no wasn't exactly a word he readily understood.

He pushed open the door and peered into the room. "Am I disturbing you?"

"Actually—" Harriet never managed to finish the sentence.

"What are you doing here?" Drew's voice was icy and he pushed onto his feet, his hands balled into fists at his sides.

Harriet's throat constricted. "Drew, I can explain."

"You know him?"

Harriet nodded and swallowed hard.

"Why is he here?" Drew turned his furious expression toward her and she inwardly cringed.

"What's going on here, Harriet?" Jonathan asked glancing over at Drew in confusion. "Who is this man?"

"You've got some nerve," Drew said before he pulled himself up short. "I thought I remembered you," he said. "That first time we met you looked so familiar but I dismissed it…"

Harriet let her gaze drop to the floor. "I wanted to tell you. I'm so sorry."

"What's going on here?" Jonathan interrupted.

"Jonathon Connor, this is DI Drew Haskell…"

Dr Connor glanced over at Drew and cocked an eyebrow in Harriet's direction. "Forgive me, DI Haskell but I don't recall—"

"You treated his fiancée," Harriet said. "Freya Northrup."

Jonathon glanced back at her and his expression cleared. "Ah, I see…"

"Is that all you've got to say?" Drew exploded, his face white with rage. "You killed her."

"I did no such thing," Jonathan said, anger causing his voice to rise in equal measure. "Your fiancée was a very troubled young woman. I was trying to help her."

"She was fine until she came into contact with you." Drew took a step toward Jonathan.

Harriet slipped off the bed and moved between the two men. "Drew, I'm sorry. I should have—"

"You," he said. "I confided in you. I told you and you lied to me. You knew all along… How could you?"

"If I'd told you, you wouldn't have wanted to work with me."

"Can you blame me?"

She shook her head.

"You came around that day, sniffing around to see if I was going to take any action against your precious Dr Connor."

"That's not what happened. I came because I wanted to see how you were. I wanted to—"

"You wanted to see the devastation you'd caused, you mean." Drew's voice was ragged and instinctively, Harriet reached out toward him but he pushed away from her and turned for the door.

"If I ever see you again, Dr Quinn, I'll—" He shook his head. "Thank you for your help in apprehending Robert Burton. But Yorkshire CID no longer requires your services."

With that, he tugged the door open and disappeared out into the hall, leaving Harriet to stare after him. She didn't blame him in the least. She'd lied to him; withholding the truth was as good as a lie and his reaction was justified.

"Well, he's pleasant," Jonathan said as he reached out to touch her shoulder.

Harriet shrugged free of him.

"Why are you here, Jonathan?"

He stared at her in mock surprise before his gaze narrowed. "I was hoping your little scare would have brought you to your senses, but I can see now that my hope was misguided."

Harriet pinched her fingers against the bridge of her nose and shook her head. "Haven't you done enough damage?"

"Poor, little, Harriet. You've chased everyone away now... I hope you're happy." He pulled open the door and left, the sound of his expensive shoes squeaked on the floor as he stalked down the hall.

With a sigh, Harriet dropped back onto the bed.

He wasn't wrong. But she had made a mistake and now she was paying the price for it.

GET THE NEXT BOOK!

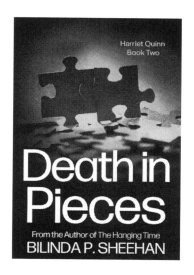

Harriet Returns in the next book in the series.
Death in Pieces

OTHER BOOKS BY THE AUTHOR

Watch out for the next book coming soon from Bilinda P. Sheehan by joining her mailing list.

A Wicked Mercy - Harriet Quinn Crime Thriller Book 1

Death in Pieces - Harriet Quinn Crime Thriller Book 2

Splinter the Bone - Harriet Quinn Crime Thriller Book 3

All the Lost Girls-A Gripping Psychological Thriller

WANT TO KNOW WHEN THE NEXT BOOK IS COMING?

Sign-up to the mailing list to receive an email every time I launch a new book.
Mailing List

Or Join me on Facebook
https://www.facebook.com/BilindaPSheehan/

Alternatively send me an email.
bilindasheehan@gmail.com

My website is bilindasheehan.com

Printed in Great Britain
by Amazon